Possession Of My Fate

Possession Of My Fate

The Three Immortal Blades

Kia Carrington-Russell

Crystal Publishing

CRYSTAL PUBLISHING

Published by Crystal Publishing (Australia)

Copyright © Kia Carrington-Russell 2016

The moral right of the author has been asserted.

Cover Design: © Angela M Hudson
All Images Used Under Licence by Shutterstock.com

ISBN 978-0-6483370-9-6

Dedication

To those who have shared with me the journey of Karla and the Three Immortal Blades, thank you. With this adventure and discovery of my characters I found myself as a woman and author. Without your support I wouldn't be where I am today. Thank you for that. To you all, I love you dearly.

1

My Destiny

A journey always has a starting point.

When I look back now, I realize how far I have come.
I acknowledge the things that I have learnt.
I cherish the friendships that I have made.
I cry at the frustration of not yet being at my end goal.
I fear the things I have discovered in this world.
But, without them I wouldn't be the woman that stands
here today.
Life is full of surprises.
I just had to learn to become open minded, and believe in
this world, where anything is possible.
I live in the world of monsters and immortal beings.
There is also light and greatness to be found.
I've discovered I must focus on that.
For my own sanity and fate, I must believe in the good.

Chapter One- Ripples

*D*ays have passed since our confrontation with Taskatae, her creatures, and Lucas's brother, Nathanial, who now lay dead. My thoughts continuously drifted to how Lucas had so quickly run away from me, scared of Tyran's hold over his soul and body. I looked into his dark-brown eyes and saw that he mirrored the emotions I experienced with Misfeata. And that was mostly fear: fear to know that we may not have the ability to contain them within; that the Elder may erode our very soul and take possession of our body; that they would leave what we had of ourselves as a mere memory, a shadow. It would always be a fight, and no matter how much he believed that it would not happen between him and me, it had now become our fate. I had only had two days of rest since that horrific day and images of his pleading eyes still pulled at my chest.

Ashley tapped me over the head, lightly knocking my thoughts away as I focused on him again. "Are you focusing?" he asked, irritated by my eagerness to escape into my thoughts. He raised his hands into fists again, preparing for my attack. I raised mine to his and we bumped fists together, acknowledging it was now fair game as we trained. It was early in the morning and everyone else still rested within the motel room of the seemingly deserted town. Both Ashley and I struggled to sleep after all that had happened, and although Scott was able to heal everyone rapidly, everyone was still exhausted from our battle.

Ashley's wounds were healed except for his eyebrow piercing, which left a small scar. For reasons that he had not yet explained he kept the scar there, perhaps in memory of the day in which we had avenged his father's death by killing Nathanial. We trained behind the motel in a small park which contained only two swings, one slide, and a bench.

He came at me and his large arms punched toward my face. I quickly blocked him and threw him to the left. I jumped into my punch, aiming at his face, but he speedily evaded me. Grabbing my closed fist and holding me beneath my arm, he flipped me over his back. I caught myself, slamming my feet into the ground so I wouldn't jar my back. I then used his arm, wrapping myself around it and flinging myself over it to attempt to lock him in a hold. He hastily let go, releasing me from the hold he had on me.

A piece of my light-brown hair blocked my vision and I blew it away, still cautious of what Ashley was planning next as I pivoted on my feet. I felt Paul's presence and I looked up toward the bench. Ashley took advantage of my distraction, punching into my stomach and brushing past my side to kick at the back of my leg. As I dropped he wrapped his arms around my neck. Not tightly but enough so I was unable to escape. I exhaled in frustration, tapping on his arm to signal that he had me. Although I could easily use my Shield to deflect him, this was a hand-to-hand combat. It was obvious I had lost because I had let myself become side-tracked.

"You need to stop dozing off or I'll start thinking that you are letting me win," Ashley taunted as he rounded on me again. I pulled my fringe over my face and tightened my hair.

"Karla!" Scott shrilly called. Ashley flicked out his hands in agitation at the second interruption. Scott waved over at me flamboyantly before tapping on Paul's shoulder and pointing to Ashley. "Go train. I have to talk to Karla."

Paul looked at him, unimpressed at being told what to do, but he raised his eyebrows at me compliantly and we exchanged places. Ashley swiftly rounded on him, unfazed by the change in opponent. Paul was a close match to Ashley when it came to hand-to-hand after all those years of training to be the best boxer in our small town of Roperia. It was all other elements and paranormal abilities that he lacked in combat.

After everything that had happened, I realized that it was Paul whom I fought for. He had been by my side for so long now that I seemed to have forgotten my appreciation for him. After Taskatae had taken him, threatening to do the same to him as she had to my father, I went into a frenzy to rescue and save him. I had never realized just how dear Paul truly was to me.

"We have a problem," Scott said, now serious as his pink eyes watched Paul and Ashley fight. My heart sank as I once again felt that this was a never-ending run. There was always a problem; there was not a brief moment where we could just rest and think of what to do next.

"What's happened?" I asked, not wanting to hear the answer. I watched Paul and Ashley as they sounded one another out before trying to hit at one another and lock each other in holds.

"I went to see Trish this morning," he admitted, surprising me because of how contentious their relationship was. She hated him. Although you would think the feeling would be mutual, I believed that Scott cared for his younger sister deeply, especially now that their father was killed by Nathanial in front of them both. They were both on their own, but Trish had never strayed far from her father's side, making me wonder where she could now go. Although I despised her as she constantly irritated me and tried to pick fights, my sympathy was with her after losing her father.

I had no pity for Max Jacket, however. He had in so many ways jeopardized Paul's life, as well as my own. No longer would we be manipulated by him just so he could gain power or knowledge.

"I have been watching her closely and monitoring where she's going. At first she was heading back home to our cottage to bury our father, but since then she has had to change her direction. She came across a large group of Starkorfs heading our way," Scott explained, staring at his nails in contemplation.

"And let me guess, they're on their way here?" I sneered in a rhetorical tone, unable to laugh at such absurd circumstances anymore. Of course they were coming toward us. After Ashley and I defeated Praytar we had single-handedly ruined their feasting habits, home, and leader. After that horritic day the Starkorfs fled. When we were searching for Taskatae and Nathanial we learned that some followed Nathanial — the son of Praytar and host of Tyran — but there was still a large amount that were not with him. Who did they follow? Those who followed Nathanial struggled to keep their human form; their feasting habits obviously were affected by the presence of a new leader.

"I'll ignore your queer sense of humor... yes, they are. Toward the castle of Taskatae, in fact, where they will find the remains of their prince and learn that Taskatae has fallen. They will follow us. You have declared war by killing both their leader and his son."

"I know," I said, closing my eyes. How could I have acted in any other way? I looked at Paul, who now sweated through his grey sleeveless shirt, panting heavily as he and Ashley attacked one another more viciously as they were too evenly matched. It was a surprise to Ashley to acknowledge that although Paul did not train as a Shielder, he could fight as well as one.

When I thought of Paul I realized that why I killed Praytar and Nathanial was partially to protect and save him. And although he could have run, and could have escaped this bloodshed and war, he stayed by my side. His courage strengthened me. *I will protect him no matter what, no matter who the enemy may be.*

"Who are they following?" I asked, trying to formulate a plan. First we would have to evacuate, creating some distance between them and us. I would have Ashley return to where my mother, Helena, Suzumiya, and Chris were hiding to confirm they were safe. For precaution they might have to be moved. I couldn't have my mother involved in this fight again, not after it broke her the last time. She despised my kind and all others who were not human. I was forced to take her parental rights away: to shelter me. I allowed her to be put into an unconscious state against her will so that I could protect her from afar.

I now had Uncle Kyle, who had been fighting against the Starkorfs for all these years since I was little, waiting to be reunited with me to help me find a cure to rid me of the Elder Misfeata who resided within me. He had been deluded by lies and false hope. Such a cure could not exist. However, just to have him by my side was a comfort.

"Karla, it's not Lucas," Scott said carefully, surprising me. I looked at him bashfully. Why would he assume I thought it was Lucas who led them? My heart instantly twisted at his name and the thought of him rising against me. I frowned, thinking of the naïve promise he once made to me: that no matter what our fates, he would not fight against me. But as Tyran entered his body and tried to possess him for the first time, I knew that it was a promise neither of us could keep. Despite this, no matter what the circumstance, I did not believe or assume that it was Lucas who led them in the hunt for my head. But now Scott created doubt in my mind. *Are we truly fated to fight and hate one another?*

"Have you ever been in contact with Eden before?" he asked seriously.

I thought of the few Starkorf names I knew and shook my head, not registering the name. "No, who is he?" I asked in anticipation.

"He was second in command in Praytar's time." Scott let the words hang heavy in the air as I thought of the education Lucas once gave me on the Starkorfs structure. He had once mentioned that Raven was daughter to the second-in-command. My stomach squirmed at the realization that it was Raven's father. My eyes widened as I looked up at him, his grim face confirmed my suspicions.

"Raven's father," I whispered with despair, realizing now that his vengeance and hatred of me ran far deeper than those who simply wanted to harness the Elder within me. This was now personal. Raven was the first Starkorf I had decided to kill. Before my birth she hurt my parents and would probably have killed them if the previous host of Misfeata, Elisabeth, hadn't intervened. She had hurt everyone around me; drained and murdered more people than I could imagine just to keep her child-like body. She tried to kill me for the reward of my Immortal Blades, Aeisha. And ever since that day I had decided to end her life — to kill for the first time — I had suffered the consequences.

It had been only days ago that I left in search of her mother, Taskatae, who destroyed my family and turned my father into a beast. Praytar's son, Nathanial, who was engaged to her daughter, all had a good reason to personally want to kill me and those who were close to me.

And now I had taken Eden's only daughter as well as his lover. I closed my eyes at the thought of the ripple effect I had created. I narrowed my eyes on Paul again, inhaling deeply and thinking only of him as my legs nervously bounced.

"We'll let the others rest for a little while longer and then we must leave. We need to place distance between them and us before we revaluate. We don't know their numbers yet. We just need to make sure we are alive and far away," I said heavily, ignoring the sinking feeling in my stomach.

"Karla, the majority of Praytar's army followed not Nathanial but Eden; he is well known for his years of service and combat, some even deeming him to be one of their best warriors," Scott explained, his pink eyes looking at me earnestly.

The wind blew in my eyes and I blinked several times, digesting this information. I looked at him blankly, trying to muster the courage I knew that would be needed. As much as I wanted to face my new opponent with determination and courage, I couldn't help but dread our next few steps. *When will this war be over? Is it in my death that I can finally be at peace?* I wondered if my death would finally end the war between the Elders.

"Eden is after me and when the time comes I will face him," I said, holding both my hands under my chin and focusing on Paul with determination. My mother also came to my mind, strengthening my resolve. "This is my fight."

Chapter Two- Eden

$\mathscr{I}$ watched Ashley and Paul for a few hours as they trained and reflected on the theory of 'what if'. I watched them with complete judgement, experiencing a nostalgic sensation and questioned what everyone's life might have been if not for this world. What would they be like within the normal living world? It was soon to be my eighteenth birthday, and yet I felt as if the responsibilities, struggle and leadership I had, exceeded far greater than that of my age. This was not something I so easily handled. And what of Paul and Ashley?

Would have Ashley been living a normal High School experience with Helena, and his father Seth still alive? I imagined them to have been a doctor and nursing duo of sorts. Would Paul still be the popular class clown of our grade? When I thought of a normal future for him I questioned what sort of lifestyle he would have had. Probably a wife and beautiful children. Maybe he would have been a boxing trainer, or a soldier. I couldn't at all imagine him to be chained to a desk in an office role.

And what of Lucas? My heart ached as I thought of him, what other life would he have had? For so many years now this was all he knew, so what life would he lead for himself? Would he have still been a cocky menace or an introverted quiet specimen?

And of my life? I would have still been working at the café, helping pay off my parent's debt and finishing my senior year of schooling. Would I have considered university and further pursue education; or simply have tried to find a high paying job to help my parent's finances. So many paths could have presented themselves in front of me, yet instead I was locked within this very different world.

"You think of foolish things," Misfeata interjected into my mind with a disgruntled tone. I didn't want to respond, but I couldn't avoid my acid like tone reproaching.

"That would have been my life if you had not desired a lifetime of entirety to fight a selfish war. I hate you," I spited back.

"I do not care for your hatred child, sooner or later I will have full control of your body, and then you are permitted to consider the 'what if's' of this evil world," she calmly responded.

"And have you never considered your 'what ifs', if you hadn't been chained to such a stupid war?" I asked angrily. In my dreams I had seen Misfeata's exterior beauty, I even questioned at one point if her heart was good. If she could have been a strong minded woman, still to have had children within her time, and live a normal life. I remembered that she had birthed children. I questioned if she loved them as much as a normal mother.

"I was never to lead a normal life," after much hesitation she continued. "I could not so foolishly delude myself like you do. I will never be human, so I do not wish for such simple things." I could feel the stir of her retreat and leave me at peace, something I was grateful for as usually she would continue spitting hateful thoughts and words towards me.

Paul and Ashley had tired, claiming truce and both approached me.

"What did Scott want before?" Ashley asked rubbing a blue towel over his sweaty face.

"We'll discuss it later," I quickly dismissed believing it was smarter if we had one small break of rest again before we approached what seemed like a never-ending battle. No matter what part of the world we might try to hide in, we would never be fully concealed. Eden was after me with an army of Starkorfs. It not only endangered my life, but those who I loved as well. This was not a fight I could avoid, but for now I only wanted a few more hours of what little normalcy and recovery we might be entitled to.

"Do you feel like resting for a little while, Karlz? You've hardly slept," Paul said stretching his sleeveless white shirt over his face. It was cloaked in sweat. I quickly diverted my gaze as I found myself staring for far too long. Usually I would reinforce I didn't need rest, and that we needed to decide the next plan of action. But after my nostalgic thoughts of the lives we could've once lived, it was what I wanted most.

Ashley also looked exhausted and needed the rest as much as I did. We trained instead of sleeping, trying to keep our mind away from the things we both feared facing. Mostly the loss of our fathers. When I slept, Misfeata would torture me. It was only because I had Scott that I could at times have a peaceful sleep.

We walked back towards the small near-forgotten motel. We were all silent, preoccupied with our own inner turmoil. Not much had been spoken about the war we fought and the amount of lives we had taken, Starkorf, beast or not. Paul's fingers snapped me out of my own thoughts as he held my hand, walking alongside me. He gave me a sheepish smile, reassuring me that I was not alone. I had so many around me, and yet I had never felt more alone. But his singular touch was exactly what I needed, for too long now had I denied myself that, thinking it was the only way to protect everyone- the only way that made me strong.

Paul and I stayed in the same motel room. At first I thought it was so I could protect him, if something crept up on us. But with his hand holding mine, I realized that it was for my own security and comfort. Never had I been so bold as to sleep with anyone, the thought made me shy. But as we both took our shoes off, Paul lightly pulled me towards his singular bed.

I wanted to pull away, from fear of what it would lead to, but red blushed over his cheeks in an innocent way. A reassurance that insisted it was harmless and only for comfort.

"It's just to rest Karla since Scott isn't here, I will try my hardest to keep the nightmares away," Paul said shyly.

"Okay," I said quickly, much to both his and my own surprise. I wanted to be held- to feel safe. Another part of my mind lingered on the thought of being embraced by Paul after I had so desperately found and saved him. I never realized how much he had truly meant to me until that day. And selfishly, as much as I tried to push him away and tell him to leave, I wanted him to stay.

He put a clean sleeveless shirt on and laid on his side wrapping his large arms around me as I had my back to his chest, my breath barely heard. His chest was warm and left a lingering warmth and comfort spread throughout me. I didn't dare move, because I was too shy and awkward to. My breaths were shallow and hinging on his every unflinching movement. My head felt molded into his bulky arm. Although the muscle was lean and hard, it was so smooth and comfortable at the same time. His fingers lightly pushed back the fringe of my hair as he spoke.

"Rest Karla, I will watch over you when you sleep," he said angelic. His words pooled into me, and no matter how frightened I was of Misfeata, I found far more strength coming from Paul in his determination of her not approaching me in my sleep while he shielded me.

*

My comfort and security was contained within Paul as I watched him sleep and his low snore seemed to ease me. I hadn't been able to sleep, no matter how much I desired it, I feared Misfeata would torture me in my sleep far too greatly. I folded myself into Paul, my face close to his and my hands rested on his chest. His large arms were wrapped around me in comfort. I found peace and a sense of rest while watching him sleep. I fought for Paul that day and as I fiddled my finger over my lips in thought, I now understood how true my feelings for him were, no matter how much I had tried to contain them and ignore them.

"Karla," Ashley said, breaking me from my trance of Paul's peaceful sleep. I looked over my shoulder almost surprised and embarrassed at the same time. Ashley didn't look at me indifferently. I was sad to know that this small time of silence and peace, of simply being with Paul was already over.

"I'm coming," I said quietly, looking back at Paul who stirred slightly at our voices. Paul was evidently tired and sleep had pulled him over. We had both been through so much, and he still didn't shake in fear beside me or blame me for almost being murdered. I was ashamed by my fear of sleeping. Paul had been tortured too, physically. How much strength could he possibly have? What was his secret to keeping it together?

Ashley left the room as I looked over Paul and stared at his hand. I reached out and looked at it significantly as if in every part of him was a residue of myself. I compared his large tanned hand to my small pale one measuring the size difference. Paul was so much bigger than me and able to protect me in other ways other than just the war we fought in. It was because of these hands that I was able to keep my sanity. Although I am broken from everything that has happened, his hand does not shake like mine, he grounds me.

As I slowly dropped his hand it tightened and moved, entwining his fingers with my own. I was surprised to look up and see that he was awake, his beautiful green eyes looking back at me. He idly rubbed his forehead messing his dark brown hair back and forth as he properly woke.

"Good Morning," he moaned, his voice dry and deep.

16

"Good Morning," I replied softly. "We have to go speak with the others." His strong arms pulled me in towards him tighter.

When Max Jacket used him as bait, I found it to be a more powerful motive than the one I had originally taken to gather my revenge on Taskatae, the Elemental Breather who called herself 'Mother'; titling herself that because she could create beasts from eggs and manipulate fertile people into creatures.

She had done this to my father, as I had unknowingly stabbed him in the chest, trying to protect my mother. A tear slid down my eye as I recalled that impacting memory of my father dropping into my arms as his figure changed and I had realized my mistake. Every day I will regret such a mistake, never able to rekindle my family.

As a Shielder, I was now the protector and had to do all I could for the shattered memories of my family.

Never had I been so scattered in thought. I now accepted Paul's embrace, scared that he may leave at any time. I never knew how tightly it was that I clung and needed him until someone had taken him away proclaiming that they would enthral the same fate upon him as my fathers.

Scott stayed close, his Elemental Breather ability able to help everyone heal quickly including himself. He had been quiet for the days spent in the motel room, unlike his usual flamboyant self. When Scott first came to me wanting to help me find my parents he was loud, obnoxious and 'fabulous' as he liked to put it. But quickly as we journeyed together I saw another side to him, a more darker and untrustworthy existence. It reminded me he was an Elemental Breather, his anger unable to be controlled easily and his want for knowledge and belief of himself being more prestigious than others overwhelmingly bright. But his abilities had saved Ashley, even after he betrayed Paul and me so deeply after changing his form into myself and tricking Paul to believe it were me which led them to a kiss that I didn't want to recall witnessing. His silence was powerful, I think reflection mostly after his father, Max Jacket. Although his father hated him, I believed that Scott still grieved for his father's death.

Paige had followed us around since we first found her near Max Jacket's home, killing nearby Starkorfs and rudely inviting herself to join us. We didn't know much about her background and Scott had once said that when entering her body he couldn't see anything- only darkness. We didn't yet know what she was or who she was but despite her bad temperament, rudeness, and irritation, she was a savage fighter. She claimed that all she wanted to do was follow the fight, and no matter how daring, or how heavily injured; that is exactly what she did. Her hatred for Starkorfs and Taskatae's beasts driving her to slaughter. Even though I disliked her remarks and attitude, and still didn't know what she was; I believed that there were many things in this world that could exist, and what she was, was something I didn't yet want to find out. As arrogant as it may have seemed, my instinct told me to trust her, to keep her close, that she was not an enemy. And the most powerful thing I had learnt in my journey so far, was to trust my instincts.

I had Ashley, who also had changed. After his father Seth had been killed by Nathanial, Lucas's brother, he barged into any battle. But now after his near death, it seemed that even he glowed with reconsideration.

Perhaps consideration for his mother, Helena who was in hiding with my mother, Suzumiya and Chris. After the ambush with the Starkorfs in the old warehouse near my home town Roperia, where Seth was killed they went into hiding. It was what led me to my first battle with Praytar, Lucas's father who was the first inhabitant of the Elder Tyran. It was the first time Misfeata had possessed me in such a way, where I then knew the power she contained when in possession of her Immortal Blades, Aeisha. If she were to have complete control of my body that day I would have been turned into a beast and my life in human form taken from me- my soul lost forever.

It was the infuriating pull she had when close to her brother, Tyran, that after centuries of fighting their hatred for one another could no longer be contained and they fought short sightedly trying to eliminate one another. And yet, after all these centuries had been unable to do so. The true way to destroy them which I had recently found out was to destroy the Elder's Immortal Blade, which have their souls intact. But still, it was something that no one knew how or is able to do.

In my search for my partnered blade, Aeisha after one of the sais were stolen from me by Taskatae's creatures I had come across Kurt to find that he were a traitor and one who worked alongside Nathanial, handing my parents over to him as gifts. When confronted by his treachery and fighting the Shielder, who was once my mentor and taught me to first use my ability, he gave me delusional words and theories.

One that my Uncle Kyle, that by fate alone I was reunited with as we both infiltrated the Elemental Breathers Annual Ball, so heavily believed in. They thought there was a way to exorcize Misfeata from me. There was an unfamiliar man named Christopher that had fed my Uncle these words, and in it, my Uncle believed in it whole heartedly. For Kurt it was in his belief that he could take that power and ruling for himself, to rebuild the Shielder's strength. But for what reason he convinced himself I didn't know, as already he had become a traitor to his own kind by aligning with the Starkorfs. But it was a belief he so strongly believed in when we talked, and one that placed me on the edge of my seat, as I knew somewhere out there he was trying to find such a solution and was searching for me. It was not Kurt himself I feared as I had already proven myself worthy of a victor in our fight, but the alliances he may have forged to chase after Paul and me.

There was mention of Sebastian's grave, the youngest Elder who vanished in flames with his lover, Carla, who was pregnant with his child. There was much uncertainty around his disappearance as an Elder cannot die unless their Immortal Blade was destroyed, but no one found the remains of his body nor blade, Sheliste. It is now only in recent days that few believed he may have not died and his blade could still be obtained at his grave. And yet no one had seen his grave nor was it actual fact that it existed.

This was only theory that Kurt and my Uncle Kyle believed in so strongly. My Uncle was trying to find a solution to give me back a normal life, and yet after looking at his tired face, ragged body and numerous scarring from fighting against Starkorfs all these years, he should know better than anyone that there is not a life for us that we could simply return to.

Since our fight with Taskatae and Nathanial, everyone now recovered. Uncle Kyle had attempted to approach the topic many times. But for now I just wanted to rest, at any time we could once again be ambushed.

It wasn't something I wanted to discuss. I thought I would be the first to jump into the direction that may dispel of Misfeata within me and yet I was hesitant to raise my hopes that it could truly happen. She had for so many times told me it was not possible.

Ashley walked back into the room surprising me as I had dazed into my own thoughts, he arched a questioning eyebrow at the embrace we had as Paul shuffled behind me to properly wake. He held himself up on one arm and looked over me with a small smile. I wasn't sure if I was still something he wanted as it was once an unrequited love. But for now I wanted Paul to embrace me, and my new acceptance put a smile on his face. No matter what darkness we had been through he could always see the brightness in it and smiled. And not to put pressure on myself, but it were as if I were his brightness right now. In words, I had not yet described to him that he was my savior. I reached out for him, it had always been my purpose to protect him, and he was my brightness at the end of every day.

"Karla, you really need to come out now," Ashley said. His blue eyes narrowed on me as I lifted myself from the bed. "Trish is here."

"What?!" Paul and I asked at the same time. Last I had heard of Trish she had been wondering around aimlessly. Scott was watching her carefully. What would force her to come here? She hated us, and we her.

"Why is she here?" I demanded. Trish hated me, disliked her brother, Scott with the distaste her father had fueled within her from a young age and hated humans mostly. She was always too flirtatious for my liking and irritated me purposefully, being the person who I first fought against when Misfeata first possessed my body and showed me the capability and strength that I had.

"Starkorfs swarmed Taskatae's castle. Trish had witnessed it, there's an army of them," he said heavily and slightly panicked as he stroked through his short black hair.

"Who leads them?" I asked already fearing the answer. Scott had spoken of this to me hours before. I thought I would have time to tell the others, before their movement would have been so quickly detected, and it was a surprise that Trish of all people reported it to us. She was probably unknowing that her brother, Scott was keeping an eye on her movement this whole time and already knew of the Starkorf army. They will search for us, we have just killed their second leader, Nathanial. Our time resting here was over, or it endangered the few humans who lived in the area. We had to yet again flee.

"It's Eden," Scott said flatly, coming in from behind Ashley, his pink eyes narrowed on me seriously.

Panic sickened my body as I realized it was not only me he would be after. I looked dauntingly to Paul's beautiful face who looked away so I could not see his expression. Paul was the one who weakened her, giving Max Jacket the opportunity to kill Taskatae. How much longer can Paul push through for my sake, why has he not left this ever ending battle, and left me behind?

20

"Karla we have to go," Ashley said gently. I flinched nervously under Paul's strong hands as he rubbed my shoulders and I looked into his moss green eyes, so tired that it was not yet over. He rubbed gently, his pink lips pulling into a flat smile.

"Everything will be okay," he calmly said. His four simple words drew a heavy weight into my stomach, swirling with anxiousness. It seemed as if Paul was waiting for this very day- The day that I would look to him for answers or reassurance instead of trying to fend for myself entirely.

Chapter Three- Unwelcome Visitor

We all met in Ashley's and Paige's room. Trish was standing near one of the wall paintings looking at it with disgust. I imagined that if she dared to dirty her black lace glove, she would attempt to wipe dust from it.

Scott was the last to walk in and kept obvious distance from his sister as he hid behind Paul. However not discretely with the difference in height between them because of his lankier and taller physique. Paul stood close to me on my right with his hands strapped over his chest. Ashley was on my left, his eyes so intense on Trish that even I might have been intimidated by such an unwelcome glare. Paige sat on the end of her bed, with one leg perched up casually as she flipped the small black dagger that was always strapped to her chest through the air and caught it. My uncle Kyle stood close to her and leant against the wall with arms crossed.

"Eden will be coming for you," Trish growled unfazed by the amount of unwelcome stares directed at her.

"We already know this," I spoke up seriously taking my leading role that was expected of me. It wasn't something I asked for, but it was something that eventuated because of the immortal within me, Misfeata. That and I was the very existence of an entire race. In my time of darkness I became emotionless and assumed the leader role, now being aware of that role, I wish I hadn't so quickly jumped into it. Every judgement and every decision I made had consequences which could endanger everyone's lives.

"Good, I don't care much for when you get killed, but I do want the location of Lucas," she announced daringly.

"What makes you think we have his location?" I hissed.

"Well you are lovers aren't you?" She clapped her hands together directing her attention to Paul. "Oh, that's right you're here to, hmm it's a shame your girlfriend gets around isn't it," she said spitefully. Paul took a threatening step forward but I placed my hand in front of him. I didn't like Trish and would happily fight her and force her to take her words back. But if I did it would only show that I felt defensive about the accusation. It is true I was confused by my feelings for Paul and Lucas, but I also knew this was how Trish would try to pull us a part.

"We don't know where he is. Why would you need to know?" I asked trying to keep my composure. Trish always made me angry and ready for a fight.

"Because it was his brother who killed my father. And as a proud Elemental Breather I will get my revenge on Nathanial's family," she said hastily, giving a sneering glance to Scott who cowered further into the background. Scott was one of the strongest Elemental Breathers I knew and yet the abuse he endured as a child had been his undoing and his weakness.

"Do as you want, we don't care," Ashley spoke up, reopening the door. "But you aren't welcome here. You have wasted our time and we don't care for your stench."

"How dare you speak to me like that. You do realize what I am. . ." Trish's snarl was cut off as Paige's hand wavered and her blade flickered towards Trish. The blade burst into flames as it glided in front of Trish's face and made a small thunking noise as it impaled the wall. Paige wasn't aiming for Trish's face. But the smile on her face said the warning was still there. Trish's eyes frenzied black as her pupils were swallowed.

"Damn it Paige, we aren't trying to burn the place down with us in it," Ashley growled. He grabbed the vase of flowers beside him on the side bench and threw the water over the flames that almost began to torch the wall.

"You're still too polite," Paige smiled. It was a menacing look but one that wasn't effective. Trish who was infuriated and for some reason tried to control her angst, scrunched up her dress.

"Like I needed your aid that much anyway. I will find him and send his head to you in a box. I can't wait to make him scream," Trish said directly to me with a grotesque smile.

She barged between Paul and me, her head held high as she summarized another filthy glance over the room. Before she had even left Paige had pulled out her backpack and started throwing odd bits and pieces into the bag.

She had already started to pack. Without words we all knew we had to. We weren't safe here. We would be tracked down and have to go back into hiding. We couldn't stay in public places like this in case the humans were involved.

"No one is obliged to follow," I said breaking the silence. "Eden is after me, he has a grudge against me. I don't want all of you fighting and risking your lives for my sake."

Ashley scoffed and reshuffled up against the pale yellow window frame close to where Paige's weapon was still embedded. He crossed his arms over his chest casually as he leant against the frame. He shifted the curtain to watch Trish's external leave. "We all fought that day Karlz, not just you. We stick together."

"Agreed," said Paul. Ashley and he exchanged and odd glance, it was one of respect. Something Ashley had never given him before. He had always considered him to be a nuisance. My heart churned with both anticipation and anxiety that Paul had been accepted. I was both happy and sad to know his existence was accepted in this world.

"Where do we go from here?" Uncle Kyle interrupted. He looked as fierce as any experienced warrior with the cuts and hardship on his face and skin. Scott offered to heal them but he said he would rather the human way. A very surreal thing to ask for, and one I hadn't experienced for some time now that my body instantly healed itself. I had much respect for Uncle Kyle, although the oldest here well comparatively, I wasn't exactly sure how old Scott was since he was an Elemental Breather and they far outweighed human years- he still treated us equally. Any stranger that looked at us from afar would notice that most of our group still looked to be in our teens. That odd moment passed through me as I searched for the small calendar I had seen as I walked in and summarized the room. I walked over to it and collected it looking at the current date.

How small it seemed, but within three weeks it was soon to be my eighteenth birthday. So much had changed since then. Everyone exchanged an odd expression as to why I was picking up the calendar. I set it back down locking contact with Uncle Kyle. He had a knowing expression on his face.

"Perhaps we should venture back to your organization?" Scott prodded at Ashley. Ashley gave him a quick assessment. The subject of where the others now hid was still very secret. That safety also held my mother in it. Even I didn't want to expose it.

"No not yet," I interjected before Ashley could. It seemed as if he were about to say the same. "We can't lead an army to their front door. They don't have the manpower."

"There is only Suzumiya and Chris left. Both of our mothers need that protection. We can't cut corners on that," Ashley said with hands still strapped across his chest. Ashley and I exchanged a nod. I wanted to see my mother more than anything right now but I couldn't risk it.

"So we just head out and do what we have always done," Paige interrupted carefree and threw her bag over her shoulder. "Let's just move on and make decisions on the road. It's not like we have much of a plan or destination right now. So we will just go with it."

"We do have a goal," Uncle Kyle retorted sharply. "Karla, we should find more information about Sebastian's grave. If we have nothing else to do, surely we can put time and effort into that. I've been trying to research for years now-"

"Come on Grandpappy," Paige mused. "Fairy-tales are for children, we fight creatures that drain and kill humans. Don't be disturbed with such magical ways to wipe that off. We need to move out."

"It's not a fairy-tale. If it's possible then shouldn't we try Karla?" Uncle Kyle scoffed at Paige's insolence the first time his more adult role to a young adolescence took effect.

"Say theoretically it is true," Paul said placing his hand lightly on my back. His touch shot a touch of warmth through me. It almost felt hopeful, but I didn't want to delude myself. To find a cure to rid of Misfeata- I didn't want to believe in such a thing in case I were disappointed. But still imagining a lifetime with her trapped inside my body seemed torturous. "Won't that leave Karla vulnerable? Say she turned back into human. Who would protect her?"

I went to argue that I could look after myself, and then closed my mouth as I realized his point.

"It's fine that we try to find this Elder's grave and all, but the problem will still be chasing us," Paul continued. "While Eden is still in ruling he will seek Karla out for a lifetime."

"You're so hot," Scott said with a promiscuous smile. "I agree with the old man, I think we should look into it, see what we can find. I am intrigued by this mysterious and shadowy figure called 'Christopher' that you're Uncle has been in contact with. He will be a great source of information." The thought of that evidently made Scott gleeful, he was after all an Elemental Breather and knowledge of the unknown was everything to them in power.

"Or just a free loving hippie," Paige scoffed with hindrance.

"Right now we just need to leave," Ashley said. Paige flicked herself off the bed and came to Ashley's side. It was odd how the two seemed rightful standing beside one another, as if they had always been comrades. I was still unsure of Paige's presence and who or exactly what she was after the warning Scott gave me. But there was a comforting feeling to have her there.

"In the Starkorf world wouldn't the politics change with ruler?" Uncle Kyle countered.

"In what way?" Ashley asked.

"Well, Eden currently has a large army following him, but they are the followers from Praytar's reign aren't they? Only a few took their loyal place behind Nathanial, he wasn't exactly deemed as their strongest leader. But isn't Lucas like their last prince or heir or something? What if he claims back that control of the army? Won't that protect us if we can come to an agreement and pardon?"

"We're not relying on Lucas to protect her," Paul said zealously. I was saddened that Lucas was now seen as a pawn in a means to protect me. The words I wanted to say died on my lips. *Besides we couldn't coexist close to one another now. Not now while Tyran resides within him. The elders within us would undoubtedly try to destroy one another.*

Everyone's opinions of him had stayed the same. Only mine had changed. I had hated him so much because of his betrayal and yet my feelings still wavered for him. Ashley had known him for almost his entire life and loved him as a brother, yet his hatred ran deep and never wavered. Why had only mine changed? Lucas was the enemy. So why did I so often have to remind myself of that?

"Right now we just need to leave. We need more weapons," Ashley pointed out. "That should be our main focus."

"Can't you just go back to your little groupie thing and get some yourself and meet us somewhere?" Paige suggested.

"It's too risky, even if I go by myself in case someone is following me. Although," Ashley paused. "I do want to report on how they are doing, after everything that's happened. I want to make sure that they are still okay. I worry about how restless Chris and Suzumiya are becoming being on babysitting duty."

"Call them now," I said also desperate for an update about my mother. "You're right but we can't risk their location." Ashley nodded and pulled the phone out of his pocket. He left the room within seconds, desperate to hear the tone of his own mother's voice.

"Now can we please hurry up? I'm getting bored standing around and waiting for you guys," Paige huffed. She reefed her small black blade from the wall and placed it back in the sheath strapped to her chest. Everyone dismissed and began to pack only the few things that had been taken out from their backpacks. We were always ready to grab and run if required. This was the way we now lived, only able to take one day at a time.

Chapter Four- The Travelers

$\mathcal{T}$he sundown arrayed an odd orange across the small town that we had stayed at for a few nights. I adjusted my backpack over one shoulder letting Paul know that I could carry it myself. Aeisha, my two sai blades were concealed beneath my leather jacket. The office clerk had given us an odd look as we paid and left. We were a mismatched group and even our clothing made us look like we were part of some bad gang. It was very different to only months ago when I was serving coffee at my part time job and studying.

We began driving with no real destination. All we knew was that we had to keep moving and put as much distance between Eden's group and ourselves. Ashley drove with Uncle Kyle in the passenger seat. I sat between Paige and Paul awkwardly. Paige's bubble-gum popping would've had me irate if I weren't half delirious from sleep. Scott sat on my lap contently in the small form of a kitten. Although awkward to know that it was Scott, a living person I knew, I still couldn't resist the urge to stroke my hand through the orange fluffy fur. He didn't seem to mind and I thought back to all those times I had done the same to him in wolf form at Max Jacket's home.

We drove for hours and left civilization far behind. My eyelids grew heavy and I found myself almost falling asleep numerous times. The small ginger kitten pawed my stomach. I looked down into Scott's pink eyes. I smiled warily, not even having to hear him say it. I was grateful to know I could sleep and he would keep Misfeata away. And so within minutes, with the low hum of the car and splashes of cold air from Pauls open window hitting my face I fell asleep. My head slowly but comfortably leaning on his shoulder as I drifted.

My head hit the back of the seat as my eyes sprang to life. Already I had Aeisha out and ready to fight at the sudden awakening. My eyes took a moment to adjust, alert but taking in what I saw. Ashley had slammed the breaks. Many people in hoods and leathered jackets surrounded the car on the pothole broken road. We all sat in the car silently taking in the numbers that stretched further and hid amongst the trees.

"Don't attack!" Uncle Kyle yelled at us before any of us jumped out of the car ready to fight. Their numbers were vast but we would still do our best to get through them. I questioned how Eden had found us so quickly. But as my keen sight focused on the warriors faces, I couldn't see any form of physical mutation. Unless these were all of higher class Starkorfs and hadn't yet mutated, I didn't register them to be Starkorfs at all. All of them had weapons strapped to their bodies, but none had them unsheathed, none of them seemed to be in a threatening manner. They simply circled us and gave us nowhere to run or escape, unless through them.

Some crouched on high branches of trees and watched us. At the center of the circle a woman approached a few steps towards us.

"Don't attack," Uncle Kyle repeated. He opened his door and stepped out, silencing me as I yelled out after him. I growled at his response, opening the hole in the roof and reefing myself out in one swift movement.

"Stay," I ordered the others. Uncle Kyle hadn't strayed that far. I crouched on the roof assessing their numbers. All of them now looked at me inattentively. I still clutched at Aeisha prepared for the fight that might come. The chilled air howled in the night as the glow of the moon streaked shadows over the road and made their ominous numbers seem to only grow.

The woman who had approached us with short blonde hair, who I assumed to be their leader watched me intensely. She summarized my poise, my figure and her stare rested on Aeisha. My fingers lightly danced on the handle of them possessively.

"It's been some time now Christopher," my Uncle Kyle announced loud enough to reach her ears. The woman looked as if she had never known how to smile. Her age verging on the same of my Uncle's yet with the same lean muscle that identified her as a fighter. I assessed her leather attire and red jacket. She had two sword sheaths on her back, buckled leather boots and a pixie hair cut that looked like it hadn't been nor needed to be washed.

Christopher. . . The name registered familiar to me. Was this the informant that had spoiled my uncle's mind about Sebastian's grave? I had assumed it to be a man.

"It appears you have many friends," Uncle Kyle said, educating me that he hadn't known his informant was part of such a large group.

I rose from my crouched position, no longer feeling as threatened or on guard. I was still cautious however, because even though I had told everyone to stay in the car they had flooded out as soon as I had reefed myself onto the roof.

"Who are you?" I asked, wary of the distance between them and us.

Christopher's lips twitched, if I had known better I would have thought she attempted some sort of welcoming gesture, a smile.

"My name is Christopher Ellaine. I am like you, child. I am a Shielder. We all are." Her tone was firm, even harsh with a distinguished German accent. Ashley and I expressed a surprised glare before summarizing their numbers again. I had never seen so many Shielder's before. I had never met any out of the institution. "And you are the descendant of Misfeata." Her words reached all of their ears as they stared at me intently, yet somehow I had the impression they already knew. Silently they all dropped to their knees in a wave around me. I circled on the roof watching their knees hit the ground. Their sign of loyalty to me, who they had never met. I looked back to Christopher who was last to drop to her knees. "We've been waiting for you."

The silence pounded against me like a silent wave. I had never experienced such a wave of devotion in any form. I didn't recognize any of them and wasn't sure of their purpose in meeting me. My only assumption and worst fear would be that because of Misfeata's blood that resided in me, they thought of me as some kind of leader.

"Please stand up," I stuttered uncomfortably.

"We are here at your disposal, we need your power. You as the descendant of Misfeata must be a part of our path so we can overthrow the Starkorfs numbers," Christopher said simply. She stood, staring at me evenly. But the rest stayed with their gazes kept to the ground. I knew they were still listening intently.

"I am not looking to be a part of the greater war," I said. "If anything right now I am of more danger to you all, your association with me will get you killed."

A cruel smirk rested on Christophers face. "Don't insult us child. I have respect for the power you have residing within you, but don't forget we are warriors who have been fighting for generations. You simply have a power that we must follow and need."

Her remark insinuated very quickly to me that although she wanted the strength of Misfeata, she evidently didn't like the idea of her power being threatened. Not that I wanted to threaten her title. But right now she made that evidently clear.

"You sought me out," I responded quickly, indifferently. A woman not far behind Christopher stood. She was very beautiful with long curly hair bound into one ponytail. It was then, as she rested her hand on her stomach I realized she was heavily pregnant.

"What my mother means to say is that we need your help. Our numbers have been dropping. We need your aid Misfeata."

"She is not her!" Ashley said coldly. The woman didn't flinch but gave him a generous smile. Christopher and her held similar features but their friendly manner was very different.

"Apologies, Karla. We require your support. We have travelled overseas to find you. We have been in search of you for some time now. We had long thought Misfeata died with Elisabeth's fall. She had fought alongside us for a long time helping us battle. She was a true warrior. With as much respect as we offered her, we require your strength."

"I apologize for my daughter, Jennifer. Sometimes she doesn't know her place," Christopher hissed defiantly.

"She can say whatever she wants," Paul said quickly. At that I gave him an approving look. I didn't believe in this aristocrat stuff.

"All of you can stand and speak," I said welcomingly. A few shuffled uncomfortably before they slowly, one by one stood unsure. I could tell by Christopher's reaction that she wasn't too happy that they went out of order with what I presumed to be her command.

"Even if they wanted to speak with you. Not all of them could. Unless you knew eight different languages," Christopher vexed. "Not all are English speaking. We have been collected over generations all around the world."

I looked at all the faces, sizes and orientations- she was right.

"How had we not known of this large group previously?" Ashley asked still looking at their numbers. There were even children. They stood by themselves, as equals amongst the adults. That terrified me.

"There are many groups around the world. Surely you didn't think you were the only institution. We simply travel. Kurt however knew of us. It just seems either you were ignorant to it, or he didn't want you to know, Ashley," Christopher added his name adding to the insecure knowledge that she knew more about us then we knew of them. "Martin."

A man of lanky build and dark tan stood forward. I squinted at his beautiful features and well-dressed attire. He wasn't a Shielder, he was an Elemental Breather. I gave Scott who now stood beside me a wavering look. He too seemed very interested in the Elemental Breather who stood beside them. It was uncommon but it was much like Scott who had joined our party.

"Ashley, son of Helena and Seth, a part of Kurt's institution- who has since fled and betrayed to source his own sense of power. Although a Shielder, no shielding ability apparent. Current survival rate within the year: fifty-five percent. Seth since deceased-"

"He was murdered!" Ashley spat offended. It was the darkest of his secrets said out loud in such an unconcerned monotone that I was worried Ashley would jump at him then and there. But Martin seemed unfazed as he continued searching amongst our group.

"Paul Stuart, an average teenage boy who specializes in the sport of boxing. Survival rate amongst his party in this war: twenty-three percent."

"What are you some analyze guy," Paul spat. "Your facts are a joke." Martin again continued unfazed.

"Paige, an unknown warrior, who isn't human-"

"Gahhh you annoy me!" Paige unsheathed her weapon from her chest and ran for the Elemental Breather. Instantly we all regrouped behind her having one another's back; although she jumped out of line and as hot headed as ever. We always had one another's back.

Five Shielder's surrounded her and she seemed trapped by what I sensed to be their shields. Others surrounded us. They too had unsheathed their blades but I could tell they were flickering back between Christopher and us unsure whether a command would be given.

"Get away from her!" Ashley ran for her and I quickly followed. A lot of these Shielder's had the ability, I was the only one who could counter it. Before Ashley defiantly went against their shield I jumped amidst them beside Paige who effortlessly slashed at their shields. As soon as my toes touched Paige's shoulders and weighed her down I pulsated my shield out, making sure not to hurt her in the process. A small pewww noise clattered amongst the shields as the Shielders were shoved back in surprise, shattering their shields.

Ashley was already on them. Although I didn't think he would kill any of his kind, I had to state it clearly. "Don't kill them!" Ashley took a wide swing at one of them and knocked them to the ground. He wrestled another one to the ground before they had projected their shield.

"Stand down!" Jennifer yelled. It was the echo of her mother's words. They all cautiously shuffled. Even the one who Ashley had tackled to the ground and was now wrestling with the man whose face he had punched. I held firmly onto Paige's shoulder, grounding her towards me so she couldn't lunge again.

"Hot headed I see," Christopher mused with her hands behind her back as she approached us.

"Your Elemental Breather obviously struggles making friends," I hissed looking at him again. Even the way he looked and his demeanor presented with acute awareness and total analyst. He watched our every movement as if noting it.

"Do any of them," she asked arching an eyebrow towards Scott. "Martin has predicted the outcome of many of our battles, his companionship for the past two years has aided us greatly."

"Mother, we need to move out," Jennifer said. Besides the large pregnant belly she still moved with poise of a warrior.

"Karla, please," Christopher said. "We have much to discuss and plus we can help protect your friends. Perhaps even send resources to better protect your mother. From what I hear you have a powerful enemy searching for you. We've already killed a few of his scouts. Its how we were able to locate you."

"What do you mean by that?" I asked worried that Eden had already located us.

"It's exactly as I insinuate. We tortured his scouts before we killed them. They had a rough idea and area of your location. They are also in search of their prince, Lucas. But I am sure you already know all about him."

She left the silence to filter the air. One by one she looked at those in our group as if evaluating us all. We need you and I can guarantee you certain protection for a larger amount of warriors than only yourselves. This is the place you are meant to be, you are meant to lead by my side."

I didn't like that assumption and one thought came to mind.

"You knew of the institution I was founded by and trained at; Kurt's group. Why did you never come and announce yourself then?"

"Because you're an asset, although deemed as the ultimate leader you are but a child. You're a source of power and Shielders will follow you anywhere. You are much a ghost as you are a legend. Back then you were owned by Kurt."

I let those words linger in sheer agitation.

"I won't be owned by anyone," I hissed thinking of Misfeata in particular.

"No you won't. You were a child then, you seem more of a woman now. A woman who can see as my equal, that right now gathering in numbers is the safest thing to do to protect those you love."

I wavered another look over my group, with my mother in particular in mind.

"We start with just a talk, that's all I can guarantee for now." I sheathed Aeisha and the others followed suit as did the rest of the Shielders around us. Everyone exchanged uncertain expressions. They began to slowly walk into the shadows of the trees and retreat to where they had come from.

"Come," Jennifer said. She now stood beside her mother, her hand rested on her stomach. Now that she was closer, I noted that her face looked gaunt and drawn. Even her hands looked as if they withered. "We camped not far from here."

"I can lead you if you still wish to drive your vehicle," Martin interrupted as he walked up casually. His pace was still elegant and stiff. He and Scott exchanged a very interested glance before Martin focused on me once again. "The drive will only be twenty-eight minutes from here."

Jennifer and Christopher began to walk towards the trees as if it had already been agreed upon.

"Wait, how do you all get there?" Ashley asked as curious as I was. I was worried about the tension that Martin and Scott held between one another for some reason or another. They simply stood there and stared at one another in an analytical way. Scott broke him a very charming smirk, certainly uncharacteristic to his charming and flamboyant self. Martin returned a more timid smile, one which matched his nature. Neither spoke, only watched.

Christopher turned around before her back had completely merged within the darkness of the night. Jennifer had already vanished.

"We are Shielder's of the purest kind. We like to run," she simply said. Within seconds her outline had completely vanished and I stood there memorizing their numbers and emanated strength. Perhaps the institution wasn't all there was to learn about my kind and their strength.

Chapter Five- To Be Found

$\mathcal{M}$artin continued to look at his watch as if calculating the time and making sure that it matched the predicted twenty something minutes he mentioned. Scott didn't change back into his kitten form. Instead they all piled uncomfortably in the car. Paul and I sat on the rooftop, our legs anchoring us through the hole in the roof. It seemed rebellious almost to be doing it. The wind in our hair sent a wild flare through us. Being a normal High School student I would have never done something so illegal like this. And yet it seemed like the smallest thing in the world now. This place and creatures had no law or rules. It was something so parallel to the human world, that it seemed incomprehensible unless I had already been living it.

Paul rested his hand over mine. The warmth of his touch seeming to spread over my entire skin against the cold chill of the wind. I rationed with the thoughts and Martins' analysis of Paul's survival rate only being twenty-three percent. That number continued to circle my mind. Such a low percentage. As if knowing where my thoughts lay, he rubbed my thumb lightly and gave me a cheesy smile. It was pointless to even attempt to talk with so much wind cascading over us.

We hit a bump and I jolted uncomfortably. Already Paul's hands were around my shoulders anchoring me firmer to the roof to make sure I wouldn't fall. I gave a small smile. Although I seemed in the eyes to everyone else here, the most powerful, Paul still protected me because he saw me as only Karla. An identity I had been fighting with and justifying over and over again, before I begin to lose myself. I didn't want to end up like Elisabeth and I didn't want to be consumed by Misfeata.

Paul returned my smile and attempted to push back a part of my cascading hair that flew into my eyes. I held his hand comfortably on my face, allowing the warmth to cup my cheek. I closed my eyes simply wanting to memorize this moment for eternity. My heart raced at his proximity and yet it felt like it was a place he would always be at, by my side.

The vehicle slowly halted and I was instinctively on alert, our small moment broken. Paul was also on alert and as soon as the car stopped he had jumped over the roof and onto the rocky ground.

There were many tents set up and I could hear in the distance running water. The cooler chill in the air indicated that they were close to a river. Trees surrounded for good coverage and concealed the open flames which kept them warm. Many Shielder's hovered around the tent openings and around the fires. With our approach, they all stood. All of them with poised with weapons and ready to fight.

A younger man approached us. He looked to be in his mid-twenties with short black hair and tan skin. He gestured for the others behind him to stand down. I didn't recognize any of their faces. They hadn't been part of the group which first confronted us. It was obvious that with his command their resolve turned more into curiosity then defensive.

"Then I assume the talk went well. Christopher and the others shouldn't be too far away," the newcomer said with a welcoming smile. "My name is Elijah. I am the third in command here. Following shortly after the beautiful Jennifer."

As he said her name his tone showed vulnerable fondness. I questioned if he and Jennifer were more than just comrades with her pregnant belly to show.

"We have the finer detail to discuss. Like figuring out what the hell you guys want with us," Ashley said. Elijah walked up to him gesturing a handshake. After much hesitation Ashley took it.

"It is nice to meet you brother," Elijah said with firmness. "Although different institutes I hope we can still get along. Times are changing, perhaps we can merge."

"Your leader makes it pretty damn clear she doesn't want to share the throne," Paige scoffed with her hands strapped across her chest. My uncle surveyed the conversation as I did. The other Shielders behind him whispered to one another. There were a few more children, younger this time. Some were still babies.

Elijah gave out a short laugh. "Yes, well Christopher can come off very headstrong but she always means well by her people. If it weren't for her, most of us would be dead."

"To that I can vouch," Martin said bypassing Elijah and walking towards the others. Ashley and Elijah continued to talk about their own institutes and the many questions Ashley had about their own travelling organization. My attention was focused on Martin and how he moved amongst the Shielders. Most seemed disgusted by his presence. I focused my hearing on him, where I could faintly hear him from the distance. He opened his hands to one of the mothers and grabbed the baby she was cradling. It was unsettling to see an Elemental Breather hold a child. There was no maternal or compassionate atmosphere to his stiff hold on the baby.

"Still no change, even after your own dietary intake," Martin said to the mother. "It may be a permanent defect. I have no further suggestions or variants you can try. This may not be curable," he said coldly to the mother. Although she looked as if she were to cry, her face held strong as she cradled the baby back.

"Please don't tell Christopher," she whispered. "Give me a little more time. Time might be the only variant we need."

"Those are your politics, not mine," Martin said unaffected. "But unless she asks me directly, I will avoid executing the truth for my own curiosity. We will see if time is actually a factor."

He walked into one of the tents, which stood out amongst the others. There was finery in the material and the flaps of it instantly closed behind, concealing the light that now flickered on from within. His tent was on the edge of the camp, apart from the rest. In this environment I could tell that for both he and the Shielder's it seemed as if it weren't enough space. I was curious as to how Martin ended up within this group of Shielder's that so evidently didn't want him here. It wasn't like our kind to mix often.

"Damn Elemental Breather," one of the women hissed to the man beside her. Scott wavered a friendly smile also hearing the comment. He was slightly taller than Martin and not as withered looking in comparison to the Elemental Breather's I had seen.

Scott walked straight up to them invading the woman's personal space.

"You know," he smiled ravishingly, looking back at the tent Martin had walked into. "Not all of us are as stiff and well, some of us are very magnificent." Scott gestured himself. He was playing with the comment, being far too gleeful. I could tell behind his usual flamboyant and carefree smile he was gesturing a point. The woman and man both looked at each other unsettled. "Do you know I can turn into a dragon and kill everyone here?" He said with another smile. He never actually had turned into one, but he once said it never hurt to try. At the threat everyone around him unsheathed their weapons.

Scott only smiled wider. "If you want to be a savage," he growled. "Then you will be treated like one."

"We hate your kind," the woman snarled back.

"And you are but a mere female Starkorf in the world of far too many luxuries if you feel as if you can speak to me or any other Elemental Breather like that," Scott said no longer smiling. His long face was hauntingly serious. Elijah continued to flash me and Ashley uncertain glances. Paige's gum popped forcing everyone to flinch. She smiled by the reaction.

"I've been aiding the descendant of Misfeata," Scott continued. "While you and your circus cart around the world. And the issue you find here is one Elemental Breather. My, my, my, now I know where all your time went. Be visual if nothing else. Go and do a guard duty or something and make yourself useful." Scott wavered them off and walked back to us. With every ounce of control they didn't attack. Elijah stared them down warily.

Scott came to my side. I expected a half smile or a wild cackle from him to break the tension. But it didn't happen.

"I thought Elemental Breathers had no loyalty to their kind?" I asked curious. I had to give the Shielder's here credit. They had far more control and order than my makeshift group who said or did as they pleased.

"We don't," he simply said. He elongated his neck to look more superior. I wanted to ask why he defended Martin, but with his closed off demeanor and arms across his chest I decided not to. I only arched an eyebrow and continued to pay my attentions to Elijah who was still watching his own people warily.

"If you could please refrain yourselves from causing tension amongst the group," Elijah asked kindly.

"You invited us here. We didn't want to come," Paige said and burst another bubble. Elijah showed restraint and hesitated to say what I thought first came to his mind. Although kind to us now I could detect he was a powerful Shielder and one who would be a fierce opponent.

It was an interesting side effect to now have. To be able to detect in other Shielders if they had the ability or not. Some were just natural and strong fighters like Ashley.

Elijah went to say something but caught himself mid-sentence as others emerged from the trees. Those who had once circled us crept out from the darkness, sweaty from their run. I hadn't expected them back so soon. Some joined in a warm manner, even giving hugs in a compassionate manner. As Christopher had said before as they rejoiced some spoke to one another in foreign languages.

Slowly Christopher and her daughter, Jennifer shortly arrived afterwards panting. Elijah hesitated to stay where he stood. His eyes focused on Jennifer as she smiled at one of the women who rested their hand on her belly.

"I thought pregnant women weren't meant to run and stuff," Paul said in a hushed tone beside me. I gave him a chastised look for his snide comment. Softening it as I realized he had meant no offence. I had to admit it was odd to see the physical exertion she was putting herself under, especially while pregnant.

"Good you came," Christopher said, less formally now. "Come inside, sit down. We can talk over tea," she said gesturing to the biggest tent in the middle. A woman placed a kettle on the fire nearby. The Shielders still watched us cautiously as we followed Christopher, Jennifer and Elijah into the tent.

There wasn't much inside, despite its exterior size. All that was in there was a swag, a few logs for seating and drawings which had been carved into the dry dirt. Sitting down on a log between Ashley and Paul, I noted that it looked like tactics and positioning. Christopher sat across from us. I could feel her intently studying me as I formulated in my mind what she had written down. By the looks of it, it was an ambush of sorts. It surprised even me to now know that I had a 'knack' for this thing.

The others took seats on the two side logs. All of us waited for Christopher to speak.

"It's an ambush we will be executing in the next few days," she started, entertaining my obvious attention. Paul and Ashley also had begun studying it and Ashley looked up at her pointing to a certain section of the plan.

"Why do you have so few here?" He asked.

"Because we want that to look like our weakest point for the bait. That way we can circle them. They will target that section of our group and we will hide a larger team in the nearby area when they fall for the trap."

"Isn't that a bit risky for those who have to persevere as the bait until the backup comes?" Paul asked.

"Yes and no. Only my finest warriors will be alongside me on the frontline. I would love to have you there too Karla. I would love to see what you are capable of," she said.

I whipped my head up from the sketching and looked at her.

"This is why you called upon me?" I asked agitated. Her expression did not change from the hard exterior she always held. Much like Martin it was as if she were studying my every move.

"No. Although we found a few traces of Starkorfs within this area, there looks to be a larger group, not just a few strays. While we are in the area we will simply rid of them as we always do. I have scouts on the lookout for them. They circle a similar pattern, so we are waiting for them to cross over again on here. When that time comes we will intersect them."

"Wait I have a question," Paul voiced. "How the hell are these things hunting people and never get questioned by humans who don't know anything about their race or species or whatever?"

Christopher darted me an angered look as if the question had insulted her. The look insinuated that Paul was uneducated amongst all of this. But it was something I too had pondered over a few times, but never had the chance to ask.

"Because," Ashley said with his hands crossed over his chest. "The dead can't speak. If Starkorfs are hunting humans then they don't survive. They usually drag off their bodies somewhere. Most are still with it enough to know to rid the body somewhere. If not a body or missing person report goes here and there. Disappearances happen all the time."

"What about the whole towns?" Paul interjected. "I've heard stories where they've taken down towns." My uncle shuffled uncomfortably at this. Paul shifted slightly understanding his implication. My Uncle's town had been wiped out, his wife murdered and the transition of Misfeata running through my veins instead of Elisabeth's began.

"You survived," Christopher said to my uncle. "Although still human. You survived despite your small township being killed. You decided to fight. Why don't you tell the young human boy why."

Uncle Kyle seemed uncomfortable by the sudden attention on him. Paul grunted with the disapproval of being called a young human boy. I too was interested in Uncle Kyle's response. I knew he hated Starkorfs because of what had happened to his wife. He wanted to 'fix' me, but I questioned if there was any other motive.

"I had tried to tell people," Uncle Kyle began with a depleted expression. "And I almost landed myself a one way ticket to looneyville in a white jacket. No one believed me. Even when I sought out answers myself, it wasn't years until I began finding them. By then I was very much on my own. People won't believe what they don't know or can't see. Sometimes the truth is scarier and people naturally are protected by ignorance. In all my time and at the very start of telling people about this world, not one person believed me. I eventually just gave up. This world for humans like us, is something foreign. Only those who dedicate their lives to it can see it. For others who are either Shielders or Starkorfs, it will always find them."

Uncle Kyle and I exchanged a long knowing look. I had been seventeen when this world had finally crept up on me. My simple bump of the shoulder with Lucas was what had triggered my world into chaos. Now the realty of that one day and encounter dictated my very fate.

"We find Shielders all over the world at different ages some unsure of their identity or how to control it. We've saved some from self-imploding. There is nothing worse for some than having an ability that they hide from the world. What makes it harder for them to understand is Shield's aren't visible. It's like having a gift you can't see. You just know it's' there."

"Karla's is visible," Paige said as she popped another bubble. She was hunched over her knees in a casual manner, leaning into the conversation unfazed.

"I have heard and that is something I would very much like to see sometime soon," Christopher said.

"So all your Shielders can Shield?" Ashley deterred her fascination with me.

"No some are like you. Simply excel as fighters, speed and stamina. We collect those as well. But most we seek out are able to Shield. We've been gathering all these members half my lifetime now, waiting for you," Christopher said to me. She hunched over her knees as Paige did. Her hands clasped together.

"Why?" I asked. Everyone had something to gain from me. They only wanted the creature that swarmed within me; the woman who was trapped in my body.

"Because we need to destroy the Starkorfs and we can only do that with you. We can only do that with Misfeata's overpowering strength."

"What about the extract of the elder, like we had spoken about?" Uncle Kyle voiced his concern.

41

"We are still looking in to that," Elijah said sharply. "But yes we think it is possible if we can find Sebastians grave and have Misfeata and Tyran in the same room as well."

Paige began to laugh. I flinched under her harsh tone. For Misfeata and Tyran to be in the same room, it meant that Lucas and I would have to be there too.

"There is no way you will be able to get Misfeata and Tyran anywhere near one another let alone in the same room without them trying to destroy one another," Paige said as she wiped away a tear of amusement. "For someone who scribbles tactics in dirt you surely are making a miscalculation on this one."

"Don't be so insolent," Christopher hissed. "We offer you an option. Something other descendants have never had. Not that any of them received their role in an ungrateful manner such as yourself."

"And let me guess," Scott deployed. "You want Misfeata's power all to yourself. You want that strength within you."

Christopher didn't deny it. Instead she looked at me evenly.

"I have been leading my people for almost twenty years now. I more than yourself stick to the code and old ways. I have dedicated my whole life to this war. You are but a teenager, this isn't something you want. You see it as a burden, a curse. If I can offer you freedom from that then is it not something you should consider?"

Everyone grew silent in the tent, waiting for my response. I choked on my words. To be rid of Misfeata, it's all I ever wanted and yet. . . "It's just a dream. It's not real. Even Misfeata doesn't believe it and I think if she had the choice to jump into a fitter host she would within seconds."

"For once we agree, child," Misfeata said to me, stirring within my stomach and creating a nauseous sensation. It put me on edge to know she could hear every conversation I had. That although I thought she was dormant she still fluttered with thoughts and consciousness. There was no real indication of where she was and when she might attempt to possess my body.

"Then she will be pleased when I find her a way," Christopher said with a smile.

The lady from outside who put the kettle over the fire walked in with a tray full of small mugs. Some had corners chipped on the edges. She swarmed the circle offering them to us. I took the hot cup, relishing its warmth. I took a sip of the bitter tasting tea regretting it as soon as I had. Christopher gulped hers down within seconds and put the empty cup beside her foot.

"Karla, what I really need you for is to both be the bait, but also we can offer you protection. You are the most prized possession amongst our people right now. We won't allow harm to come to you. But we also need you to bait our enemy. I've heard through sources that his pure focus is only on finding you."

"You are talking about Eden," I said, resting my own cup on the ground. Christopher frowned. She seemed almost surprised by this.

"No, I was talking about the last descendant of Tyran- Lucas," she said. My heart stopped and a cold chill swept over me at the mention of his name.

"Eden," Christopher hummed over the name in thought.

"He is the second in command is he not?" Jennifer added.

"But since the death of Tyran has been supported by a lot of the followers, his numbers are great," Elijah added as they factually spoke to Christopher.

"Two birds with one stone," Christopher simply hummed. Already I could see that her mind was processing thoughts and tactics. In that moment I couldn't think of any plan or response. Because only one thing settled in my mind. I didn't want to question it because I didn't want to voice the opinion out loud, where everyone would ridicule my thoughts.

Lucas is looking for me?

Chapter Six- Secrets

*N*oises hummed around me faintly as I lie ragged on the
uncomfortable ground. We agreed to set up camp nearby Christopher's
group. We still kept our distance and Paige stayed outside on watch. We
could never be too cautious. Although they were Shielders, we had met
far too many traitors before.

I stared at the roofing of the tent with sleep deprived and dry
eyes. I wished that I could see the stars through the material. It was a
cool night and the sleeveless shirt I wore seemed to feel invisible. The
chill went straight to my bones. It was pleasant but it felt frightfully
human. It was Uncle Kyle who laid restlessly beside me. The others
shared their own tent. Paige was to soon rest in here as her and Ashley
swapped over shifts. Our tents were always crowded yet we had
become accustom to one another.

I stared at my Uncle who was part of the reason we were here.
His face was rough and tired. I wondered what he looked like before he
immersed himself into this world. I imagined he could've been very
handsome. The pain and unhappiness was evident in each painful
looking crevasse and scar. It was as if I was looking at a reflection of
myself. Would this be my future? Was this the expected unhappiness I
would live?

Or would I be forced into an unnatural existence in the world
where I was forced to drain human life like Misfeata had done to
Elisabeth? Such a contradiction considering the very creatures she
hated she used the same ability as them. I felt a pang in my mind, like a
forceful shutter of consciousness. It was Misfeata, offended by my
thoughts.

I shot up into a sitting position unable to stay in the tent that
now made me feel claustrophobic. I grabbed my leather jacket and
rolled the thin blanket off my jeans. I walked outside. Paige gave me a
wavering look but continued to stare out into the sky bored. She was
leaning up against a tree with hands crossed over her chest.

I felt a faint presence around us and touched my hand to the ground absorbing its information. It was a presence I knew, a familiar one. I retracted my hand, having only made contact with it for a few moments, it had already begun to drain and blacken the grass.

I walked into the direction that I felt Paul's presence. He wasn't that far from the camp and as I crept closer I heard the running water of the river nearby. He sat on its edge under the bright moon, skipping rocks across it while eating an apple. I watched him for a moment, absorbing the vision of his broad shoulders. Would his age soon reflect the raggedness of Uncle Kyle? Was he fated the same because of me?

Christopher spoke of a choice to be able to rid of Misfeata but I was too scared to have such hope. But when I saw Paul, I wanted that hope to be real. I wanted to be able to live a normal life, no matter what that might entail.

I walked over to him, grabbing his attention as soon as I stepped into the light. He gave me a small smile, but the dark bags under his eyes showed me he hadn't had much sleep. He threw away he core of his apple and held out his hand to me. I took it and sat beside him. We sat beside one another comfortable with fingers entwined.

It felt like such a relief had parted from us since I found him in Taskatae's castle. After almost losing him, I couldn't bear the thought twice. I had always fought for Paul and as much as I fought his presence within this world, it was the very reason why I hadn't yet given up. Sitting here beside him, with fingers intertwined- felt so natural.

"You couldn't sleep either hmmm?" He asked pushing back a part of my fringe. Memories of our old life came to me, of when we both were only students. How much I disliked him at the start and how we grew closer. How charming he eventually became before this hell broke loose. Where would we be now?

"Five years from now," I started. "If we had normal lives where do you think we would be?" He shot a charming smile. One that too much reminded me of the cockiness of Lucas.

"Well let's see, it's your eighteenth in only a few weeks. So that would make you twenty-one-"

"That would make me twenty-three," I interrupted. I returned the smile when I realized he was mocking me. I felt foolish to still have these moments to be embarrassed by such a tease. It was nice to know we still had a light-hearted teen relationship. I hadn't known romance my entire life. This was all new to me and I didn't even know if this was the thing to label it as. All I knew was that my heart pounded for Paul and I always wanted to protect him, and that I too felt safe around him. I felt that with him here I wouldn't lose my sanity.

"You would be twenty-three," he continued with a smile. "And I would be twenty-four. Hmmm I want children, but maybe not that young." I stiffened in my seat. I had never even thought of kids, but it was something that could definitely never happen for me. Not while Misfeata was dormant within me and could possibly be passed down into my child. I went to hesitate but he ushered me into silence.

"Just go with it," he said. "This is of course is a make believe world assuming you want me in it," he toyed. "I think you probably would've gotten sick of me by the time we graduated, but hell I still would've followed you to the ends of the earth."

"Why?" My voice crept out more pathetic than anticipated. "Why me?" I repeated trying to sound more inquisitive than desperate. He shrugged his shoulders in response.

"I don't know Karlz. There is something about you. You work hard, you believe in what you do, you're selfless and even when you don't admit it you want someone to look after you. I can't help but feel protective of you. You're strong, smart and absolutely beautiful. I just, I couldn't look at you without adoring you. It's just how I feel about you. I had always noticed you but palmed it off as mere fascination and that you intrigued me. It's why I never tried anything. I didn't think it was fair to toy with a girl like you. But when I actually started getting to know you. I just kind of fell for you. And now there is no going back from that nor do I ever want there to be. We've been through a lot you and I and I would never take that back. I just wish I could somehow help you get the normal life you want and deserve. I still want to make sure that no matter what we go through that I can still make you smile. I don't want you to be miserable for the rest of your life."

My heart pounded at his confession. The sincerity of his voice gave me goose bumps. The green of his eyes were earnest and felt as if he looked into my very soul. He didn't look at me as a source of power or the elder within. He saw me as Karla. Somehow in this makeshift world, still as the same girl who he had known since High School.

Slowly my hand crept toward his jacket. I didn't know what I was doing but I let my body take what it felt like it needed, no matter how selfish that was. I pulled him closer towards me, looking between his lips and eyes to see if what I was doing was okay. I needed Paul. I wanted to confirm that everything he spoke was true. And although I believed his words, my body pounded as if there were only one way to validate.

Slowly he tipped his head down to reach my level. I closed my eyes, being navigated by touch alone. The heat of his breath filled my lungs. I was breathing in his very essence and warmth which was too much like Paul. His lips brushed over mine and were surprisingly soft. He gave me a small kiss on the lips which gave me a small buzz. My lips parted as did his, wanting more of that kiss. His tongue took dominance as did his large build. He cupped my jaw, kissing me as he laid me down. He hovered over me as I tugged down on his jacket wanting him to be closer. I wanted to feel his body rub against mine.

I panted between kisses as what started to be slow and steady, became so much more. His weight that pinned me to the ground felt like it was the only thing that kept me to this earth. Paul's leg rested between my thighs as his other hand cupped my hip.

His lips were surprisingly soft in comparison to his rough tongue. He nibbled at the bottom of my lip, both painfully and teasingly. He kissed down my neck, giving me a moment to take a deep breath. My eyes burst open as I saw the moon, wanting only to see his beautiful face once again. His lips found mine again and his kiss was more savage. The faint trail of his kisses down my neck felt as if they were on fire themselves. Every lingering touch he had left an imprint. And my body craved more.

This was amazing, Paul was amazing and everything else in the world didn't matter. Only Paul. I had always only wanted to protect Paul. His masculinity surrounded me and I was engulfed by the pounding desire of my body- where kisses wouldn't quite make the cut.

A low cough snapped us out of our heated moment. Both Paul's and my head shot up as Uncle Kyle rested beside a tree. I flushed red with embarrassment. Paul shaded a slight red but nowhere near as badly as me.

I looked away for a moment unable to contain my pounding heart or my embarrassment that Uncle Kyle had caught us. It felt so childish. I felt like such a teenager. This moment reminding me that was exactly what I was. Paul looked down at me with a cheeky grin. I couldn't help but return it. He leaned back up offering his hand to help me stand. He stayed where he was sitting with a sheepish smile.

"You better go before we get in trouble or the 'talk'," he said. He still held my hand smiling. He pressed a kiss to my knuckles before letting go. "Goodnight Karla."

I leant down and kissed him on the lips again, taking him by surprise. My body just lunged for it, even if it did feel like a bit of a rebellious act in front of my Uncle.

Paul looked back at me still stunned. I felt suave as I said. "Goodnight Paul." He smiled again and watched me leave.

Before completely vanishing into the trees I called out to Paul. That one thing that still grounded me and would always rest on my mind. "Tell me later what we would be like, if it were different." I walked backwards watching his smile. If our world were normal and we were both early twenties; what would our planned future be?

"I will tell you every day from now on if you would like," he called back.

"Come on love birds," Uncle Kyle grumbled. I blushed red again in embarrassment. My heart still beat rapidly and I seemed to have a bounce in my step. In this moment I wrapped myself with a shroud of possibilities.

*

I gained no sleep when returned to my bed. My mind hummed over the memory of Paul's lips on mine. His every lingering touch, his warmth, his breath, everything replayed in my mind like a heated swirl. I found myself even hiding under the covers embarrassed when I thought of how far it might have gone and Uncle Kyle intruding on us. It felt abnormal to be having such immature thoughts with everything that havocked around us, and yet I was grateful for this youthful feeling that tormented me with embarrassment.

It was different to when I kissed Lucas. I felt sick when thinking of Lucas and comparing him with Paul. But, the difference was so evidently there. I felt for both of them, of which I already knew. My kiss with Lucas was hot and passionate- rushed in the chaotic world that challenged and tore us apart, even amongst the betrayal he had laid upon me. With Paul it was different. It was sweet, it was sensual. It anchored me and made me feel like the old Karla, the one of which I had since forgotten. It was nice to feel that vulnerability in the unknown considering I had to be guarded with everything else in my life. It was beautiful even. His touch was slow and controlled, considerate of how I was reacting and how far I wanted to go.

I now stood in the nearby trees on watch since taking over from Uncle Kyle's patrol even though he wanted to do my shift as well. Dew had begun to form on the greenery around me. As soon as the sun began to break, the chill got even colder and instinctually I wrapped my arms tighter around myself under its pinch. I bounced lightly in the one spot sensing that someone approached me. It was a fellow Shielder from the camp. It wasn't much surprise that it was Jennifer who came with a very fitted and warm looking blanket over herself. It still seemed odd to see such a heavily pregnant woman in these circumstances.

"Good Morning," she smiled taking a position at my side. We stood beside one another looking into the direction of the rising sun, being in awe of its slow ascending colors. "I hope sleep treated you well."

I had long forgotten the way of idle chat. She didn't seem uncomfortable by my silence. She only watched the sun with me. She noticed my sweep of her stomach which she patted her hand on and she countered a smile.

"It's odd isn't it? Seeing me as big as a whale. A lot of our women here do the same. If anything we find it more stressful to be less a part of the group and action," she smiled. "Don't worry we are sturdier then human women."

I studied her face which up close appeared more fatigued and older than she did with her usual youthful glow from a distance. She looked drained and exhausted with black bags under her eyes. To me it looked like she slept as much as I did. I wanted to ask if the child was Elijah's but withheld from being nosy.

"I've never seen this many Shielders. I never thought to think that, well, we even had children," I said. I felt foolish once it left my lips. But, it wasn't something I much considered. We were all warriors, weren't we? How were we able to have children and raise them in such an environment?

"It's a wonder. There are far more Starkorfs than there are Shielders nowadays. You've probably only ever seen their women, but none can bear children because of the draining mutation," she said sadly. "Do you think it is possible, that although born a Starkorf that they can change? Do you think a Starkorf could revert back to being a Shielder?"

Her question caught me off guard. Her eyes had a certain longing and curiosity. I wasn't sure if she was asking me this or if it was an answer she was seeking from Misfeata. I had for too many times questioned what it would have been like if Lucas was a Shielder, or if he could ever change. To keep his youthful appearance I knew he had to still drain living creatures. Even though he said he didn't drain humans anymore I was still saddened by the life he had to live. I dropped my gaze to the ground, uncomfortable as if she could read my thoughts.

"I don't know the answer to that, sorry," I said honestly. Her shoulders slumped as if her hope had vanished the moment I said it. "I pray that is the case. I really do." I could feel her inquisitive gaze on me, but she said nothing further.

"My mother means well," she continued as she rubbed her belly. "She just lacks in people skill. She has actually been very much looking forward to the day she found you. Although she doesn't show it, she has much respect for you."

"For me or the Elder that lays within me," I snapped. I avoided apologizing. I wasn't sorry for expressing the pressure I felt on me. I knew how they all looked at me and that they only saw it as a means of power.

"Both," she said. "My mother had known Elisabeth and fought alongside her. Elisabeth was a natural leader. Head strong like you also. But even she struggled with the curse of having Misfeata within her. Our kind respects those who host Misfeata, for most of us, we all know it isn't as glamourous as some describe it to be. I could never imagine sharing my body with someone else."

Those words lingered in the air as we both sensed another person approaching us. They hovered along the edges of the trees not coming closer.

"Just Elijah checking up on me," Jennifer said not with fondness but slight irritation. Again, I didn't want to question their relationship.

"Your mother seems to have interest in possessing Misfeata for her own gain," I pointed out. Much like Kurt wanted the same, if even possible. Jennifer gave a weak smile.

"My mother is one of the strongest Shielders I know. She has only ever fought for our kind and made sacrifices in every step she's taken. She's forward but honest. Harsh but also fair. She only wants to keep her people safe and her opinion is by erasing the Starkorfs, she can do exactly that. She is one of the true forms of what and how a Shielder should be acting in regards to Misfeata's following."

She slowly sat down on a nearby log, uncomfortably doing so with her swollen belly. It was odd to see her move so easily and like a warrior, but in this very moment she seemed to be just a heavily pregnant woman.

"You don't view it the same?" I asked. The way she described 'in my mother's opinion', described that she had her own. She looked into the direction of where I could feel Elijah's presence. She has a very serious and sad expression.

"I don't think everyone, of either race feels the same. I think that not everyone wants to be a part of this war and kill aimlessly for the rest of our lives. We have divided into two different races but we were all once the same. I would like it, if somehow, someday we could coexist however we want. There is so much evil in the world already, I don't want to be a part of that darkness anymore. A life is a life, I don't want to take anymore." She locked her eyes onto mine. There was a heavy moment of silence between us as it felt like suddenly we were thinking the exact same remorseful thoughts. *How many lives had we taken?*

"But I very much doubt I will be here in that time. So I hope Karla no matter what happens in your future that you can lead accordingly and make a difference." She sat up uncomfortably again and rested her hand on my shoulder. "You are the last descendant of Misfeata. People will naturally listen to you. I hope that you can use that differently to what Elisabeth did. She hated the Starkorfs more than anything. She wanted the same as my mother."

"Why was she so hateful?" I asked. I had to know what it was the spurred her on to fight every day. I questioned if she ever drowned in the voices and faces of those who she had killed. Jennifer looked surprised that I didn't already know the answer.

"In the time of the great wall, one hundred years ago; where Shielders, Starkorfs and Elemental Breathers were segregated from humans- was the time of Elisabeth's rising. She was your age and studied at the academy. From what I heard it was a very different world behind that wall. The Starkorfs killed her family in search of her, this was before she even knew she was a descendant of Misfeata. When they killed her father, who was the barer of Misfeata- she became the new host and last generation. Her family was slaughtered and eventually before the wall collapsed, so was her lover."

The words lingered heavily. I had never known that and still I didn't know much of this before time and the wall that encased everyone. Elijah now impatient began walking towards us.

"Ironically," Jennifer continued before he was visible. "Her lover was an Elemental Breather. It's ironic that even Elisabeth once thought race wasn't an issue."

"Jennifer its cold out here," Elijah interrupted. Jennifer scoffed slightly.

"You don't have to babysit me Elijah, I am fine." She dropped her grip from my shoulder. "When you are ready my mother would like to see you this morning. She is going to ask you to join us on the ambush we discussed yesterday. I personally hope you say yes."

She gave me a warm smile before following Elijah's lead back to their camp. I waited until they were out of hearing distance before I confronted Scott who I knew had been standing there for some time now listening in on the conversation.

"It's not Shielder," Scott said seriously as he walked up to me and stood where Jennifer once was. There was still slight tension between us when we stood alone. I hadn't yet pushed past his betrayal and still didn't know if I ever would.

"What isn't?" I asked incredulously.

"Her unborn child. It's Starkorf." I looked at him shocked. I wanted to argue that his joke wasn't funny but saw the certainty on his face. I looked back towards the direction that they had left in and the sun continued to rise. I flicked over the many things she said about Starkorfs and when she questioned me if I thought they could ever change. Most of all, the image of her exhausted expression and face came to mind. Her fatigue wasn't from pregnancy, it could very well be from the draining of the unborn child.

"Will she die?" My voice came out a little more high pitched than I had hoped. I realized then that I liked Jennifer.

"Yes."

Chapter Seven

$\mathcal{I}$ waited for the others to wake, which wasn't long after I could fully see the sun. Even after sleep they all still looked tired. But that was only a side effect of this life. I turned red when I saw Paul walk out of his tent and childishly looked away towards Paige. Scott who was standing beside me arched a questioning eyebrow and simply said a knowing, "Oh?"

I gave him a harsh glare which stifled him enough not to ask what happened or when. A sheepish smile stretched over his face as he lazily shrugged his shoulder before straightening out his pink suit. It still irked me that even though we all "roughed" it and only had a few change of clothes amongst the essentials we survived off; that Scott still had a trunk full of fine clothing and more than what would have once fitted in my own cupboard at home.

I once questioned him about it and he gave me a baffled look as if I had lost my mind by questioning it. He simply reminded me that I was a Shielder and he was an Elemental Breather and of course I wouldn't understand. Vanity quite simply was something I would never understand.

"I only want to go alone this time," I said to the others. Paige made a dramatic sigh and threw her hands in the air.

"Can we just go and kill something already? I am so damn bored playing politics," she poised. Ashley started a small laugh.

"You only encourage her," Uncle Kyle said. "Karla, I've known Christopher for some time now. I should be coming with you."

"No," I said firmly. "Actually I only want Ashley to come." Ashley seemed to perk at that as if in that moment I had chosen him to be the captain of some sports team. "We are talking from institute to institute, there are some decisions I can't make on behalf of Ashley."

"But I-" Scott began. I gave him an effective look. I looked at Paul who was the only one who hadn't protested as if expecting the same from him. I blushed red as soon as I made contact with his beautiful green eyes. The flashes of the night before flooded in front of my vision. He too looked away with a sheepish smile.

"Well, that's awkward," Ashley said in a brotherly manner. "Let's go before I start teasing the both of you," Ashley continued. He went to grab me around the neck and ruffle my hair but I projected my Shield so he couldn't touch me. He slapped on my Shield in slight frustration of using such a trick against him.

"You don't play fair," he said as he began walking to the others' camp. It reminded me of the time when Ashley had tried to gang up on Lucas with a mouthful of bubbles and Lucas had used the same trick. I pushed that thought down and looked at my group giving them all a reassuring look.

"I will only do what I think is best for us. If you disagree when I get back then we won't do anything at all."

"As long as you agree to the fighting then I don't care," Paige said as she sat down sharpening her blade.

I gave Paul another glance before I hesitantly left them behind. He wavered a shy smile which seemed so unlike him. For all his confidence and experience in these situations he seemed just as shy as me. Scott watched us intensely as if watching some soap opera with glee. Paul gave him a condescending glare. The rift between the two perhaps unbearable, although they avoided the subject and tension of what happened between them. Paul evidently could not forgive him, of which I didn't blame him. Paul was both humiliated and almost died because of Scott. No matter how fond Scott have been of him, he still put his life in danger.

"Come on super Elder," Ashley mocked as he waited for me ahead.

"Shut up," I sneered. He knew how much I hated people commenting on Misfeata instead of me. He smiled when I gave him a light punch in the arm.

"What do you think she wants now," he said now serious as we walked.

"She wants us to fight with them," I said.

"Of course she does," he said putting his hands in his pockets.

Instead of meeting Christopher in her tent she appeared to have already been on her way to see us. The Shielder's behind her appeared to be packing up camp already.

She seemed in a hurry as she approached us. "They have already started movement sooner than we anticipated."

"I never agreed to fight alongside you," I said.

"Let me break it down quickly and sweetly for you," she snapped back in obvious haste. "We can offer the rest of your members in your institute protection, including both of your mothers. I would advise that right now they stay with us instead of their current location. If you are being sought out I can guarantee you they are searching for your mother as well. If they can use anything against you they will. We can protect them here." She didn't give me a moment to interrupt. "Karla, I have been fighting these battles and games my entire life. They will come for your mother. Suzumiya and Chris can join the battle. I can only imagine how frustrated they are getting by bunkering down for so long. All I ask is that you join us on this mission right now and cooperate with our organization. See how you fit in and to find out what Lucas wants from you and so we can anticipate the movement of Eden. I will not let harm come to you, but my people could really do with your strength."

One of the males began stomping out a few of the small flames that flickered. Already their tents had been packed. I looked between Ashley and Christopher aware that a lot of the Shielder's eyes were on me in anticipation, including Jennifer's and Elijah's. Admittedly I too wanted to know why Lucas was actively seeking me out. Ambushing this group of Starkorf's might tip me closer to that. Amongst all, the security of my mother always took priority. And although I thought she was once safe far away from this war, I heeded the counselling that she might be in more danger now than ever before.

I gave Ashley a direct look. Without asking him for his advice he nodded his head, obvious with his mother in mind also. "If I bring them to you, where can I meet you in three days' time?" He asked.

Christopher snapped her fingers and a Shielder came to her side with a map. She circled four different spots. "This is where we are intercepting the Starkorfs." She circled one spot. "In three days' time we should be here," she pointed to another spot. "Be visual if we are not there then we had to change direction for security measures, then you go here." She pointed to the last spot. "Worst case scenario if we can't find security in either of those two places then this third one is a city where we can meet in public."

Ashley memorized it and nodded. He looked at me, with the pace of how quickly the situation was forming. "I will have to take the car so I can get there by today."

"Okay," I simply said.

"We run, you're human companions can't keep up," Christopher commanded stiffly. "They will have to go with him, my people won't hold back their pace for them."

"Uncle Kyle and Paul," I said to Ashley.

"They won't like it, but it has to be done," Ashley confirmed.

"Done. Hurry we leave in ten minutes," Christopher hasted and turned to her people to continue orders. It was obvious that her scouts had returned information to her, obviously her target was a little bit faster than she anticipated.

Ashley and I went back towards our own camp. "Will you be okay with just Paige and Scott?" he asked.

"Don't worry about me. Just look after the others," I said. "This is the right thing to do isn't it? For our mothers?" I asked him showing my vulnerability. I couldn't meet his eyes as I asked him instead having a quick look at the scar which was healing over his eyebrow where his piercing once was.

"I wouldn't have agreed to it if it weren't. As selfish as it might be, it's what I want protected more than anything."

"I agree," I said. If I had Christopher's word and promise that they would be protected I couldn't deny the appeal of having an entire army of Shielders protecting them over only Suzumiya and Chris in hideout. "I haven't seen my mother since I tricked her." I thought out loud. I had taken away her parental right to protect me, so in return could protect her. I wondered how angry she would now be with me.

"We do what we have to, to protect the one's we love Karla. It's not always glamorous," Ashley said with a serious expression. He no longer looked like the playful young man I had first met. He too had changed and aged within only the past few months.

"How did it go?" Paul shot up from the log he was sitting on. They had already packed our camp.

"That was quick," Scott remarked as he filed his nails and looked up at our entrance for only a fleeting second.

"I don't have much time to explain but Ashley can explain on the way there. We are splitting up for now. Scott and Paige with me. Paul and Uncle Kyle with Ashley," I said.

"What, why? I'm not leaving you," Paul urged.

"I'm with the boy," Uncle Kyle said angrily. "I am still your Uncle and will always be here to protect you."

"It has to be done," Ashley shot back defending me.

"We will meet back up in a few days. You are going to get the others. It is safer here for them than being on their own."

"You're mother?" Uncle Kyle asked almost bewildered. It had been many years since they had seen one another and I don't think either would be prepared for that confronting moment.

"Yes," I said taking the first descent breath I felt like I had since deciding this plan of action. "I need to go now."

"Wait where will you go? Karla please," Paul said, standing in front of me and grabbing my hand before I can pull away. I looked down at his hand that caught mine unable to so quickly tell him the plan. I knew he hated it when I endangered my life and fought. The rush of who I was flooded over me. I was basically immortal.

"I am going to fight," I said strongly and locking onto his green eyes. "I will be fine Paul." Before he could argue I cupped his strong jaw silencing him. "Please," I begged. "I need you to look after my mother. It's only for a few days, I will see you again." It was also a silent prayer for him to stop pushing to be by my side. I didn't want him to be a part of this fight. Martin's voice rang in my head. *'Paul Stuart, survival rate: twenty-three percent.'* "Please Paul."

His hand slid around my waist and he dipped his head down to my height giving me a heated kiss on the lips. He rested his forehead on mine as he spoke to me. His eyes still looking into my own.

"I want to protect you more than anything," he said heatedly.

"Likewise," I whispered and pressed another kiss to his lips, no longer shy or red about it. "Trust me."

After much hesitation he pulled away from me. "I'll always trust you." It pained him to let me go.

"We will see you in three days time," Ashley said as he began walking towards where we had hidden the car. I nodded at him and Uncle Kyle, who surprisingly yet still reluctantly followed him. I think he too realized my mother was far more defenseless than me.

"Three days," I repeated to Paul and let go of his hand. "Look after yourself until then." I walked away from him with Scott and Paige already waiting. I looked over my shoulder where Paul still watched me leave. He was the image of someone who had just been abandoned. My heart pained at the site. I never wanted to be parted from him. Especially in such a rush where we couldn't properly say goodbye. Although I reminded myself only three days, I knew anything could happen in that time and three days could very easily turn into three years if we managed to lose communication.

"Alright," Paige bounced gleefully. "Finally some fighting."

"You're an animal," Scott simply stated as he dusted off his jacket after scraping it lightly against a branch.

"I hope you don't expect me to exert myself," he scoffed to me. "I would much rather cheer on the sidelines."

"If everything goes smoothly you won't be needed. I want you to focus on something else for me." This piqued Scott's interest. I scouted around us to make sure that no one else was within hearing distance.

"I want you both to find out what you can about Christopher's group. She's too busy focusing on me and what I am doing. When we make contact with the target, I want you to find out some information for me. I want to know where Lucas is and why he is looking for me."

"This group isn't necessarily affiliated with him. They might not know anything," Scott said. "And besides, I thought you didn't like the way I gather information?"

When he said 'gathered' what he meant was torture. I didn't indulge on his humorous tone as if I were crossing over to the dark side with him or something along those dramatic lines.

"It doesn't matter if they are affiliated with him. Lucas is still their Prince. Surely they would've heard something. I don't like how you obtain information, so do it another way."

"Ahhh, in other words as long as you don't see it, you don't have to worry about feeling guilty about it. Or what lover boy thinks." I shot him a filthy glare for antagonizing me.

"Shouldn't you focus on Eden?" Paige asked casually. "Maybe taking over this army and leading it yourself?"

I stopped in my tracks and looked at her. "I have no intention of leading these people. And if you hear anything about Eden, then report it to me as well. We need to make sure we are still creating distance."

"Oooh how alternative," Scott squealed. "I feel like a double agent almost. Wait," he stopped in his tracks, realization dawned on his face. It mixed into a disorientated shade of fear. "How are we getting to this place?" I smiled in response, knowing he wouldn't like the answer.

"We run."

"Nooooooooooo," Scott said dramatically. "I don't want to be a part of your pack of wolves."

"Ironic for someone to say when they can turn into one isn't it?" Paige retorted.

Scott gave her a daggered look. "Don't be jealous of my beautiful fur," he simply retorted and looked away. "If I break a sweat, I will most certainly be annoyed."

Chapter Eight- Agreements

$\mathcal{T}$here was so much coordination in everyone's placement and structure. There were five separate groups when running. The center was where all the weak and children stayed. The other four groups taking both sides, front and back. The pace they ran was phenomenal and there was no hesitation as they all ran as one. It is exactly what I imagined it to feel like if a part of an animal pack of some kind. The snide remark of a 'wolf pack' from Scott came to mind.

I was within the front group and ran beside Christopher. Jennifer led those who were segregated to the right and Elijah to those on the left. They expanded further out having 'fielders' to make sure that the group wasn't endanger. I now understood why the others couldn't have kept up, this was beyond human pace.

I never truly realized the stamina a Shielder had in comparison to a normal human until today and this group trained every day of their lives for this. Scott had vanished as soon as we had started. I assumed he had turned into some kind of bug and rested on someone while they ran for him.

The children in the center concentrated hard to keep up with the adults. They didn't struggle but few rest breaks were given to them. I was surprised that they were able to match the adults, or simply the group ran slower to match them. For the mothers who had babies or toddlers strapped to their backs, seemed to move with such stealth that the children weren't at all bothered by a few of the jolts and jumping over woodland.

Even I began to feel exhausted by the end of the day where the constant running began to burn my legs. When we stopped for a short break my body quickly restored itself. The only one who wasn't with us was Martin. Jennifer said that he didn't run and couldn't keep up even if he had tried.

Instead he often moved forward without them and purchased supplies and items they were in need of. He only took two other Shielders who could be trusted alone with him. In other words, two

Shielders who wouldn't try to harm him. Apparently he was meeting with us before the ambush. His element was used by Christopher before each attack, briefing her on the odds and ratios of separate plans of attack. I personally thought it was foolish that she planned her attack on statistics and analysis of the situation. But then again, I hadn't yet witnessed the results of Martin's element.

The running eventually became a blur. All that gravitated my existence was the pounding of my own feet and heart. The race of fellow Shielders running beside me hummed in the background noise as if a part of me. I no longer thought or complained. I just ran aimlessly and quickly through the woodland where I imagined no human ever knew to exist. It felt so primal.

It had been dark already for a few hours until Christopher finally halted the group. Most of them fell exhausted, mostly the younger ones who were now praised by their parents or mentors. They began instantly setting up camp and fell into a very evident routine.

Paige slumped into a nearby tree evidently exhausted. I wasn't yet sure what she was but it appeared that even she struggled to keep up. Scott still hadn't remerged, which had me wondering exactly where he had gone.

"I'm fine Elijah." I heard Jennifer say. I scanned amongst the group to find her. She was hunched over against a tree panting. Her legs looked as if they were about to give way. "I'm just tired as is everyone from the run."

Elijah fumbled around her. He whispered to her quietly checking to make sure no one else heard. It was times like this I was grateful for my sharp hearing. "But it's different in your case. That vile creature inside of you-"

"There is nothing vile about my baby," Jennifer snapped. She was still hunched over with hand on her stomach as she maintained her breathing. Her deathly stare froze him over. He went to retort but decided it was best not to.

"Karla," Christopher said over the group, wavering me to her. "Come this way dear." Men with axes in their hands and piles of wood in the other cut between us setting up a fire. I made my way to her. Paige naturally followed looking like a bodyguard of sorts as she gave everyone an eerie expression if they stepped on our path.

"Now I want you to get plenty of rest tonight. We leave early tomorrow morning. Don't feel separated from the group. I have Thomas over there setting you both up a tent. You're Elemental Breather shouldn't be too far away."

"Scott?" I asked.

"Yes he went with Martin. They shouldn't be too far off. Make yourself comfortable and tomorrow before we analyze the situation we will also go over the plan. My people only need a few hours sleep to restore. Hopefully with luck, Lucas will be affiliated with this group and close by. To be able to kill him and destroy Tyran will be something of many blessings."

"Lucas and I will not fight," I said outright. With her confused expression I tried to cover my outburst. "What I mean to say is he won't stay around if he knows I am close by."

"Well yes, I recall you both used to fight alongside one another before his treason came to light. It's inevitable for you two to fight. Don't be distracted by companionship. He wants to kill you. Never make light of that."

"He doesn't," I quickly said. That one defined response must have shattered my strong demeanor. Her face lightened.

"Please don't tell me you think you two are friends or old comrades or something childish like that?"

"I do not," I said recovering myself.

"Then why the hesitation to fight him? It's not like you will be fighting him anyway. I know the pull Misfeata has, she would instinctually possess your body." I scowled at her very meaningfully.

"That is exactly why I won't fight him," I growled. "I don't care what you consider to be normal or okay, but I am not willingly allowing her to possess my body. *I* will avoid confrontation with him at all costs."

"What a selfish act," she retorted now tilting her head up at me and peering down on me. She looked like a disapproving mother. "Perhaps you should reconsider your tone and angle if you want the protection of your mother guaranteed."

"You have already given me your word," I growled. My hand instinctively rested on the hilt of Aeisha, in case this ventured to a fight instead.

"Nothing is for free. Your power is needed. And here amongst my people we only focus on one thing. You need to align yourself with that."

"I never chose to come to you. I don't need you," I hissed.

"Don't mock me," she snarled. "You are but a child chucking a tantrum. Obviously you haven't seen enough of this tainted world to realize I am your best hope."

"What are you two talking about?" Jennifer crept into the conversation, wary of her mother. "Mother I hope you are not offending Karla."

"Be quiet you insolent child," Christopher snapped harshly. There was a glint of pure hatred in her eyes in that moment. "Children who do not heed advice will always get hurt. I am here simply to prevent it."

I could feel that the tone was more directed to Jennifer's pregnancy because she protectively placed her hand on her stomach. Christopher barged past her walking towards those who set up tents.

Jennifer smiled warily. I still didn't have the courage to ask her about it.

"Your mothers a cow," Paige said loudly. A few of the Shielder's around stopped and gave Paige a side glance before continuing their work. Jennifer only smiled with a slight sigh.

"Perhaps menopause," she mused.

"You protect her too much," Paige said unfazed. "Even if she were my mother, I would've hustled her to the ground by now." I wanted to scold Paige for how openly and loudly she spoke but I knew even if I had she would be unfazed.

"Oh we have hustled a few times," Jennifer said with amusement. "But I've learnt to trust my mother. No matter how bizarre the situation or her judgment, there has always been a reason. She simply lacks people skill."

A large group of Shielders gathered and began to walk into the trees. "What are they doing?" Paige asked nosily.

"They are hunting for meat tonight," Jennifer responded. Paige's expression changed into an innocent glow.

"Then that is the party I want to be a part of," she gleamed, already walking away.

"Do you yet know what she is? Even Martin can't figure it out," Jennifer asked curiously. I imagined it put a lot of people amongst this group on edge to have a foreign alliance.

"No not yet," I sighed behind her. Even if I had I might have withheld the information from Jennifer. "But I feel at ease with her around. Surprisingly. We don't overly get along much but she has risked her life more than once to protect me and those I hold dear."

"Sometimes that is all the evidence you need in this world. It shouldn't always be dictated by race," Jennifer said, still looking at Paige as she argued with one of the men who tried to refuse her coming. He quickly gave up. Jennifer looked sorrowful and it made me more curious as to how she became pregnant with a Starkorf child. I had a feeling that it wasn't forced. The question was on the tip of my lips before she returned to me with a fake smile, covering up her expression. "I better go get some rest before tomorrow."

"You're coming to the ambush?" I asked surprised.

"Of course. I am second in command here. I just won't be a part of your group. I will be leading my people from the side. Don't look down on my skill because of my swollen belly," she mused. "No one wants to protect this child more than me."

Jennifer walked away, greeting a familiar slender figure as he approached. Both Martin and Scott walked silently beside one another. It seemed beautiful even. Both were very elegant and beautiful, like all Elemental Breathers. Neither exchanged words as they walked through the Shielders who snarled under their breath at their presence.

Martin took it a little more graceful than Scott who pointedly stared at all of them with a charming smile. He even winked at a few. "Jealousy is a curse." He even mentioned to one of them. Martin veered right into the crowd of Shielder's who prepared their tents. Scott and I met, our greetings very different.

"Why hello sweet cheeks," he said dazzled.

"Where have you been?" I hissed under my breath looking around me to see if anyone else was listening. He looked around less than discreet, mocking me.

"I was gathering information, like you requested from me." A beautiful smile flashed over his face. "And I didn't want to be a part of your weird tribal run thingamajig. Too primal for me."

"So what did you find out?" I asked him as we crept closer to the outer edge where I began unpacking the tent material. I wasn't expecting any help from Scott. We kept our voices low so no one could hear us.

"Not a damn thing," Scott said annoyed. "That Elemental Breather is both boring and quiet. I would've communicated better with a mouse. Talk about one sided conversation. Yes. No," he mocked as if repeating Martin's monotone. "Sometimes he just ignored me. Me out of all people?!"

"I couldn't imagine," I mumbled.

"I know right," Scott said with his thumb nail in his mouth and lightly chewing on it in agitation. Something I had never seen him do before. "So when is this showdown happening?"

"Tomorrow, we fight tomorrow," I said preparing myself for what would come. It was ironic, no matter how many fights I had now been involved with. It seemed that no amount of mental preparation even fixated the butterfly feeling in my stomach.

"Well then, I will stay with you, so you can get some rest. But prior to that, please make sure this filthy tent gets a rinse over or something. I don't want to have to beg Martin to let me be a part of his more glamourous housing."

I growled at his dramatics. He acted as if nothing at all had ever happened between us. As if betrayal had never seeped in to our odd friendship. I didn't even know if I would consider it as that, perhaps comradeship was the correct word. No matter the case, a few hours of proper rest with Misfeata being blocked from torturing me in my sleep sounded perfect. I was satisfied by how little I had felt of her recently and hoped that this was a form of either her depleting inside of me or of me finally gaining control.

I gasped in shock as the swell of her reached my throat and I felt as if I couldn't breathe. I tried my hardest to push her down, but she flooded me in one clean unsuspecting sweep. Everything around me became dark and hazy and I felt as if I were trapped in a dark room. I was only able to see everything through my eyes, yet not mine. Not under my control. I screamed in rage, trying my hardest to take back control. She had been resting and waiting for this moment of ease to sweep over me.

"I think I can handle her tonight," my lips said. There was definitely a more mature tone to my voice. Even Scott eyed us evenly for a moment. I hoped that he could tell the difference, but there was a factor Misfeata was attempting this time, that she hadn't all the others. She was trying to act and sound like me.

"Well okay," Scott said no longer judging. "Let me know if you need me. Until then I am going to watch these people flutter around and wait until they've started a fire for me."

Misfeata watched him leave. I felt the smugness of her trail through my entire body. I screamed inside, trying my hardest to barge through the barricades she had put up to trap me. I never considered that a full day's run and physical exertion could also factor into my weakness. She had been waiting for this moment for me to weaken my defenses and believe that she was gone.

"*Ssssshhh little one,*" Misfeata said. "*You don't have to fight anymore. You can rest like a good girl now.*"

Chapter Nine- Unexpected Truths

It was easy to fade in and out of consciousness while trapped within my own body. It was like being contained in a glass prison. I could see everything happening around me through my eyes. But the movement of my body was foreign, the jolt of every step was hard to register as my own. Misfeata charmed her way through the Shielder's. Because they were already in awe of me and Misfeata who laid within, they kept their distance.

I was surprised that Misfeata hadn't announced herself. It was after all her that they idolized and wanted, not me. Instead she still impersonated me. No one as of yet could tell the difference. The scenes around me faded in and out. I was losing consciousness and then I would come back to consciousness from utter darkness and nothingness. I would witness that we were amongst trees practicing by myself. Misfeata was training with Aeisha, reinforcing her full control of my body. I would fade out and then come back. She was laying down in the tent, staying awake like I did to make sure I didn't reclaim my body while she slept.

No matter how much I screamed and pushed back against her, the barricades were hard. I was completely trapped and consumed by her. Again I faded out into utter darkness. It was exhausting screaming and trying to claw my way back. I wondered how I had done it so many times before. Perhaps it was the adrenaline of the fight that enabled me to do so. Or when her mind was focused on only Tyran I was able to flip it when she lost a moment of control. But right now she was focused, she was in control and she possessed my body.

The morning was a blur and Christopher responded well to my sudden willingness to do and agree with her tactic and plan. The Shielders circled Christopher and listened to her every word and command. It took a huge amount of concentration for me to focus on what the plan was. I continuously faded in and out. From the information I gathered it was as she described the night before. I would be a part of the frontal team, the 'bait'. It was only me and another two Shielders, which was Elijah and another tall and strong looking male. Paige protested and wanted to be on the frontal, not because she wanted to fight by my side, but simply because that seemed like where most of the fighting would be.

Christopher was recently meant to be a part of that group but with slight manipulation from Misfeata she agreed she should lead the back-up team. Martin who was also amongst the group analyzed the increase of statistics every time we changed or altered a new motive.

Jennifer took one of the sides. Another male taking the other. And then a fourth group to take the behind. The scouts had gathered that there was about twenty Starkorfs, less then what they first predicted. Their numbers will still enough to gather information from. The goal was to kill them before they attacked a town. Christopher planned this so it also created noise amongst the Starkorf world to letting them know that her group was in the country and on the hunt.

It scared me how much Misfeata relished being a part of this group and although she liked Christopher's lead and charge, she had every intention of taking that leadership. Still I didn't know why she pretended to be me. Misfeata was their elder, their god one would even say. Instead she played out to be me which infuriated me even more. It made me sadder to know that no one differentiated between us.

It was only Paige that Misfeata noted to be cautious of. There was a certain awareness in Paige that forced us both to believe, that just by looking she knew. But Paige didn't confront or question the matter. Perhaps I was wrong and only hopeful.

I faded out of consciousness again. If I wasn't actively trying to focus and stay attached I'd drift within seconds. When I realized I was drifting, I reappeared to notice we were once again in a completely different time of the day and positioning. It was a nightmare to watch my life flash in front of my eyes. What if I never reappeared from consciousness? What if I was lost forever? Not even the emotion of anxiety and stress seemed to bother me here. The only heightened expression that seemed to disturb or interfere with Misfeata's determined focus was rage. Only when I lashed out at her in rage would she feel me inside of her. Just as forcefully she would push me back down, which was rather painful. It felt as if she was pressing down on my brain, until I would submit from fear of it exploding. I knew it wasn't my brain but it was my consciousness and existence which scared me even more.

I came to consciousness again, already having missed the travels and how we now got here. Beside me was Elijah and the man who I had met before, Thomas. I realized alarmed, that already we were positioned to be the bait. Misfeata lightly tapped her fingers on Aeisha, excited for the challenge that would come. I wondered if she would lash out with no mercy and kill all twenty by herself, just in show of strength or if she would play herself down as to what my capabilities would be and watch how the others handled it.

There was a hum of pleasure that mused through her body- my body no matter how disconnected I felt from it. She relished in this control.

Misfeata looked over the open road. We stood in the center of it. It was the main road which connected to the small town about twenty minutes away from us. A few farm houses surrounded us, few and far in-between. But they had long been deserted. Some looked as if they had been burned to the ground. There was a haunting feeling about it all. It felt like they had been attacked before. In the distance on our left, where Jennifer's group hid the entire barn and houses looked as if it would creak and collapse within seconds. Paint peeled and the open fields of crops were long forgotten and dead.

There was even a post nearby to our right, highlighting where once a bus stop curated children to go to school. That was no longer used. The heat of the day burned at my skin. Further past the openness of the day was woodland of which we had come from. This was where the other groups hid amongst. It made more sense to me that Jennifer's group should've been the backup group, considering she was closest.

"You are new to all this fighting right?" Thomas asked me. "Do you ever get scared? You were just a High School student before weren't you?"

Misfeata tried to contain her amused expression. Instead she simply replied, "I adapted."

Thomas didn't ask further questions. No one here knew me. No one understood how I would usually act. What I feared most was Misfeata knew, more than anyone else. We had now been sharing the same body for almost a year. She knew me inside and out, even my darkest fears and secrets were exposed to her. How would anyone ever tell the difference? Could even Paul or my mother tell the difference? Surely they could, but even as I thought it I doubted it. What if I were trapped forever?

Misfeata crouched to the ground now impatient. It wasn't evident what she was doing because there was no grass to kill. She concentrated through the cement of the road. Thomas and Elijah watched unsure of what she was doing. They couldn't see her shield because she concentrated it beneath the cement and into the earth. She didn't care if they held judgment because she was the elder and creator of how they first existed. She found no fault in her own power and capability.

Misfeata waited impatiently as she focused on our surroundings trying to feel presence further on. A pump of adrenalin coursed through her when she felt the presence of the anticipated twenty. The numbers that she didn't expect were the ones that were already behind us, heading towards the town and on the sides. That group of thirty were well on their way and almost reaching the town. They had bypassed the side groups and avoided Christopher's group entirely. It seemed that this frontal group of twenty, might have been their own bait.

"There are more than twenty," Misfeata shot up within an instance. She began to command and altered the plan as it should be. "You," she pointed to Thomas. "Inform Christopher, her group is to reach the towns people, immediately. Elijah, inform those on the sides and have them expand to those who are waiting in the back."

"What? How do you know?!" Thomas asked suddenly more alert.

"Do not question me," Misfeata snarled. "Now go. Both of you." Elijah had a pending look. Obviously struggling with the commandment from me and not Christopher. He hesitated to leave.

"And what about you?" He asked. A smile crept on Misfeata's face. She pulled both of Aeisha's blades from beneath her jackets. The pulse and connection of her gems and soul fulfilling her with power and greed.

"I will take care of the twenty," Misfeata ran forward without hesitation. She could've waited for them to reach her. But it wasn't befitting for her hasty style. She wanted to destroy them now, excited to vanquish their numbers. A small challenge, but one she accepted to 'try out' the control of what she considered to be her new body.

Their snarls could be heard in the distance, which only propelled her further amongst their masses.

To them, they would have only seen one teen girl. To Misfeata, she had already located their vital organs and cuts that would take them down in one clean sweep. It was a collision of one Shielder against

Starkorfs. But she wasn't just any Shielder, she was Misfeata; the Elder that created this war. She would dance amongst them with ease, slaughtering them in a grotesque gleam. This was her world and one she relished in.

In the middle of the road she collided with the first, dodging their blade and slicing Aeisha across her throat. The gurgling noise of her last breath seemed to anchor me more than it did Misfeata. In comparison to Misfeata's shield theirs were near non-existent. Misfeata hadn't yet projected hers, she wanted them to get as close to her as possible so she could watch the life dim out of their eyes by her own doing.

She slashed another across their chest, forcing him to take a step back. She spun between that man and the one who jumped behind her, outstretching both arms elegantly and piercing both in the chest, with one clean swift movement. She reefed her blades back out and flipped back through the air, beside another. She countered their axe, taking note of the scarring over their mutated face. I couldn't even tell if it were man or woman.

She spun close to the ground, slicing their ankles and enjoying the sound of their barbaric scream. As the Starkorf dropped to the ground she came up and punched his jaw, creating a shattering noise. The Starkorf drifted in the air and hit the ground hard, foaming from the mouth as his body jolted inhumanly.

She dodged to the left as a new attacker tried to spear her. She matched the pressure of his Shield so he was still able to stand in close proximity to her. She countered them all differently, making sure they still attacked at full force but in a close position so she could still strike for the kill. Before focusing on the one who just attacked her, she looked over her shoulder and flung Aeisha towards a Starkorf. She focused her shield on Aeisha, so it shattered that Starkorfs shield and pierced her right in the eye instantly killing her.

The axe made a terrible screeching noise against Aeisha. Misfeata punched the Starkorf in the stomach winding her and slashed Aeisha across their throat. If I could have closed my eyes I would have at the sight. Misfeata was unflinching in her kills. She loved the thrill of it and the satisfaction to know she was superior. In her mind, she was elegantly executing the murderers. I wondered if she ever took reflection upon herself and realized that right now she was the murderer.

'Hunter,' she corrected in my mind. 'I am always the hunter and they are my prey.' She revoked Aeisha which was impaled into the Starkorf on the ground.

The bloodshed was a blur and over in mere minutes. She didn't rely on her Shield or executed any mercy. It was only brutal force that she used. Nineteen of them now lay dead on the ground. A few of the Shielders from the group had now caught up in aid of back up. Before they reached Misfeata, she scooped the shirt of the last standing Starkorf who was terrified by her. He scampered backwards on the ground, terrified as she approached. She lifted him by the shirt with one hand. He had already lost his weapon. This Starkorf was only young, naturally young with no defects.

"Where is the prince?" She snarled. She wanted Lucas's whereabouts so she could destroy Tyran.

"No one knows," he stammered answering what I thought to be honestly. A sigh of relief swept through me as he couldn't answer her. He didn't know.

"Where is Eden?" She snarled again. She was now only wanting to quench the thirst of her killing spree.

"We're not aligned to either. I don't know," the man stammered.

"Not good enough." Misfeata pierced his chest, watching him as the light dimmed out of his eyes. She reefed it out with such savageness, angered that she had no answer. She spun to the group of six Shielders who came to aid her. They searched the viciously murdered bodies on the ground. Most of them kept a mutual face, but two of them had expressed their fear and disgust. This was the war we fought, yet to have killed twenty in such a short time and so savagely, represented Misfeata's true nature.

"Well don't just stand there," she snapped. "Dispose of these bodies before humans stumble upon them."

"Karla?" One of them questioned. Misfeata reared her head at the woman who spoke.

"Yes," she scythed. "Where will you be going now?"

"To the town to save the people of course," Misfeata responded. Her savageness almost broke the usual audit of my own voice. But it was still my voice and face she wore. She began running towards the town. Although she wanted to protect the humans and stood by her pledge, she still held the ulterior motive in hope to find Lucas's whereabouts.

After minutes of running she finally reached the township. The time hadn't prepared neither of us for the worst. In the main street of the small town which would have held no more than one hundred people, death surrounded us. Of both humans, Starkorfs and some Shielders. Misfeata no longer ran, searching the faces of the humans who she had failed to protect.

This alone grounded her savageness and I could feel the tender touch of grief reach her cold heart. Only few were Shielder's but still the numbers of dead humans far outweighed either of our race. In our peripheral we could see the outstretched hand of a child, holding on to their teddy. Misfeata didn't dare look further as the guilt already sunk in. Her rage was now gone.

Their skins were tainted light blue from being drained. A few were scattered on the main road alongside the bloodshed of the fight that had happened. In the center of the town some human bodies were seen through the glass windows of stores. I had hope for those who lived on the outskirts, but when I searched the grim faces of the Shielders who began to 'clean up' the bodies so no evidence was found, I lost all faith.

It wasn't my proudest moment, but as Misfeata reflected on her own grief and her inability to protect these humans, I navigated my full force against her. It was as if grasping her mind with my hands and pushing her down, swapping our own darkness. She fought, but wasn't prepared for my side attack. I felt as if I had fallen in to my own body. No longer being a bystander. I took a shaky step, of what had felt like years.

"Karla," Christopher said snapping me out of my own moment of relief to now possess my own body.

"Yes," I said. My mouth felt dry and my voice felt foreign to me. I looked around at the bodies again, trying not to cry. Never had I seen an attack of this magnitude. This was a whole town. Much like the attack upon my parents those many years ago before I was born. This would have been the very same scarring experience. "We failed." I said almost inaudible.

Jennifer also looked grim. "It was a miscalculation on my behalf. I will bear their lives not easily. The twenty?" I looked at her slightly shocked that she so easily moved to a different subject. I didn't believe that she was heartless but questioned if this was what was expected of a leader amongst our kind. I nodded my head. She acknowledge their death.

"Impressive," Christopher said.

"Are there no survivors?" I asked, my voice coming out shaky.

"Not that we have yet found," she said factually. I was stunned by her reaction. It was one that was very familiar to Misfeata's. Even though protecting humans was the pledge of all Shielder's the two leaders here seemed unfazed by them as casualties, or simply focused more on the slaughter of Starkorfs. "Please excuse me." She touched my shoulder slightly with an amendable expression before walking away.

I staggered for a few more steps, deciding I could no longer bear to be a part of the town. I began walking back into the other direction from which I had come from. The flashes of all those bodies and the smell of blood replayed in my mind. I don't know for how long I was walking, but eventually I found myself near the old house and barn where Jennifer's group originally hid.

Still staring at the ground as I numbly walked to no place in particular, I heard a mumbling noise. I perked instantly grabbing both of Aeisha.

"No you mustn't." I heard Jennifer's voice weak. There was more mumbling in what I assumed to be Jennifer weakened and defending herself against a Starkorf and I could detect a Starkorf in the house. I located a side window jumping for it and projecting my shield around me so the glass wouldn't shatter. I rolled onto the white and dusty tiling of the kitchen landing elegantly.

I located both Jennifer and a Starkorf hidden in the corner of the room. I went to throw Aeisha at the man before Jennifer's scream halted me.

"No, Karla. No," she said defiantly standing in front of the man protectively. My eyebrows knitted in confusion. The tall Starkorf stood in front of her protectively.

"I won't let you hurt her," he said proudly.

"No Karla, please," Jennifer said trying to break past him. I found the man's hand protectively pressed against her stomach. Suddenly it dawned on me. I was still crouched on the ground, my blade in the tips of my fingers. We all breathed heavily for only a moment as we all tried to gather our own thoughts.

"Karla," Jennifer said reasonably. "He is not an enemy."

"He's a Starkorf," I snarled savagely as much as Misfeata would. After the scene I had just witnessed and the humans dead, I also found myself detesting their kind.

"No, please. I know you don't believe that. You out of all people know there can be exceptions," Jennifer pushed past him, but his hand never left her stomach. I could detect that he was using his Shield against her belly so he physically wasn't draining her. I thought of Lucas as she had said it. How had she known that? I didn't need her to say it, I already knew. This man was the father of her child.

"Inside!" I heard someone call out from the road in the near distance. It wasn't something that could yet reach Jennifer's and this foreign man's ears.

"The others are coming," I informed them, sheathing Aeisha. I don't know why I didn't try to kill him. I don't know why I excused him, but I couldn't be deterred to think anything else by how strongly and beautiful Jennifer believed in that one simple line: *"You out of all people know there can be exceptions."*

"You must go!" Jennifer said as she began to push the man.

"Jennifer please come with me. I can't do this anymore, I can't be without you," he said with tears streaking his eyes. "I want us to be together, I want my family."

She pressed her lips to his so passionately that I looked away embarrassed that I was still in the room.

"Please, don't ever risk coming here again. I love you so much. Now go," she whispered. "You shouldn't have followed me here." I remembered that their group had now travelled many countries and had only recently ventured to my own. In a way it was seemingly romantic, but even I knew it was a love that should never be. I pained at the thought with Lucas in mind.

"I will always follow you. I love you Jen," he kissed her again as the shouts of the others became closer and louder. His lingering hand left her stomach as he skittered out of the room. Before leaving he looked back at me. "Protect her from her mother. Please protect our child."

I hadn't even responded before he fled into the back door and across the open field and into the bushes. Only seconds later Elijah had burst into the room.

"Is he here?" He flared angrily, kicking in one of the doors and searching for him. I instinctually stood in front of Jennifer who straightened no longer in her romantic haze but in her warrior feat.

"Drop it Elijah," she said ruthlessly. I had never seen Elijah so frantic and uncontained. Suddenly all of the pieces to Jennifer's mystery child clicked into place. Elijah's jealousy and hatred very evident of the

Starkorf who he despised the most. More Shielders swept in to the house scanning.

"Where is he?!" Elijah yelled coming closer to us. The others uncertain as to what the argument was about and I gathered that perhaps this romance and the true father to her unborn baby was a secret.

"You have no right to-" Jennifer took a step forward in front of me but her knee buckled. I caught her just in time before she hit hard and unsurprisingly Elijah had already jumped the island counter and swept her in his arms as well.

"It's draining you isn't it," he said almost in tears, his zealous demeanor now gone. He said it so low that only we could hear. "You shouldn't keep pushing yourself. Please."

Jennifer panted harshly, steadying her breathes. After a few heavy gulps of air and her face evidently looking gaunter every time she did so the paleness of her skin began to redden again. "I'm okay."

"It's not okay," Elijah said, his voice distraught. "It is killing you."

Jennifer smiled faintly. "I hope that one day you will respect my wishes Elijah." She pressed a kiss to his cheek as a tear dropped from his eye. She looked at me with the same amount of respect and love. "Thank you for hesitating and trusting me," she said to me. She used both of us for support so she could stand, finally being strong enough to do so herself. "But I don't want to make right now about me. We have lost a lot today. I could only hide here and wait. I can already sense our defeat. Did they take over the entire town?"

Elijah looked to his feet in mourning. "Yes." Jennifer cupped his cheek so he would look at her. There were cuts on his face and arms. "Then let us go mourn for those who we couldn't protect."

Chapter Ten- Revolution

*H*ours passed and everyone hurriedly swept the town clearing out the bodies. No matter how much of the evidence they tried to hide, I questioned how they could possibly avoid being caught for such an act. The blood had begun to dry and the town now held an abandoned and ghostly demeanor. I wondered how many of those now dead still lingered around in the afterlife screaming for this chaotic day. I was sad to know that not one person had survived, total execution.

"How do you not get caught when doing this? How does no one find out?" I questioned Jennifer as we stood beneath a shady tree, a fair distance away from the scene. We looked over the town from a small hill while the others still busily worked. As much as I wanted to be of assistance, I couldn't bring myself to hauling dead bodies like they were nothing. I knew the others mourned for the human loss, but in a sense I realized this was also standard for them. How many times had this chaos happened?

"You would be surprised how many Elemental Breathers are in high positions, especially when it comes to business and media. It is the Elemental Breathers who prevent coverage on this sort of thing. As if it totally never existed," Jennifer said. I gave her a wary look, although I didn't doubt it, I struggled with imagining Elemental Breathers happily working with humans to cover up for Starkorfs and Shielders.

"I don't get it, they hate all races other than their own and to be honest I've never exactly come across a 'modern' Elemental Breather. They're all traditional and fancy," I said honestly. I couldn't look away from the work happening not so far away from me. Would this one day be expected of me? If I am unable to save humans, will I have to drag their bodies instead?

"It's ironic you say that. I heard that one hundred years ago, behind the great wall within Elisabeth's time, that Elemental Breathers and Shielders worked happily together against the Starkorfs. Obviously that trust was broken once the wall was broken. But the Elemental Breathers have always sought out order in this chaotic world. It was in fact an Elemental Breather with the help of a Shielder who created that wall to barricade and separate our world from the human one. No one knows the identity of those two members however. It's scary to acknowledge how little we know and yet this is just the way of things." She rubbed her stomach contently, circling it in a loving manner. I couldn't help but ask, no longer finding the discomfort of seeking answers.

"Your baby. . ." I didn't even know how to manage or end that thought. I neither wanted to accuse or upset her. She countered a sad smile.

"My baby that I cherish so much, has a Starkorf father. Genetically it obviously took the Starkorf trait over the Shielder's," she placed another smile. "But I do not begrudge either. I am very happy with having the opportunity to give birth to the child which I love to the man who I love so much. No matter what he is, we neither want to be involved in this war." I let the silence fill the air while I thought about this. The images of Lucas inevitably appeared. How many times had I questioned whether a future was possible with him? It was so taboo in this world, and yet Jennifer had done exactly that with no regrets.

"Elijah and your mother?" I asked. I knew how Elijah felt about this. He loved Jennifer that much was evident, and this child would take away that very woman. Her mother however, I could only imagine the hatred she would have for it. "Does your mother know it's not Shielder?"

Jennifer offered another bittersweet smile. "At first when I had found out, no one knew of my affair with Kingsly. When we had first met he saved my life. Against all the predictions and hatred my mother fed me to believe of their kind, he was the only person at the time who could have saved me. Elijah and I had a falling out, he has loved me for as long as I can remember as teens. I ran away and when far enough, I had realized I had stumbled into Starkorf territory. It was Kingsly who had found me. So beautiful and elegant to the eye, and in every way not a mutated energy thieving Starkorf. He safely got me out of that environment. I was still young and not strong enough to fight off that many Starkorfs. It started off as curiosity for the both of us. Because of all the Starkorfs within that country and area, we stayed there for a few months hunting them. So every few nights I would sneak off to meet him," she smiled as if reminiscing. "And then one day, I kissed him. At first it burnt and it seemed almost insufferable. But then we realized that if we both projected our shields we could still have that contact, that touch and sensation. I have never had a passion like it run through my veins. So much raw tension and desire." I drifted off into my own thoughts about this kiss Lucas and I had shared. It was of similar tension and passion. Breathtaking and in the moment, magical. It pained my heart to both remember it and feel it on my lips now. "Even when we travelled he continued to follow me. For years we kept in touch, escaping and finding one another when we could. I love him more than I could ever express to anyone within my own group." She sighed sadly. "Elijah was the first to find out, finding me with him. When I found out I was pregnant, I was both terrified but also over the moon. My mother unsuspecting of it, assumed that Elijah was the father. Much to my appreciation, Elijah has lied for me and the rest of the group consider the same. Only Elijah and I know the truth, however I suspect my mother knows."

"How do you think she knows?" I asked curious.

"Because she has tried to kill Kingsly. He is a fine warrior himself so was able to challenge her head on and both escaped unscathed. But as you can see my baby sometimes has the draining effect and she has noticed it. She even once told me that if a defect within the child is evident when it is born, that she will kill it."

My throat and chest tightened at her words. I whipped my head to scan her face, nothing but sadness and pity remained.

"My mother knows," Jennifer continued circling her stomach. "If I die, I am scared for my child. Because my mother will do exactly that if she finds out it is a Starkorf. I have pleaded Elijah to save my baby and to look after it, but I know how deep his hatred for both this child and Kingsly is. Karla, I don't know what to do. I'm not even scared to lose my own life, but only to leave my child in this world unprotected amongst my own people." A tear began to slide from her eye and her bottom lip began to quiver. She wiped the tear away with an apologetic smile. "I am so sorry, hormones make me cry at almost anything now."

"I won't let them do anything to that baby," I said strong willed. I could never let them harm a baby, just because of how it was born. It was a baby it knew nothing better. I couldn't bear to watch such an injustice.

Jennifer's face lit up with hope. She grabbed my hands within seconds holding them close to her heart. "Please Karla, promise me you will protect my child. Please, the only one who can do it is you. You are the only one strong enough to prevent my mother from getting to it.

Please," her voice broke. Her wide eyes scanned mine for every glimmer of hope they chased.

"I promise," I said disheartened that I was the last hope she felt she had. I was disappointed to know that she didn't have the support that she should from her family. What kind of person could consider killing a baby? I thought about the woman who held her young baby and Martin analyzing it. She had asked him for more time, so that Christopher wouldn't hurt it. What sort of world was this where 'ridding' of a defective child was okay? When did this twisted sense of justice start? Was this Misfeata's doing? I felt her slightly stir within me, as if the ringing of her name had awoken her. *"The weakest only ever slow the rest down. There are sacrifices that have to be made."* I slammed into her consciousness as painfully as I could, but it rebounded and hit me harder. I squinted at the instant migraine it gave me. I was so infuriated by her response but still her ability to protect herself from me was far greater than that of my own. I didn't even respond through words. She could sense and drown in my hatred of her.

"Why don't you run away with Kingsly?" I asked thinking that to be the safest option.

"We have tried," she said in another cracked tone. "Before we came to this country. We had tried. And he was almost killed. I can't let him die because of me. I want him to survive so when the time comes he can take our child. I need him alive and well. I will slow him down and my mother and Elijah will find him. Kingsly is strong but he can't stand against all of my people. Either way, no matter where I am, within his arms or amongst my people, who are still my family- I will die. My baby which I love so much will take all the energy I possess, that is the fate of baring a Starkorf child. I have come to terms with that and still would not change it. Just please promise me that you will protect my child and help it safely to Kingsly. Karla, my mother will kill him."

"Him?" I asked. An adoring smile ventured on Jennifer's lips.

"I just have a feeling. My child will be a boy. Please protect him," she pleaded with me. I didn't hesitate with my response. This was something I couldn't deny anyone. I wasn't the most maternal but I could ask my mother to aid me in looking after this child until I found Kingsly. If these were Jennifer's wishes I would happily oblige. My only regret was that Jennifer would not survive to see her own child. I wanted there to be hope and tell her she might survive. But I had heard of the stories, I knew in this gory world that it wasn't how it happened.

"I will protect her with my life," I vowed. "No matter what." A huge relieved smile stretched over Jennifer's face and she embraced me. Her large stomach pushing against my own lightly.

"Thank you so much," she cried happily. Her embrace was tight yet gentle at the same time. "You are an amazing and beautiful strong woman. Not because you have Misfeata within you. I know the others idolize you because of her. That is not the case, stay true to who you are. Your sense of justice is right Karla, in a world where many don't see the same. Never let Misfeata overcome you. I know the curse you bear and I can only sympathize with your struggle. You've sacrificed much but it is only you who has both the power and voice of reason. You can change all of this," she said pointing towards those who busily carried away bodies.

"I can't and I don't know how," I admitted suddenly uncomfortable with all the kind words, but heavy meaning she had behind each one.

"You once fought alongside the prince, Lucas, didn't you? Are you able to make him see the same way you do? Can we not all work together in this new generation? He is still young, perhaps mouldable. You must change it Karla. Only you can do this."

I opened my mouth to respond, but fell short. I felt the presence of someone walking towards us and cowered away from a response. I didn't know what to say. It was as if Jennifer knew that Lucas and I wavered a strong bond. But how could she know that? And now, with everything that had happened between Lucas and I, if we tried to even stand close to one another the Elders within us would try to kill one another. There was no escaping this fate. The flash of his alarmed face and pleading eyes came to mind. That day when he scampered away from me and took Borac, I knew our fate had changed. No matter how much he promised that he would never hurt me, it was a promise that could never be kept, even when we both wanted it to be true.

"Jennifer, Karla," Christopher said from the distance. "We are about to start the mourning ceremony if you would like to make your way down."

"Of course mother," Jennifer said. I couldn't help but give Christopher a fierce look knowing what expectation and death sentence she had put on her unborn grandchild. I thought no one was evil enough in the world for that, but here stood the very strong warrior, who very easily could do that- thinking of it as a source of weakness and evil.

81

I walked with Jennifer to the place where a large heap of bodies had been piled up on wood and dried leaves. I looked away at all the purplish figures where some were still wide eyed.

"You must watch," Christopher said as she came to my side. Now all her people stood around the carcasses watching on. "This is something we could have prevented, but we were too late for. It is both respectful to wish them well in the afterlife, but take responsibility of us not making it on time. Their deaths are on our hands." I went to respond but choked on my words. I did feel guilty for not saving their lives and for not countering the Starkorfs plan. Christopher nodded. Four men walked closer and lit their thick sticks which burst into flames. They wedged them in amongst the pile off wood, until the flames began to enlarge. I sensed all around me that all the Shielders projected their Shields. I too did the same and looked through my grey ripples that swirled around me, unlike the rest who were invisible.

"We project our Shield both in respect for those lost," Christopher said, focusing on the flames. They reflected a golden spark in her eyes. "And also so we don't have to suffer the most hideous smell anyone can come across, and that is human flesh."

Looking between both her and the flames and the rest that mourned around, I fell into suit. This was a grotesque world and I now truly understood that this was larger than just me and my inner struggle with Misfeata. There were incidents all around the world like this where humans were being killed and it was simply being swept aside as if it had never happened. Although mourning for them now, how could this world and war possibly be justified?

Jennifer's words rung so true in my mind. I had to start a revolution of sorts, to try and make an impact or change to these old ways that both Shielders and Starkorfs were slaves too. And that started with finding one person- Lucas.

Chapter Eleven- Selfishness

*W*hether it was deemed as disrespectful in their beliefs or not, I couldn't stay to watch and didn't want to know how they next discarded the bones. I knew that they were doing something different with the Starkorfs bodies, but even then I had no interest to know. This wasn't something I wanted to be a part of and so I ventured closer to the farmers properties which were now so barren.

I stood in the center of the road, where I previously prepared for today's battle. No, not me. Misfeata did. That very expectation of how today would go was entirely different to the outcome. I had never even thought of an outcome like this to be possible. But the one factor remained. There was a flaw in our plan and we hadn't spread out wide enough to detect or prevent the Starkorfs getting around us. This was a failure that cost many people their lives.

My impatience only grew further. I sat in the middle of the road, watching the sun set. I had a yearning to have Paul close by to hold me and tell me everything was okay, like he always did. I felt an emptiness without his presence. I questioned how he would process everything I just saw and how he would appear to be unscathed by it, where as I emotionally struggled to handle it. It left me with a bitter numbness and sense of loneliness. I began to hate myself for how much I depended on him and that I expected his embrace to be the only thing that could assure me that everything would be okay. The reason why he'd been in this war for so long, was because I had always wanted him close. Without even realizing it at the start.

As time moved on, so did the group. Eventually, everyone was ready to leave. Scott and Paige segregated amongst others, but still stayed close to me. I walked with Christopher, Jennifer and Elijah taking the lead. There wasn't as much urgency in our steps. We walked a fair distance before we began to run. I noticed that our numbers had dropped and two of those children who came to fight alongside us no longer walked with us. I tried my hardest not to think of where they had gone. I knew where they were and what has happened to them. Some

Shielders had red bloodshot eyes from what would have been hours of mourning.

Eventually Scott went with Martin in the car and the rest of us ran back to where the camp was. Hours later, after running through the wild we arrived at our camp. Scott and Martin were already there. It appeared that the news hadn't yet reached the other Shielders who stayed back as Martin and Scott being Elemental Breathers would have kept to themselves. They at first looked cheerful. Their expression then changed from hopeful to an instant expression of mourning.

They looked through the members searching who had not made it back. I dipped my head in shame, infuriated that I couldn't save them. Christopher in a clear loud voice spoke six names. Those were the six that no longer fought beside us. There was very little emotion. A few walked away into the trees by themselves, and a few comforted one another; but mostly they tried to hide any emotion they might've had.

Christopher walked straight into her tent, closely followed by Elijah and a few others who fought with us today. I ignored the hierarchy and did not follow suit. I couldn't bear being around the others right now. Instead I walked into the trees asking Paige to stay back who attempted to follow me. Still I didn't know where Scott had vanished to. Paige surprisingly respected my wishes and walked the other way by herself into the night.

I continued walking unable to stop, I just continued to walk further and further out moving aside branches that were at my eye level. I rested against the trunk of a tree looking past the grey clouds that drifted and at the stars that didn't shine as brightly as they should have.

I was alert as soon as I heard the snap of a branch. Yet I felt too tired to stand, I just waited for the threat to appear. No matter who it was I knew I would manage. For this moment, I just felt like I no longer had the fight in me. I was so tired of fighting and didn't even want to begin to think about the restlessness I felt about losing myself to Misfeata.

I rested my hand on the ground, absorbing the information it fed me. The moist ground quickly blackened as I killed it. I noted that only one Starkorf walked toward me. I waited for him patiently, my hands pointedly ready on my blades for his attack.

To my surprise it was Kingsly who walked out. He put his hands up in a nonlethal manner. Not fully letting my guard down I too relaxed my posture with no real intention to fight unless I had too. I simply didn't have the strength.

He waited for a moment, awkwardly standing there in his posture.

"You're that girl aren't you? The one who has Misfeata in her?" He asked after a few moments of silence. My lack of response curated the answer he was after.

"Shouldn't you be worried about being so close to the camps?" I exhaustedly said. "I'm sorry but I don't know where Jennifer is right now." After another long pause he spoke again.

"I actually wasn't here for Jennifer, I am here for you. I know of a guy looking for you, to find your whereabouts." That grabbed my attention as I could only think of two people who would be seeking me out. There was both a stir of hope that this man would be my connection to Lucas, or anxiousness that he was a scout for Eden. A third occurrence struck me that Kurt was also trying to source me out.

"Tell me Kingsly, are you an enemy of mine?" I asked with a threatening tone. It sounded something like Misfeata would casually say, but in my current mood and demeanor it was the most fight I could gather in my tone.

"I only side with Jennifer. But I think if she trusted you enough like today, then that means that you too might have the same ideal as Jennifer and I. I am only new to this area, but I have met a group of followers who are scouting for the prince who has Tyran in him." Instantly I whipped my head in his direction. It was Lucas who he was following. I tried to not convey my hope in that, still playing a very casual demeanor.

"Where is he and what does he want with me?" I asked.

"Apparently he just wants to talk with you and-"

"That's impossible," I quickly pointed out. "We can't be close to one another without the Elder's trying to kill the other." In my tone I must have given something away because he gave me an incredulous look.

"What if I told you that he found a way to put that to a halt?" His words felt heavy in the air. So much hope filled me. I fantasised to be able to talk to Lucas, to see if he was okay. To even possibly reach out to him. It was painful to imagine as reality sunk in. And then I thought of Paul, I still cared for him so much with all my heart but I couldn't deny my yearning to still see Lucas. I felt like a traitor to both of them.

"That's impossible," I whispered dipping my head in shame by the mixed emotions that tore through me about both Paul and Lucas.

"It isn't. What If I could guarantee you a meeting with Lucas in two night's time? A place where you can both talk without trying to kill each other?" Kingsly said. It was a dream I had long tried to hide. It was something I wanted more than anything. The way we parted on that faithful day had tormented my heart ever since. If there was a glimmer of hope to see him and not have the Elders possess our bodies, I couldn't deny my greed and desire for it. I yearned to see Lucas again, despite the enemy territory that came between.

I couldn't completely give in to my hopeful glimmer. Even I couldn't think of a way to supress Misfeata or Tyran. There was none. This could be a lie, a trick even. On that very same night will be the moment when I'll be reunited with my mother, Paul and the others. I couldn't let any of them know that I was meeting with Lucas, and how this could possibly be a trap. I looked into the sky where an owl circled beautifully low towards us. "How do I know you are speaking the truth?"

"Because I won't do it for nothing. I want something in return," he said honestly. Much to my surprise it made me believe him. Everyone had their own selfish desires to fulfil, it made it more realistic in this world.

"What is it that you want from me?" I asked him looking to my left where I could sense someone slowly approaching. "Someone is coming so you better make your request quick."

"I need your help to keep Jennifer alive. I need you to somehow use the Elder power you have so our child won't kill her." It escaped him as a plea and he had dipped his head down to me. "Please you are my last resort, I have researched everywhere I could possibly imagine. I don't know where else to go."

"My powers don't enable me to do that. I don't know how to fix that." The person was now verging closer and we only had a few moments left. He noted our urgency.

"Please do everything in your power to make that happen. I swear to you I will find Lucas and organise this arrangement so you can see him. Just please try your best to save her." A noise in the background broke, our time was now over. He looked into the direction it came from and began seeping back in to the trees.

"In two days' time I will find you and take you to your meeting place. Just please, please save my baby and Jennifer." He ran into the trees before I could say anymore. I had a hollow feeling of surprise and shock that someone believed my powers were so godly. But I couldn't deny his desperate tone, he really had run out of options. I continued to stare into the direction he fled to thinking of how it were plausible I could save Jennifer. Secondly, I questioned how very real my chance of meeting Lucas now was, but under no circumstance could anyone else know. The only person I could tell, in case I disappeared was. . .

"This is depressing," Scott said as he came out of the treetops. The exact person I was thinking of.

"You aren't very quiet amongst the trees," I noted. It was odd that even though he had betrayed me once, he still seemed to be the only person I could tell about my meeting with Lucas because I knew no one else would agree or so easily let me go.

"I didn't mean to be quiet. You and that Starkorf were the ones sneaking around here, not me." I wasn't even surprised that he knew.

"You were the owl," I said thinking back to the owl I saw circling in the sky. That must have been Scott spying.

"I was the owl," he simply said. "So are you going? Even if you don't know this method of 'sedating' the Elders?"

"I don't think I have much of a choice," I said defensively.

"Everyone has a choice. What's your objective for meeting him?" Scott often changed his personality from serious and powerful to flamboyant and overly charismatic. It was something I had become accustomed to. It surprised me how much I still trusted him even after his betrayal. Then again both he and Paul had almost died in my very arms. I suppose that was the reality for me to not begrudge them too harshly because they had both almost died for their association with me.

"I just. . ." I didn't know if I dared say the words out loud. "I just want to see him. With this war and everything set aside. I want to fix it so we never have to fight again. But mostly, I just want to see him."

"Paul will be coming back that night. He'll question where you are," Scott said. "A heart doesn't always so easily choose what or whom it desires does it?" I gave him a questioning look. He often teased me for my mixed emotions between Lucas and Paul. They were the two major factors in who I was today and why I fought. Yet, still after everything that has happened, my feelings for them both were so strong that I struggled to challenge either.

"Have you ever been in love Scott?" I asked curiously. He only thought about it for a short time with a decisive answer.

"No. I have been fascinated by many. But not love. I think love is when you meet someone you are willing to sacrifice things for or even throw your body as the Shield in the middle of a fight for, with consideration of the world we live in. I've never met anyone close to who I would do that for. Then again I am elegantly selfish and may never love anyone more than myself," he joyfully said in a wicked laugh. I raised my knees towards my chin and hugged myself in thought. We pondered in comfortable silence.

"I want to see him," I hesitantly said. "But it might be a trap. I need to know that you have my back in case something goes wrong. Just in case it is Eden and not Lucas."

Scott rested his hand on mine with an odd expression of fondness that we didn't too often share. "I will watch over you," he simply said in a low hum. "I'm just saying, your boy toy isn't going to like it, and my gosh can you imagine both your Uncle's and Ashley's response if they knew! How scandalous," Scott shrieked in excitement. He began rambling on about make believe situations that forced me to believe he had watched far too many soap operas and TV teen romance shows. I looked back to the sky where a real owl now hovered in the sky. I was choosing to see Lucas again, but lying to the rest to do so. I had no right to judge Scott for his previous betrayal when I was selfishly doing the same.

Chapter Twelve- Inner Turmoil

$\mathcal{D}$espite Scott staying by my side promising I would have a restful sleep without Misfeata affecting me, I tossed and turned and was unable to do so. Flashes of bodies and blood flashed across my mind repetitively. Even when I hid under the blankets I found no closure. I was even jealous of Paige who was unaffected and slept peacefully. I feared what sense of judgment she had if she were able to sleep so easily. She often made it known how much she loved the fight, but even this seemed too much.

Scott read a book in the dark, his eyes glowing a mystical yellow, representing the owls' eyes who he transformed back from. It was obvious he needed no lighting with those eyes, he could see clearly in the dark. I stepped out eventually unable to clear my mind. I washed my face with cold water, splashing it over me in hopes of waking me up. The only grateful thing I found with Misfeata being in my body was that although I obtained hardly any sleep I was somehow able to still function. I supposed that was a part of the rapid healing as well, or something like that. I gave up on questioning my bodies' capabilities and gifts for some time now. It no longer even felt like my own.

A nauseous swelling rose within me and my legs buckled in fatigue. I screamed silently and cried as my hands naturally grasped around me. It was hard to focus when my body shut down. The blood that pumped through my veins frenzied and fought one another. My every organ slowly stopping and reaching my demise. Through the pain I had to try and think clearly, something I was now accustomed to. I gathered my Shield within me as quickly as I could and let it combust around me. Dirt spilled around me from the wind and blowout of my shield. The adrenalin that pumped through my veins averted my death.

For a moment longer I whimpered into the dirt, coughing in to it as I tried to gather my shaking body. The healing already begun. But right now, here closest to the ground in a pile of a dirt, was literally where I felt I needed to be. Although amongst tents and with the thought of someone coming out and seeing me in such a state, I didn't care. I was tired of fighting and sick of seeing dead bodies in a broken world. I no longer wanted this existence. I never wanted it, but now it was worse- I was struggling to find the fight and desire to live.

When I rescued Paul from Taskatae's castle and lost my consciousness, I walked on the edge of life and death. I had that choice, and even now I questioned if I regretted it. I didn't because I wanted to protect those who I loved most, but I also grew tired of this constant battle.

Slowly I pushed myself back up and took a few wobbly steps until my body had rebalanced and it were as if nothing had happened. I started my long walk which I hoped to clear my mind, if anything I only continued to roll over the same thoughts. There was no escaping my mind. If it weren't Misfeata making me miserable it was my own constant thoughts.

Eventually hours later, I came back. The sun had only risen for a few hours now but already everyone was very energetic. It appeared that I had come back during their training. They all fought diligently. The younger members fought ruthlessly with real blades against one another. There weren't many children, but I found it startling to see them of all ages sweating as profusely as the adults.

Christopher fought with Elijah, it appeared to be more of a dance than anything. Their weapons clashed together with force. A lot of them trained in hand to hand combat. A small child surprised me when he flung himself over his adult opponent in one swift movement. With as much force as possible he plunged his knife towards the man's chest, hovering above just before contact, showing his control and ability.

A woman sat down with a three year old, teaching her how to project her Shield. There was such a wild and electric feel pillowing the atmosphere that it was hard not to want to train. I saw Paige in the corner of my eye exempting a bored expression. I walked over to her, her eyes almost lighting up as she saw me in hope of what I would offer.

"Do you want to train with me Paige?" I asked. Even though she was older than me, her entire demeanor lit up like a child's would.

Fighting hand to hand combat with Paige without my Shield was not easy. Although she was small, she was both swift and strong. Countering her punches left bruises on my arms, or so I imagine they would have if I still bruised. I noticed that we became a spectacle to some and that they watched us closely. I had never fought against Paige, only alongside her and I truly valued her strength more now than ever. I knew she was strong, but this strength she held felt both comforting, yet strangely familiar. I couldn't pinpoint where I had sensed this fighting form from before.

At times we were equally matched, but then other times I would get the upper hand. This annoyed her even more and she became near savage. At times it seemed she had forgotten that it was only practice. Only twenty minutes into it we were pulling no punches and elegantly flipping through the air and striking with all our force. Our sleeveless shirts clung to our body from sweat. Our leather jackets thrown off long ago.

Scott and Martin sat beside one another in silence, both of them studying our moves. It was a bit unnerving but I didn't have much time to focus on that when Paige's fist was coming my way. The thing about training and fighting was I loved it. It was a moment where my body just acted and my mind didn't rush with thoughts or issues it just tides with the fighting, taking one step at a time to become the victor.

After about an hour, Christopher's clapping broke our form. Paige and I both panted harshly, exhausted by what was meant to be a small workout, but became so much more. I eyed Paige before looking at Christopher. Still I had no idea what she was. I felt that she was not an enemy and I could rely on her. But I worried because I knew she wasn't human and for some reason her fighting presence reminded me of someone and I didn't know who. I had never noticed it before.

Scott uncomfortably picked up a small towel with two of his fingers, it was evident he was grossed out by touching it. He offered it to me and I grabbed it wiping over my dripping face. He seemed grateful to have rid himself of what he thought to be filthy. I peeked over the towel at Martin who still studied me intensely.

"Very nice match," he said with very little praise in his tone. "Both of your forms are interesting. I have noted it," he said. I wanted to spite back that no one had asked him to do that and I didn't like my fighting technique being analyzed but Scott had already spoken up.

"My gosh, you sound like a damn robot," he sighed loudly. Martin didn't waver his gaze towards Scott. He simply stood and walked towards other Shielders and began analyzing their fighting technique.

"Very nice," Christopher said with another clap. "You even made a spectacle of yourself in front of my fighters. Could I be so lucky as to challenge the all mighty host of Misfeata?"

"I'm not some trial you can stage your strength against," I said annoyed. "I refuse to fight you. I only train with my comrades."

91

"But I am one. I am also a Shielder, Karla," she said annoyed after being told no. I imagined it wasn't something she was used to.

"No, I am still waiting for the rest of my institute to arrive. I will only practice with them. I don't want to be some strength that you try to overthrow or compare with or impress in front of your people. I fight only for what I want and who I want. I don't fight when or because you want me to."

Her narrow face hardened further. The evident aging in her face was stern. Not many people overheard our conversation, but it didn't prevent the annoyance that displayed on Christopher's face.

"You may want to watch your tone with me and remember that it was I, who has allowed your members to come back into our protection. You might want to fall in line soon," she snapped before walking away.

"What a cow," Paige said beside me wiping her own face. "She might not be able to fight you but I'm up for it." She threw her towel at Scott who shrivelled into some tiny creature before it could touch him. When he reappeared in his natural form his eyes shot daggers at her.

"Don't worry about it," I said to Paige and grabbed her arm. A coldness swept through me and a moment of dark hit me. She pulled her arm out of my grip as I looked at her somewhat dazed and unsure of what I had just felt. It was as Scott said, I felt emptiness. Yet it felt so familiar. My expression must have conveyed my confusion because she walked away before I could question her anymore.

I saw that the mother with the ill child drastically changed direction as Christopher walked towards her. She was relieved when she realized she hadn't spotted her and hid in a tent. I watched how they trained and took particular interest in the little girl who still tried to concentrate on practicing her Shield. It was odd for a child so young, being so grounded and having such control. Not that it replicated through her Shield but evident on the little girls face. I remembered the first time that I had practiced my Shield. The first time I thought it was beautiful and was not terrified by it was when I sat on an open grass hill with Lucas. He took my hands in his leather gloved ones and made sure I applied pressure to them when we monitored my progress.

Back when I had been so amazed by what I had created and what I could do. That moment shared with Lucas felt like a lifetime ago. I idly thought about what idea he might have had so we could talk with one another without the Elders trying to possess us. There was a possibility of not seeing Lucas, and I had to lower my expectations. That by tomorrow night I could both see Lucas and have Paul return to me. My stomach gutted at the thought of seeing my mother. Would she be happy to see me or angry by how I had last departed with her?

I was also nervous to see Helena, Suzumiya and Chris. I wasn't sure if Suzumiya still hated me as passionately as she did before I left the institute and if Helena was still grieving after all these months since losing Seth. I wondered if they had yet found out about Kurt's betrayal. I could only assume so because Ashley continued to report to them.

Within hours everyone began to pack up their belongings and we began slowly venturing to the spot where we would meet with the others tomorrow night. It was at a slower pace, one with consideration for the wounded. I had almost forgotten that although Shielders, their wounds still took a little bit of time to fully heal. Martin and Scott still left in the car with a few of the Shielders who were prioritized. It was still intriguing that they walked everywhere and only relied on the car for a few supply trips and to transport Martin who couldn't keep up with their usual pace.

It was eerie walking with them. No one said anything, utter silence. Only the crunches beneath our feet were heard. I no longer had an inkling of where I was anymore. I only followed the rest, like we were a herd of animals. Paige was evidently getting annoyed by the slow pace as expected of her. We eventually set up camp for another night, where Martin and Scott hadn't joined us. I laid wide awake reforming the same nightmare memories in my mind. I couldn't fall asleep in case I ventured into Misfeata's world.

However with very little sleep the nights before and a day of walking, no matter how strong willed I thought I was, my body gave in and I found myself in the grasp of Misfeata's world.

Chapter Thirteen- Longing To See You

The noise of a clock continued to tick. It was the only thing I could hear in the darkness where I lay. Tick, tick, the suspense of every second was a nightmare in itself. I was paranoid and frightened, considering all the things she might do to me here. And yet, Misfeata had not yet appeared. Tick, tick, tick. A loud noise swelled my ears as the clock chimed eight.

I counted each and every haunting decibel. Still blackness. Nothing. The vast emptiness surrounding me could have hidden anything. I was in a defensive stance waiting for hands to reach out to me or for anything unnatural to come. A bright burst of colour reached my eyes, making me squint at the sudden change. I raised my hand trying to dim its blinding effects. Misfeata stood there idly, her back turned to me as if looking into the distance. When my eyes adjusted, I realized she stood on the hill of which I first identified her in my dreams; when she showed me how her little brother, Sebastian was killed.

I didn't want to stand by her side, but I also stood uncomfortably still in the darkness, the only image for me to walk towards was the one which she stood in. She hadn't yet made a violent move towards me so hesitantly I began to walk towards her.

She was as beautiful as always with her fiery red hair and beautiful green gown. She simply stood and looked over the hill to the town which she once occupied. I stood beside her looking her up and down, measuring our size difference. It was odd to know that a woman far taller and elegant than me resided within my body. She didn't look fierce or threatening here. She simply looked like a beautiful woman staring into the sunset.

"I often come back to this place and memory," she said giving me a quick glance over. "Thinking of how this all started and where we had gone wrong." I didn't say anything. I was still waiting for her hands to reach out and strangle me or for some mustered beasts to attack me.

Her lips twitched into a small smile. Of course she had heard my thoughts.

"We weren't naturally a violent breed. We were once peaceful and happy," she said.

"Could have fooled me," I said sassily. Her gaze never lowered but her neck straightened further as if she thought my comment were insolent.

"I too wish this war could end Karla. But the only way for that to truly happen is with the death of my brother, Tyran."

"And what after that?" I said quickly, interjecting before she could say anything else. "Once you've killed him what happens then? What happens to you? What happens to the war? This war you have created isn't just about you two anymore. You have built hatred between two entire races which has consumed them into a continuous war. The whole point of your kind was to protect humans yet it is because of your war that they are in danger."

"I have lived for over three hundred years. I have witnessed how everything has eventuated and become as it is. Never think you know more about this war than I do, because I have been fighting it a far greater length than you have," she hissed. "The decisions I make have always been for the better of my race and unfortunately a young girl like you could never understand those sacrifices that have to be made."

"I know too well what sacrifices I have made for this stupid war," I hissed with the flash of my father's death coming to mind. Tears swelled in my eyes but I held them back fiercely to not show my weakness. "Why have you brought me here Misfeata?"

She let the slight breeze sweep through us for a long time as she contemplated and continued to look over the township. "Because I wanted you to know that although I am a monster, and I know this, that I too have moments of reflection. I too get tired of fighting in what seems to be an endless war. I do what I do because I believe it is the right thing to do. Eventually when I claim your body completely as my own and those days are closing in," she threatened. "Your sacrifice wasn't for nothing and that I am grateful for the gift you have given me."

I scoffed at her in disgust. "I will never let you win and claim my body. It isn't some sacrifice that you can justify, I will never allow it."

She gave a weary smile. "But you tire of the fight, and when you do that is when weakness shows. I have fought for over three hundred *years now, I am far more durable than you. Make the most of the time you have Karla Grey. Your time is coming to an end."*

My mind felt as if it were tearing apart as the world swarmed around me in darkness again.

I gasped harshly as I rose out of my sleep. I cradled my knees panting harshly and wiping away the sweat that made me feel sticky and gross. I took a few more shallow breaths, my head pain now gone. I shuffled uncomfortably and looked over at Paige who had pounced awake beside me because of my sudden outburst. She was fully alert with blade out of her sheath. She summarized the tent and looked at me.

"Just a nightmare," I said. She hesitated and searched the tent again and then nodded satisfied that was all it was. My constant and unimaginable nightmare. Not daring to sleep again I walked out into the warm night. The breeze felt cool on my skin and felt as if little icicles replaced the sweat.

To my surprise, Jennifer was walking back from the trees. She was startled to see me until she realized who I was. She walked up to me with a faint smile.

"Sorry," she whispered. "I thought you were someone else. I have something for you actually." She began to fiddle in her leather jacket and pulled out a small piece of paper. "I have a message for you."

I didn't have to guess who she had made contact with in the woods. I also had a suspicion as to who the letter may have come from. She gave me the piece of paper and held my hands between hers.

"I know what Kingsly asks for is unreasonable," she whispered so no one might overhear if they were awake. "He will still help you but I've told him your powers don't reach that far. All I ask is that you make sure my child reaches him. I've accepted my fate." She gave me another sad smile before walking away and left the note in my hand.

She slipped into her tent which was closest to her mothers. I looked over behind my shoulder to find Elijah watching me. If I recalled correctly it was his time to be on watch. He exchanged a haunting expression with me. I further crinkled up the note she had placed in my hand doubting that he could have overheard or seen the exchange but still uncomfortable by his watching eyes.

I walked into the trees looking over my shoulder every now and then to see if he followed. Much to my surprise he hadn't. When I felt safe enough to do so, I leant against a tree and opened the letter. It was in the unmistakable writing of Lucas.

Karla,

I hope you are doing well. I am sorry for the way that we parted last. You had for so long described the sensation to me, and even my father had so many times told my brother and I what to expect. But, I don't think there is any amount of preparation in the world to avoid the experience of having Tyran enter my body for the first time. I promised to you that I would never hurt you. And I still very much intend for that. But, I can't deny that impossible growth of hatred, not towards you- never towards you. But the one that rivals between the Elders. I think I've found a way for us to talk. We need to. I want to protect you at all costs. I know Eden is in search of you and I want to banish that threat for you. I also can't deny that I too am looking for a way that we can get rid of this curse. Although I am considered as the most powerful Starkorf currently, I have never felt weaker. There have been so many times now I've struggled against Tyran. Is this how you have suffered all this time? I am so sorry for having triggered it. Everyone desires this strength, yet I wonder if they had a taste of this curse whether they would still want it.

I want to see you, more than anything. The only thing is, the way that we might be able to supress the Elders will be very painful for us in return and will leave both of us exposed and vulnerable. We will be at a point where we can't fight if we were to be ambushed. I have gathered enough security on my behalf to cover us both if an enemy catches us off guard, but I have to request that you come alone. I know Ashley and the others won't agree to this and I can't risk that they might take advantage of me in a weakened state. Please come alone. It was by chance that my men were approached by Kingsly, who claimed to have known where you are. I was surprised to hear of those who you have connected with and their numbers. Unfortunately Eden's followers still far outweighs both your numbers and mine. But slowly I am gathering my own. I am keeping tabs on Eden's location. Karla he's getting closer. You must keep moving. Tomorrow night Kingsly will fetch you and escort you to our meeting place. I apologize for the insufferable pain you will go through to see me. But, it was the only way I could think of.

A few droplets of ink from the calligraphy pen had dripped near the bottom of the page before his next sentence as if he were thinking for a while as to what he would say.

Karla, I haven't been able to stop thinking about you. I am so sorry this is how it has become.
Please come tomorrow night, I beg of you.

Lucas.

I stared at the note blankly with a mix of emotions rolling inside of me. I feared it was a trap and that's why he sought me out alone. I was anxious as to what he meant by insufferable pain just to see him and why hadn't he elaborated on why that might be. I was pained by the words he had used and the devotion to the promise that he made. It broke my heart. I felt treacherous towards Paul for having such conflicting emotions. But I couldn't deny my urge and want to see Lucas. I wanted to see him more than anything.

I grew wary that Eden was closing in on my location. It would only be a matter of time until he found out where I was. I could skip oceans to run away from him and still be found. But I didn't have the numbers to go against him. I hated that I thought I needed the numbers, like it was a true war. I didn't want anyone putting themselves in danger for my sake. This had begun because I had decided to kill Raven. My first murder and that is what it was, I had killed someone with my bear hands. I looked down at my shaky hands in disbelief of all those lives I had since taken. Raven had tried to kill my family and killed hundreds before. No matter if I tried to justify it that way, the reflection of my own sins still appeared. There was no coming back from the things I had done. And then that pang and longing for Paul to be here resurfaced once again. I so badly wanted him to hold me and tell me that everything would be okay.

Tonight, I reminded myself. *Tonight I will be able to see Paul. I will see both Paul and Lucas.* And the anxiety only grew.

Chapter Fourteen- A Fleeting Moment

*T*he day went extremely slow as I struggled with the undermining thoughts of how tonight could possibly go. We would soon reach the destination where we were to meet the others. I would be reunited with my mother and see those who still remained at the institute, but that was after I first saw Lucas. I wanted to inform the others because I knew they would disapprove my arranged meeting with Lucas, which was why I had to leave before I saw them first. This was something I had to do on my own.

Again, it was only silence that we walked in. There were a few halts of the group so scouts could inspect the surrounding areas. Christopher had an overwhelming sensation we were being followed but after inspection, it wasn't the case. I questioned if that was simply paranoia and caution curated after all the years of battle. I too often did the same.

I was reunited with Scott who silently waited with Martin and the few Shielders who had already begun to set up camp. It wasn't night yet, but it would only be hours until the moon would be showing. I couldn't help but avoid that hurdle of nausea as I waited patiently for the others. I questioned how far away they were and if they would arrive before I left.

When night came and they still hadn't arrived I decided it was time to go and walk around idly hoping that Kingsly knew where to find me.

Before departing from the camp Jennifer, who was helping one of the other women teach her child to walk gave me a knowing glance. Paige assessed me as she always did when she knew something was happening without her knowledge, but I didn't feel safe with telling her this secret. It appeared Ashley and she had become close over time and I couldn't risk her telling him or looking for a fight either.

I walked over to the sulking Scott. When he saw me approach he gave out an unearthly whine.

"Why must I still reside like a barbaric person? I feel like I am losing both hygiene and my identity." He pitied himself with sadness. A few of the Shielders shot him a disgusted look. His look only reflected the same of which they gave.

"I'm going for a walk. I might be a while," I said. I knew he would understand my ulterior meaning.

"Eww, you've been walking all day and yet you still want to walk. That sounds like far too much exertion. Is it a walk I should be a part of? Do you want to cry on my shoulder or something grotesque like that little Shielder," he said meekly. Scott continued with his theatrics which countered anyone considering my disappearance odd because Scott was making such an obvious big deal about it. Somehow it deterred their interest.

"No I want to be alone," I said shrugging him off before tucking my hands in my leather jacket and walking away. I knew that he would come looking for me within hours if I hadn't yet returned.

"Karla?" Christopher said in confusion as I was walking towards the trees. "Where are you going? This is the night your group will be coming to this place? We need to reassess our next move. I believe my people would appreciate you being here for it."

"I will be back shortly, I just need to clear my thoughts," I said annoyed by her as she blocked my path.

"No, perhaps you misinterpreted. What I am saying is, you can't leave right now," she said directly. I seized her up, my face close to hers in the most intimidating manner I could. I couldn't help but feel the anger swell in me. It was a deeper anger that I wasn't sure if it derived from me or Misfeata. I knew she hated being told what to do more than anything. It was an identical trait in both her and Christopher.

"You do not own me," I hissed so my breath lingered on her face. I could sense her Shield within her building and I did the same. At any moment either of us might strike out at the other. She obviously hated her authority challenged. I noticed that others around us had stopped to stare. Whether my rebellion was a form of disrespect or challenge, I didn't care. I wasn't owned by anyone. I was challenged by Misfeata every day in the same sense. This was her own power struggle and not one that I wanted to be a part of. She still hesitated to do anything, so I simply walked past her knocking her shoulder. I waited for her retaliation but to my surprise no matter how angry, she didn't lash out.

It appeared that the almighty host of Misfeata was shown immunity of some sort to disobeying orders. I continued to walk into the trees and woodland. Long ago I feared racing through such a scenery by myself. Now it just felt natural to be alone and in the dark. After walking ten minutes away from the camp I crouched to the ground and placed my hand on the dirt. Obviously it had been raining recently because it appeared muddy. I absorbed the information it fed me getting a sense of where Kingsly might be. I felt the presence of all those at camp. I wavered on the off chance that in the very far distance there might be people coming closer towards that camp. I couldn't sense whether it was the institute or not. It made it hard when none of them could Shield so I couldn't detect that ability. I was wary of the presence, wondering if I should go back to report it. But the camp should be safe and even if it were Starkorfs, the scouts would announce an alarm before they got anywhere close.

To my right, I sensed a lone Starkorf walking idly in the woods. I could only imagine it to be one person, and that was the very person who I sought out now. I approached in that direction until I hid behind a tree. I waited for the person to walk past me so I could assess whether it was Kingsly.

When he walked past unsure and unable to detect my presence I called out to him, scaring him from his tracking of Christopher's group. I had to give him credit for his ability to follow the group without being detected.

"Kingsly," I said. He jumped sliding out his sword in a quick manner and on guard. I didn't worry about unsheathing my own. I simply stood there with my hands crossed over my chest. When he identified it was me he put the sword away. He carried on his back a small backpack which took my interest.

"Well I guess this makes it easier for me to find you instead of me trying to call you out. How did you know I was here?" He asked. After asking it he shook his head. "It doesn't matter, I guess you are the almighty Elder so you would have heaps of tricks up your sleeves."

"I'm not an Elder," I said with interest as I leaned over to see what he had in his backpack when he dropped it to the ground and begun to unzip it.

"No you're not," he said. "But because of the Elder within you, this is what is going to make this hurt. *A lot.*" Still with eyebrows arched I watched him as he pulled out his contraption. Instantly I retracted my interest as I saw the red glow of the gems. It was as if the pain had already begun. I recalled that excruciating pain that gems of similar make to Tyran's blade and soul had on my body. Praytar, Lucas's father had imprisoned me in it and it became unbearable and I could hardly move. It both weakened my state and scorched my skin, unable to naturally heal as I always did.

The gems were in the shape of what looked like a thick studded collar. Realization dawned on me.

"No. . ." I said in disbelief. It was both a plea of my own and a warning from Misfeata who had suddenly arrived. She very forcefully tried to possess my body. *No! You will not do that to me!* She reprimanded.

"Can you deny that it won't work?" Kingsly said. "Lucas told me that this was the only way and you wouldn't like it." I looked at him in disbelief if he knew the pain I would go through with that on then he wouldn't so casually approach me with it.

"You want to chain me like a dog with a studded collar?" I gasped in shock. "That very object-"

"Will take Misfeata away," he said. "Lucas is doing the same to keep Tyran at bay." I looked at him in disbelief. I couldn't stand the thought of Lucas wearing the contraption either.

"This is madness. I won't even be able to walk let alone defend myself," I said in sheer horror.

"This is the solution I came with. But every moment you waste is another moment that he will be suffering. When I left he was about to put this on himself. I will walk you to him. I suppose really, with this item, it comes down to trust. Do you believe and trust Lucas or don't you?"

I don't know what my expression conveyed but no matter what it was Kingsly looked at me evenly waiting for me to come to my own decision. He didn't know anything about Lucas's and my past, yet like Jennifer I think he had made a conclusion himself. But even I didn't know if I trusted Lucas. I trusted Paul undoubtedly. But Lucas and I had such a betrayed past that in my right mind I should decline the offer and tell him to go to hell. And yet I couldn't race past the thought of Lucas being in insufferable pain, waiting for me. I didn't want him to be in that pain nor did I want this to be the only solution as to how we could talk. Would we even be able to communicate properly while in so much pain?

"I won't allow it!" Misfeata cried out to me. I closed my eyes and struggled to push her down. She couldn't venture any closer to control. In a rebellious notion my mind was made up.

"Can we wait until we get closer to him, before I have to put that collar on?" I asked.

Kingsly seemed to sympathize. "We can. I don't know what the distance is from him that you can still control yourself. Only you two would know that. Better to put it on before you reach him and lose control."

"I think I know my limit," I said with regret that I would soon have to willingly put it on. "Take me to him."

*

Misfeata was reacting stronger within me. She was both trying to possess my body so I wouldn't put the contraption on and also because she was reacting to nearing Lucas. He might not be able to sense us now in his weakened state, but I certainly felt him. We had been running now for thirty minutes until I had to catch myself on a tree unable to run any closer. It was too unimaginable. I couldn't contain her for much longer. I wanted to scream and run back but I knew what had to be done.

Still clinging to the tree I nodded to Kingsly. Knowingly, he unzipped the bag and brought out the collar. It looked more like a clamp as he brought it closer towards me. He would simply clamp the metaled gemmed contraption around my neck. It looked too thick for me to possibly break in such a state. I leaned away from it already feeling its draining effects.

Misfeata clawed within me and started a pounding migraine. She tried to weaken me and take what she could. I shook my head nervously and closed my eyes, on the verge of vomiting as I tried to push her away. In one clean sweep Kingsly clamped it around my neck.

I screamed and dropped to the ground. It felt as if every gem in that collar pierced into my neck and was bleeding me dry. I felt as if my very life source was pouring into it and scorching me like any Starkorf would if attacking me. My screams sounded inhuman and I found myself in a foetal position clinging to myself in pain.

At some point Kingsly picked me up and began carrying me. No matter how hard I tried to keep myself awake the pain had got the better of me and claimed my sight.

It was a familiar voice that woke me from my darkness. I woke up in pain, so much pain, but I felt so exhausted that the pain had a numbing effect now. I felt completely drained. It was painful for me to find the strength to open my eyes.

My lips had said his name in a whisper before I could even see his beautiful face. "Lucas," I whispered. I opened my eyes and found myself to be hunched on a comfy chair. By the looks of my surroundings we were in some small cabin where a fire was lit. There was a chair across from me where I imagined he should have been sitting. But instead of finding him there I continued to look around to find where his voice came from.

"Karla," his voice was pained and rough. It was barely audible. I weakly looked down at my side where he was sitting on the floor with his gloved hand over mine. "Karla," he whispered again. I gave him an approving smile as he rubbed his gloved hand over my face, reaching out and tracing my cheekbones.

"I'm so sorry to do this to you," he said in a pained expression. "It was the only way I could think of." His every word sounded as raw as my throat felt.

"Will we always be a slave to this," I asked trying to slightly move so I could edge closer to him. "Is this the only way we can communicate?" He stroked my cheek again. No matter how much pain I was in, that lingering sensation was felt above all.

"I hope not," he said honestly. "I've been trying to find a way that we can get rid of this. But it will end in either one of our deaths or researching more in the theory of Sebastian's grave."

"You don't believe that too do you?" I croaked in despair. I still hadn't given in to the temptation of such a thing to be real. I couldn't allow myself to relish in that thought of happiness.

"Karla," he croaked. His beautiful brown eyes were serious and remorseful. He brushed one of his hands weakly through his hair, as he always did when unsure of what to say. "I have no other option. I have to believe. I can't give up on a way that might be possible."

"Misfeata said-"

"And Tyran also. He also says it's impossible," Lucas said. That moment left me silent. Tyran speaks to him, of course he does, like Misfeata speaks to me.

"How are you fairing with it all?" I asked. Lucas was now the only person in the world who I could connect with over this. I cursed in pain as a shot ran down me. I had over exerted my movement and suffered for it. He tried to reach out to me quickly for balance but ended up doing the same to himself.

"It's not a lifestyle I want for myself. It's hard to keep him away," Lucas said honestly. "I can't deny this extra power though, it's almost unchallengeable." He was silent for a moment before looking at me again. "Well except you, you are the only one strong enough to challenge me." There was another long pause between us as I faded on the verge of losing consciousness again. "I wasn't sure if you would come."

"I wasn't sure if I would either. I still worry that even at your order, your followers will attack."

"They won't!" he defied quickly. A shot of pain struck through him as he gasped and tried to grip the collar. "They obey my orders. There are less in numbers than what I thought there would be. A lot either created their own small group or followed Eden. I won't let him touch you. I will reclaim my people for the better." His gloved hand traced my lips. I wanted in so many ways to be on his level. I shuffled slightly, using all my strength I could to slip off the chair. It wasn't an elegant fall but one that positioned me beside Lucas. He cradled me into his arms and between his legs. My back and head rested on his shoulder. It felt both unnatural yet natural at the same time. I avoided touching his bear skin so he wouldn't drain me. Even though he was fully covered and it defeated the purpose when the red gems drained me. His color glowed the same green as the ones that were attached to Aeisha.

"I want this war to end," I pleaded. It seemed ironic, so many people thought we were the only answer to concluding this war and yet we had no idea how to stop it and what to do. We could only steal this moment in the middle of it all, and who knew it may very well be the last.

"So do I, I will find a way. I promised that I would protect you and I will keep to that, even at the risk of my own life. I was the one who dragged you into all of this," he said stroking back my hair slowly. I nuzzled further into him embracing his smell. I slightly turned so I could look into his eyes. Looking up at him I questioned how cruel fate was that we could never have an existence together that wasn't so painful. I again couldn't help but ask that one question which always wavered my feelings for Lucas. Were these truly my own feelings or simply the connection that we shared through the Elders?

"If it wasn't you someone else would have found me," I said wanting to stroke his jaw longingly. I couldn't of course, his skin would instantly drain me and I was too weak to produce my Shield into my fingertips. I had for so long wanted to be like this with Lucas yet the guilt continued to wash over me and remind me that this was wrong. This was different to the embrace that Paul and I shared. How could I do this to him? How could I do this to either and yet my longing to touch them both and make sure they were alive and well was too compelling for me to ignore. I never knew when it would be the last time I touched either or was able to speak with them like now. What if eventually Misfeata did completely take over, could these be my last few memories?

"I am looking for Kurt," Lucas said hissing as another shot of pain struck through him. "We don't have much time here so I will tell you everything I know. When I find him I will learn everything he knows about Sebastian's grave, if there is an answer or a solution somewhere close I need to try Karla. We both do."

"I fear believing in something that will never happen," I said honestly. "I can't get my hopes up."

"Karla, is this the life you really want? Are you happy with this kind of life? If you had the decision would you choose this ability or revert back to human?" I stared at him for a moment dazed by his sudden question. I had always mentioned and thought about my old life, but never had I thought about reverting back to it because I thought it was something I would never be able to do.

"I want to take your suffering away," he said wiping over my cheek with his leather glove. I clung tighter to his shirt insecure by his question.

"I'm tired of fighting," I said honestly. I hadn't yet admitted that to anyone so openly. "And I don't want to fight you. I don't want anyone fighting for me. I'm tired of being cautious and paranoid. I don't want to fear people chasing me any longer. I don't want this existence." I choked in a jagged breath which was so excruciating as the gems around my neck felt as if it constricted and choked me. I then realized instead that I was bordering a panic attack. I took another shallow breath realizing I had awoken my true feelings and declared them loudly. I was having an anxiety attack. No matter how strong I had to be and no matter what battles I always faced, I was still a teenage girl. I never wanted any of this. Flashes of my father came to mind and I choked horrifically again. I clung to the collar of claustrophobic. I felt as if I couldn't breathe.

Lucas spoke to me through it but I couldn't help but be overwhelmed by what seemed to be the first moment of grief I could pass without the threat of Misfeata taking advantage of me. My gasps were unnatural and I thought I was dying.

I don't know how long I was in that state for but Lucas was there to wipe away the tears and rested my head against his shirt as that insufferable fear came to my mind. I cowered into him, my shoulders hunched as I cried. Some of the tears were unable to come as I was so physically exhausted already. My cries slowly turned into whimpers before I was able to calm myself down.

"Hey," Lucas said tilting my head up. I didn't have the strength to fight him and looked into his brown mournful eyes. "I will find a way. No matter what happens between you and me, I will find a way for you to escape this suffering."

He leant down and kissed my shoulder. He was unable to kiss me directly as neither of us could project our Shield. But even through my leather jacket I felt both warmth and affection.

"I will also protect you from Eden. It was never his army to lead in the first place," Lucas said defiantly.

"Do you want to be in charge Lucas, with all this power, is that what you desire?" I asked meekly. He gave me a cocky smile, although sluggish it was still the very typical smile I remember of Lucas from all those times ago.

"You were born and accustomed to the human world, Karla. This is something I have always been in anticipation of. This is what I was born for. It's not for greed or strength that I want to claim that throne. It's only because like you said, you and I can make a difference. I want to lead my people in a new light. I too don't think we should continue these generations of war. I have a feeling something far greater then ourselves will go against our race. And when that happens, I hope both Shielders and Starkorfs can align."

"What do you mean?" I asked sceptically.

"It's just a feeling," he said pressing my head back to his shirt. I nuzzled into it comfortably. "We must depart soon. We have both been gone for far too long."

I clung to his shirt even tighter. "Just a few more minutes. Just a few more like this, please." His grip tightened around me and I imagined it was the extent of his strength. I still ached from the collar strapped around my neck and it was hard to stay conscious through the pain. No matter how painful it was we both desired this extra time.

Kingsly came into the room and collected me from Lucas. Lucas and I stared at one another longingly saying nothing as he pulled me away. What else did we have to say that we hadn't already? Neither of us wanted to say 'Goodbye' in fear that it was the final goodbye we might say. We had to believe that we could see one another again. Although I wanted to argue with him, I knew it was time. Kingsly carried me out of the room and ran with me into the trees. The heavy jolt of his run felt like shards up my back every time.

"Far enough," I croaked. He gave me a quick assessment before resting me against a tree and taking off the collar. I gasped loudly, the cold air hitting my lungs as if it hadn't felt such freshness in so long. I sat there for a few minutes hunched over and feeling my body thrive once again and rebound from the pain it was suffering from.

In the near distance I could feel that all familiar presence which stirred Misfeata. I began to walk into the opposite direction of Lucas in case I was wrong about my proximity and Misfeata would awaken. I could sense Tyran from this distance. I imagined that Lucas were doing the very same as me now and staggering away.

"Thank you," I whispered to Kingsly. He pointed me into the direction of my camp.

"Would you like me to escort you in case someone comes across you in this state?" He asked gentlemanly.

"No. I will be back to my full strength within minutes. I can take it from here," I said with a bitter smile. I continued to walk into the direction he pointed me to, tripping over the trunk of a tree. I was grateful that Kingsly had already departed and not seen it. The walk which was very slow to start with became a faster pace until eventually, Misfeata was at her full strength. And she was not happy.

Chapter Fifteen- Weakling

$\mathcal{I}$gathered all the strength I could mentally before venturing back into the camp. I could sense others amongst them now, and the amount of new arrivals matched the institute. I was excited to see my mother after so long but nervous as to how she would react after the last time I had seen her and took away her parental right. Secondly, I didn't know how to face Paul. My feelings for him were true and I felt like my contact with Lucas betrayed him.

I felt two people bordering the camp and allowed them to approach me first. Chris had his usual upbeat walk, where his dreadlocks bounced around. His dark skin looked paler making me question how much sunlight he had actually seen over the past few months. Suzumiya's bright colors in her hair seemed slightly faded but the red and blue were still evident. Her cat like eyes narrowed on me, but not as they used to. They were no longer filled with the hatred she once harbored for me.

"There she is," Chris said with an upbeat tone as he approached me and threw his arms around me in a friendly manner. Surprised, I hugged him back patting his back lightly. Suzumiya rolled her eyes at his greetings.

"As you can see not much has changed on our end," Suzumiya said. Chris let me go and swept an approving look over me.

"Damn you are all bad ass Shielder now aren't you. I feel like you used to be a little cub that we trained and now you're all grown up." He had a large cheesy grin on him, one that would usually have macaroni cheese sauce spread over it. He blew a bubble of gum and placed his hands in his pocket.

Suzumiya looked uncomfortable and unsure of what to do. I wasn't sure how to interact with her either. We had a lot of tension in the past and there had been times when she had even tried to kill me.

"C'mon Suz," Chris said and slapped her on the back to nudge her forward. She took a few unbalanced steps forward but still pulled short of touching me. I didn't take it personally, she just didn't seem to be the kind to hug openly.

"I apologize for the things that I have done in the past and that I did not believe you," she said bowing her head in respect. She awkwardly held out her hand in the approach of a handshake. Hesitantly I took it, it was as awkward for me as it was her.

"You've been guarding my mother these past few weeks. There is nothing to be forgiven for," I said. She looked up at me with acknowledgment. A silent agreement of where we now stood, hand in hand with appreciation for the other. It had been some time now since I had last seen them both, I had almost forgotten what they looked like.

"The others are waiting for you," Chris said moving aside so he and Suzumiya could walk alongside me.

The fire crackled as I searched through the masses to where my Mother was. She was the woman who I wanted to see the most. I searched until Chris pointed her out to me. I first saw Helena. She looked frailer than before and it was her that noticed me first. She gave me a warm smile. Paul and Ashley were helping her dish some sort of stew. Beside her, was my mother who at the same time looked up.

"Mom," I said. My footing had stopped to my surprise and I just stood and stared at her. It felt too good to be true seeing her right now.

"Karla," she whispered. Paul took the bowl that she was dishing out of her hands and she stood up within seconds. I ran to her eager to finally be reunited with her. I hugged her no longer apprehensive to what she would say. I didn't care for the lecture because all that mattered was that she was finally here.

"Mom," I said again with tears streaming down my face. She hugged me tightly and patted down the back of my hair. She kissed my cheek and rocked me back and forth as if I were a small child. At this point in time, with the gaping hole I felt in my chest, I felt exactly like that.

"I am so sorry for what I did and that-" I gushed. She pressed her finger to my lips sshhing me.

"Don't ever apologize if you feel like it was the right thing to do. I am just so glad I can finally see you." She embraced me again. I opened my eyes now noticing Uncle Kyle who had a bemused expression on his face. If I hadn't known any better I would have even thought I saw him wipe away a tear.

"Now come along, we are making a scene," she said grabbing my hand and pulling me towards the food. A few of the Shielders had stopped to watch us in bewilderment.

"There goes your mighty strong reputation," Helena teased. With the sense of a second mother I stretched out my arms and hugged her as well. "Hello Karla. It is nice to see you are doing well, dear." She said in her English accent. She certainly felt frailer and she looked tired after the loss of her husband. But like my mother at least they still had Ashley and me. When pulling out of my embrace with Helena, Ashley gave me a skeptical look.

"I'm not hugging you," he toyed with me.

"Shut up," I laughed lightly wiping away the last tears. It had only been three days and yet it felt like a lifetime since I had seen them.

I looked over to Paul who collected my hand and pulled me into an embrace. I clung to him tightly taking a comforting breath. In these arms everything felt right, which only made me feel further guilty for my visit with Lucas. He kissed the top of my head and held me tighter.

"It's good to see you in one piece," he teased. He gave me a very charismatic smile before leaning down and kissing me gently. It was soft and tender, but still enough to take my breath away. I reopened my eyes and gazed into his mystified green. When I looked at him everything was calm and right. "I told you everything would be alright," he said rubbing over my fringe to make it cover my face with a playful smile. It was always that one line that I needed to hear the most.

I still clung to his leather jacket and looked over everyone who helped with the meals. This was in a sense my new family. A new kindle of fire lit within me making me question why I ever had that moment of weakness. These were the very people I wanted to protect. So how could I ever possibly stop fighting?

A scream broke our happiness as we all looked to the Shielder who made the noise. It was the same woman who I first saw with the baby that Martin was assessing. One of the older Shielders had taken her child. I pushed through the crowds which avoided looking her way. I blocked the man who had taken the child. I couldn't help but push aside the nagging feeling that something bad was going to happen.

"What are you doing with that child?" I demanded.

"I have no fight with you," he said unsettled by my confrontation. Although I think it was more so that I was the host of Misfeata, their 'holy leader'.

"Then return the child," I chased.

"But Christopher-"

"I do not care what Christopher has told you to do, return the child," I said. My tone sounded far more mature than it usually did. I briefly looked at the baby which was bundled in yellow. It looked perfectly healthy. The man looked hesitant before me. In the corner of my eye I could see that Jennifer and Elijah watched idly. Elijah went to step forward to what I imagine to reinforce Christopher's reign, but Jennifer held him back. Everyone had gone silent and I could sense that Christopher now approached.

Having no time for chance I gently but quickly took the child away from him giving him a scornful look. I returned the child to the blubbering mother and stood in front of her defensively in time before Christopher reached us.

"What is the meaning of this?" she snarled. The others had now gathered around us. Scott looked interested in the theatrics and stood closest beside my mother. Naturally she stood by my side. I imagine as any mother would if their child were being lectured by an older adult. But the game here was different, it was I who far outmatched Christopher.

"Why are you taking her child away from her?" I demanded.

"You do not come into *my* camp and start making demands," she snarled.

"This isn't a demand," I lengthened in height and pulled back my jacket slightly, revealing Aeisha. "If you ever attempt to touch this child and harm it, or any child here for that matter, I will kill you myself."

Christopher's eye twitched. "You are that of a child, even if you possess Misfeata don't try to compare your strength against my own of which I have been fighting for years," she snarled.

"Don't threaten my daughter," my mother said taking a step forward. It was the last of Christopher's patience and I pushed my mother aside in time, pushing her into Paul's arms who grabbed her and held her back.

Christopher's projected Shield shattered under my own. It wasn't with ease, she was extremely powerful. As she came at me I grabbed her throat and rose her in one swift movement above my height. I projected my Shield forcefully against her throat so she struggled to breath. This wasn't my complete doing. Although I was mostly in control of my body, Misfeata was there, as if the pinnacle to

112

this action. Even my tone audited more like hers. And crushing her windpipe, I would have never thought of something that savage.

"You do not challenge me!" It was Misfeata's snarl ringing through. Children hid behind their parents. Some of the Shielders went to react to their leader being harmed but hesitated. Suddenly I felt the difference in hierarchy.

"Karla," Paul whispered. I gave him a side glance that could have cut through ice. It was Misfeata's immediate glare. But it was enough to rattle me back into the comfort of my own skin. I had never experienced where my movement was both hers and my own. A sudden realization dawned on me. Were we becoming one?

I dropped Christopher who elegantly caught herself from dropping, she only gasped once and rubbed at her throat. "You never attack my mother again." I said before turning my back on her and walking away.

"Well, that was fun!" Scott said with a laugh and nudged Martin who gave him a disapproving sigh.

"Quite the young Shielder you've turned into," Chris said gleefully with a bouncy beat. "Now let's get some food I'm starving."

"Come on Karlz," Paul said throwing his arm over my shoulder and pulling me towards the food. I looked over my shoulder to the woman who cradled her child crying. Jennifer now crouched beside her stroking her hair. She looked up at me with a satisfied gleam. Although she couldn't say out loud in front of the others, I would have imagined her to be mouthing 'thank you'. "You did the right thing," Paul said grabbing my attention again.

"I don't know. . ." I said thinking of the violence I displayed and the confusion I had that it was both Misfeata and I at the same time.

"Hey," Paul said wiping my cheek. "I mean it. You just saved that child's life. All of us would've done the same."

My mother and Helena spoke to one another in whispers. But I heard a few lingering words of 'baby' and 'protect'. I held onto Paul closely again looking over my shoulder. What would have they done to that child?

Chapter Sixteen- Unexpected Departure

$\mathcal{O}$ur institute, if it could still be called that was segregated from the rest of those in the camp. We stayed within our own tents away from the rest. That night was eerily quiet. Although everyone continued what it was they were doing after the incident between Christopher and me, no one spoke and I wasn't called forth to her tent to talk tactics.

Paul and I shared the same blanket in the same tent alongside Paige and Ashley who had disappeared for a walk by themselves. My head rested on Pauls arm as he traced little circles on my arm in a comforting manner. We both stared up into the roof of the tent. I still wished that I could see through it to look at the stars. My mother, Helena, Suzumiya and Chris shared the other tent. Somehow Scott had convinced or blackmailed Martin into sharing his more stylish tent with him.

I wanted to spend as much time with my mother as I could, but I was part of the group who did the rounds so the others could catch up on sleep and I didn't want to wake her. Uncle Kyle was currently doing his round.

"Where were you tonight?" Paul asked. I felt a lump rise in my throat. I neither wanted to tell nor lie to him. I shuffled so I could rest on an elbow and look at him. My hand rested on his chest. He pushed back a piece of my fringe as he studied my face seriously.

"I saw Lucas today," I said shakily. I examined his expression as a hint of frustration fixated through him. He hesitated before stroking my hair again.

"I thought if you both made contact that you would try to kill each other," he said bitterly. It was far from the reaction I thought I would receive. Paul hated Lucas and by visiting him I was endangering my life. Yet Paul didn't lecture me like he normally would. He would have known I understood the risk I was taking and willingly accepted.

"He found a way to stop that temporarily," I said.

"How?" He asked with a jealous tone.

"A collar formed of Tyran's gems," I said thinking of all that pain. His face instantly lightened and he cupped both sides of my face lifting himself up. I cupped his hands which so tenderly touched me.

"Karla, are you kidding me. You told me the pain that brings you. How much pain were you in? Why would you put yourself through that? Especially when no one was there to protect you. Why?"

"He's the only one who knows this experience and can truly understand the same pain," I said. Paul gave me a heartbroken look. No matter how much he wanted to protect me, this was something he could never fully understand. I tightened my grip on his hold. "Paul, I think I am starting to lose to her." It came out as a whimper. His eyes widened as he knew who I was referring to. "She took over my body for almost an entire day. And tonight," I choked on my words. "Tonight it was neither me nor her talking, but both. She told me I'm running out of time Paul," I choked. He hugged me tightly and I hid my face in his neck.

"You will never lose to her, sshhh," he said stroking my hair.

"Paul, I'm so scared. I don't even know who or what I am anymore." He continued to brush my hair and pressed a small kiss to my lips. I kissed him back wanting all my worries to seep away. He returned that hungry kiss, his tongue leading the way which vanished all my concerns. His tender touch rested on both my face and hip as his grip tightened. I rose onto my knees, bending my neck down to kiss him.

He took away all my worries and fears and brought me back to this very human experience. No draining, no fear and only something so bitter sweet I was scared it would vanish before me. I rested my hands gently on his face as I fastened our kiss. His tongue kept pace with my own. My kisses were desperate and in return I felt that same touch from Paul. The fear that this might be our last memory that at any point anything could happen made me hungrier for him.

His deep moan stirred something more sensual in me and he bit down on my bottom lip in a playful manner. I pulled back for a moment surprised by it, realizing I enjoyed it and wanted so much more.

I pressed my lips to his, wanting to touch his skin, to feel his heat radiate. This was the very touch and feel that always comforted me. I wanted to be closer to that, closer to Paul. I grabbed the bottom of his white shirt, stretching it over his face and returning his hungry kiss. My fingers lightly trailed his chiselled stomach and muscled arms, enjoying as he flexed to lift me and sit me on his lap.

Neither of us broke our kiss as I continued to circle my hands over him, remembering how he felt beneath my touch. He was so masculine, so safe to be with. I circled his shoulder blades digging my nails in slightly to remind myself that such soft skin had lean muscle beneath. He grunted slightly between kisses as I did so.

Paul in return lifted the bottom of my shirt and lifted it over my face. A part of the collar got caught on my chin and I giggled at his not so smooth move. He smiled cheekily back at me with a slight red across his cheeks. In one clean swift movement he flipped me onto my back taking away my laugh and knocking me in surprise. Perhaps the gentle Paul, could also be rough.

With a devilish smile he pressed his lips to mine again. His fingers trailed down my neck and over my chest. He continued to trace down, his touch was sensitive and tickled me slightly. He traced down to my hip bone holding on tightly as he began to trace kisses down my neck and along my collar bone.

"You are so beautiful," he said in a hot breath before pressing another kiss to my lips.

I hungered for Paul, for this moment that we were in. This beautiful and very teen moment. I felt alive again and somehow only Paul could make me feel that way.

A loud horn echoed throughout the woodland and we both straightened up, our spell broken. The horn echoed again as we both grabbed our shirts and put them on. Paul had grabbed the sword beside him as Ashley burst through the tent entrance. I had only just put back on my shirt and was now putting on my leather jacket. Under any other circumstance I would have been embarrassed.

"There are Starkorfs close by. There's not enough time we have to fight!" He said. Paul and I followed him out. Already Uncle Kyle had gathered my mother and Helena.

"Take them as far away as you can," I said. "Into the opposite direction."

He nodded taking my mother away. She reached out for me and for that moment I wanted to make something very clear.

"Mom, I love you so much. But please trust me," I said grabbing her cheek. "I am the strongest one here and I can fight. I will protect you and everyone else here." I expected her to retaliate to tell me that it was a mother's duty. But instead she gave me an eerie expression before letting Helena usher her along. Helena looked like a fierce warrior as she had to in moments like this.

Suzumiya and Chris looked hungry for the fight. How long had it been since they went into battle? I signalled for them to follow me. The horn blew again echoing. Screams began to rip through the children and wild barbaric noises came from the trees as if a war cry. An owl swooped close by and Scott suddenly emerged in his usual form.

"It's Eden," he simply said. "Their numbers are vast, I don't know how long we will hold them off for."

"Long enough so the others can escape," I said pulling out Aeisha and running towards the screams. Ashley and Paul were close by my side. Paige was already meters ahead. Suzumiya and Chris took the back and somewhere in the sky, I imagined that was where Scott would be.

The night streaked with shadows as little moonlight illuminated the battlefield. We reached closer to the camp until we were confronted with our first mutated Starkorf. It lunged for Paul, creeping out of the darkness. He easily flicked it off and Suzumiya had already jumped on it piercing its heart. Her fighting still reminded me that of a cat. Chris toyed with his nunchucks, deflecting any Starkorfs who might have tried to attack Suzumiya's back.

I countered the two Starkorfs who tried to attack Ashley and I, breaking through both of their Shields so Ashley could easily go in for his strike. Although the Starkorf was fast, he wasn't fast enough to re-project his Shield and Ashley had already landed a fierce strike to his neck.

The second one I circled and slashed his back, not willing to make the final blow. I was tired of killing and didn't want to further the blood on my hands. Although I couldn't justify my hesitation because he stumbled towards Suzumiya who elegantly pierced his chest with her blade. Wasn't I leading him to death anyway?

Paige slashed through her opponents in front not giving me the chance to see if they were Starkorfs who had the ability to Shield or not. If she were striking them down, obviously not. She wasn't human, but nothing about her announced that she was a Shielder in secret either.

We made our way through the numbers, quickly being pushed back towards the tents of the Shielder's camps. Now only the warriors fought, the younger and weak having been taken away. Some of those who were still weak fought defending their people. Christopher and Elijah were at the front of the imploding ambush. As I struck at another two, still weary of Paul's position, Scott dropped into wolf form beside me and ripped at the throats of two mutated Starkorfs who had tried to creep towards Paul.

"There are too many," Ashley gasped as he jumped back beside me and lunged towards another Starkorf. The Starkorf projected its Shield and threw back Ashley. Before it could jump on him, I countered my own pulsating Shield and shattered the Starkorfs. Before striking at it, Paige had already jumped on its shoulders and stabbed its neck, falling down and rolling elegantly as the Starkorf gasped for breath. She rolled towards Ashley and collected his hand instantly pulling him up.

Chris's tone pierced my hearing as I looked towards his direction disorientated. A Starkorf held him by the throat pinning him to the ground. I raced over to him, projecting my Shield and bursting through its own. I grabbed its shoulders as I jumped over it, using all the strength I could muster, which so readily and inhumanly came to me. I flung the Starkorf over my shoulder and far into the trees, where I heard its neck snap as he landed awkwardly against one.

"Well, well little one, we finally meet," a voice exposed itself. I spun around to see a well-built man who looked no older than thirty. I didn't have to question who it was and I knew his age was not that of thirty.

"Eden," I growled. He reformed his charming demeanor into a snarl. He was heavily armored, despite rumors of him being one of the fiercest Shielders and stronger fighters of his kind.

"You killed my daughter and now I am going to kill everything that is dear to you and make you watch," he chimed. I quickly found Paul who was close to Ashley and Paige. From this distance I knew he was safe with them. I just had to make sure that Eden stayed away.

"Our numbers far outweigh yours little one," Eden said with very little urgency. He embedded his large sword into the moist ground resting his hands on its handle casually. "Tell me host of Misfeata, when you sleep at night can you see my little girl's life pouring away, do you repent for your sin and what about that of my lover? She was no weakling."

Two Shielders approached Eden, very swiftly he flipped his sword from the ground and sliced them both in a graceful spin, one that I didn't expect from such a bulky framed man.

"I am excited to see what you can do. The Elders are not the only way to source power. My love Taskatae might have made a few modifications on myself. I am intrigued to see how they match against the Elder, Misfeata." He ran at me and I waited for his attack preparing for the fight to come. So many around me continued to fight and to my dismay this was a losing battle. There were too many of them. If they

118

burst through our security here then they would reach the others of which we protected.

I looked for the largest group of Starkorfs I could find and instead of countering Eden I ran towards them. I had to take out as many as I could. Eden traced my steps.

"Running out of fear little girl," I heard him say. He was held up for only moments as a Shielder attacked him. The Shielder fought him keeping to his pace. I focused only on that group.

"Fall back!" I yelled at the Shielders who surprisingly responded quickly to my command. Urging for the strength that I could only gather from Misfeata I jumped two meters high in the air and into the chaos of twelve Starkorfs. I didn't want to kill. And there was no part of this that made it easier. I spun in a circle amongst them building my Shield within me and releasing it into a combusted bang. The wind from my Shield blew against and shook the nearby trees. I staggered in my step for a moment exhausted by my ability. I fell into line quickly sweeping through them and attacking all those that came at me. Only few hadn't been knocked off their feet and now those who had gathered I danced through. It became a motion. Just a feeling of how and where I should strike. One by one I cut through them, reminding myself that their sacrifice was justified so I could save my family.

Family. My father who I was once unable to protect. Suddenly more Starkorfs burst from the trees. I countered the one's I fought trying to count their numbers but unable to. Tents were being trampled. Some lunged straight through tents to get to any Shielder they could get their hands on. Christopher and Elijah currently held off Eden as he only had eyes for me. His frustration evident.

Suddenly from the side another burst of Starkorfs flooded in. I angled myself to see where Paul was when I kicked a Starkorf back. I punched another across the face making her stagger and fall into a tree.

The Starkorfs who came from the side weren't attacking Shielders they were attacking the other Starkorfs. It took me a moment to realize what was happening because I couldn't accept that we were being aided by Starkorf's until I saw Kingsly's face who cut through a few of the Starkorfs. He found his way by my side and I knew where this group had come from and who right now seemed to be our savior: Lucas.

I wanted to scan to see if he fought alongside us but knew it wasn't possible. He and I couldn't gather in the same place without our chains and pain.

"Where is Jennifer," he asked huffed as he axed through one of the Starkorfs. They continued to pool through the trees as it seemed never ending. I pointed into the direction of where they fled and he ran towards there without hesitation. I continued dancing through their crowds, slicing at their shins to make them drop and unable to move instead of killing them. Sometimes I couldn't be so lenient and had to go for the kill.

A chain wrapped around Paul's ankle and he began to get dragged towards a hungry Starkorf. I propelled towards him running to his aid. Elijah jumped in before I did slicing through the Starkorfs arm and chopping off both hands. The screech that came from its mouth rung through my ears in a piercing shatter. Paul ripped off the chain as if it scorched his skin.

"We need to fall back," Christopher said. "Leave this other group to fight." I searched to find Eden, but noticed that he had already vanished. My stomach began to churn as Misfeata arose within me. I pressed my hand to my stomach ushering her to go away. This meant only one thing, Lucas was near. When I pinpointed him, longing to get closer, I sensed that Eden was headed in his direction. I wanted to go to his aid, to fight my own battle against Eden which I had brought upon myself. But I knew I had to run away. I couldn't let Misfeata take over because she would only focus on killing Lucas.

Christopher put her fingers in her mouth and whistled loudly. Slowly her members began to fall back and Lucas's Starkorfs were able to hold them off. I could sense that some were scattered amongst the woods and feared that like last time, some had escaped us. I gathered Paul as we all ran back towards our weaker ones. Bodies of both Starkorfs and Shielders were everywhere. Some still gasped in pain and were alive, but barely.

We ran fast, leaving the remaining Starkorfs to fight amongst themselves. I felt like a coward for doing so but understood why we had to. Our first priority was our own kind. Other Shielders reached there before we had and killed the few Starkorfs who had gone through.

I heard in the distance with my sensitive hearing Jennifer's cry. Around her I sensed a foreign Starkorf. I raced through the trees to witness her strike, impaling the Starkorf with her own sword. Surrounding her were six Starkorfs, seven now including the one of which she had just killed. She dropped to her knees, besides the one Starkorf which I did recognise.

"No, no, no, no," her cry continued. "You can't leave me. You can't leave us," she screamed wildly as she beat down on Kingsly's chest. He was unresponsive. Paul had reached my side and watched on as I did. "Don't leave me!" she screamed savagely. She wrapped her arms around his face cradling him close to her chest. I could sense that still naturally she projected her Shield from the touch of his skin. I wondered if she even knew she were doing it.

Elijah ran past us and dropped to Jennifer's side. "Jennifer we must go." He reasoned as he stroked her cheek.

"Get away!" she screamed violently, knocking him away.

Christopher walked out witnessing her daughter's state. Jennifer began to whimper.

"Momma!" She cried. "Momma, please no." The act in itself reminded me of the same emotions that arise in me when my own mother is near, that natural pleading and desire of comfort. "Momma," she cried her accent coming through thicker. Christopher looked over Kingsly in grotesque.

"Elijah, drag her away if you must," Christopher said harshly.

"Momma No!" Jennifer said. Elijah swiftly struck Jennifer at the back of the neck collecting her before she hit the ground unconscious. He collected her in his arms with a pained expression. Although he wanted Kingsly dead, I very much doubted he ever wanted to see the fierce Jennifer in this state. He walked over Kingsly and began to run from the scene, towards where everyone else fled to with Jennifer bundled close to his chest.

"Karla, we have to go, some will be following us," Paul said placing his hand on my arm and pulling me away.

A piece of silver grabbed my attention and I walked over to Kingsly. Around his neck was a silver cross. I snapped it off his neck and placed it in my pocket. I could never bring him back to life for her, but I could offer Jennifer this as a gift. My heart pained to see Kingsly with blood that pooled out of his mouth, still with determination on his face. He would have fought fiercely to protect both Jennifer and his unborn child.

I bent down and closed Kingsly's eyes making sure to project my Shield lightly so his skin wouldn't drain me. No matter what his kind, he was a good man.

"C'mon Karlz, we have to find the others," Paul said reaching out to me. I took his hand and followed the others. Screeching noises in the near distance continued to tear at my hearing. Suddenly there was a loud bang and the whole earth rattled underneath our feet. Paul pinned me to a tree, to stabilize me and protect my front. We both looked over his shoulder where flames ripped through. Another bang rattled and it was evident that either grenades or bombs were being used. I remember the first time they had used such a tactic on us, in the boot of a car. Ashley was baited by his mother who was tied up in front of the warehouse. If it weren't for Lucas, Ashley would now be dead.

"We have to keep going," I said grabbing Pauls' hand and finding the others. The explosions offered us a little time to escape. We ran for an hour, following Christopher's orders.

When we arrived to the place she sought out, it was over a large river which had one large boat. I hesitated remembering the last time I was on water and how that almost killed Lucas. I now had bad memories of almost everyone dying. Everyone linked to me had now faced death.

"The others are already on the boat," Elijah said. He no longer had Jennifer with him which made me believe he had already put her on the boat. The boat looked worn out, but still functional. It had a large pale wooden deck around it with green railings. The inside was completely concealed with no windows. Some Shielders stood outside both on the dock and land, guarding in case the Starkorfs came for another surprise attack. I imagined we only had a few hours if that between us.

"Everyone is here Karla," Ashley said grabbing my attention as he walked out from the large wooden door of the two story boat. "Your mother is inside. She is safe."

"Wrap it up," Christopher said clapping her hands and then whistling. The guards began to back onto the deck and Paul and I shuffled on to make sure not to be left behind on this departure. Wherever we were going. It didn't matter, for now, we were no longer on land where Eden could find us.

2

Lost State

There is a point that we reach where we no longer
recognize ourselves.
We hate ourselves for some of our decisions, but know
they had to be made.
I am no angel, but I am certainly not the devil that lay
within me.
I am tormented by the many voices that impact me and not
all are my own.
I am losing myself.
I don't know who I am anymore.
I am terrified I might adapt to that ulterior ego.
I might lose my sense of justice and morale and be
poisoned by this world and its influence.
I'm scared of the monster I might become.
I'm scared of losing myself all together.
Who am I and what do I stand for? Why don't the answers
come to me straight away?
Am I already too far gone?

Chapter Seventeen- Rushed Plans

At first the irritating whistle and hum of Scott woke me, but it didn't at the same time. I was at an in-between conscious state. How long had I been out for? I panicked as I realized what that 'inbetween' state was. I was already familiar with this sensation. My consciousness banged up against Misfeata's but it was already too late. What had happened? When had she possessed my body? Misfeata now walked on the deck looking between the slow motion waves of the river and the moonlight. I felt strangled and like I was suffocating. When had she taken over my body? How had I not known? For how long had I blacked out?

"Karla," Paul's voice ventured behind me. My eyes trailed over Paige who was situated at the tip of the boat, well balanced and poised as she sat on the edge. With a sigh of agitation Misfeata spun. I realized she was still trying to imitate me.

"Yes Paul," she said in a sweet tone with eyelids battered. It was an exaggeration of a doting character and it was insulting that she thought I acted in such a way.

"You really should eat, it's been two days since we've been on ship. Please try to eat," he said offering a bowl of something that upset Misfeata's sensitive nose. She avoided scrunching it up in distaste. *Two days? I have been unconscious for two days?* I slammed hard against her consciousness, trying to grasp the control of my own body. It felt as if Misfeata simply shrugged me off.

"I will later, okay. Go inside I've gotta talk to Paige for a little while, mmhmmm k?" she dipped her head to the side in a sweet manner. Paul watched her for a moment. I hoped that he knew it wasn't me, she didn't even sound like me, but with my tone and face how could anyone differentiate between us?

Misfeata turned around irritated. *Gahhh, stupid boy!* She hissed internally.

"Hey Karlz," Paul said forcing Misfeata to spin again. She made sure to keep her distance.

"What?" Her tone was flat and it was apparent she couldn't avoid letting out her irritation.

"Have you hurt your back or something?" He asked worried. Misfeata slightly crinkled her face, unsure as to why he would ask such a thing.

"No I feel perfectly fine, why?" She asked trying to speak in the tone and manner I would. This time she had actually began to imitate me very well.

"Oh nothing. It's just you seem to be walking a lot stiffer than usual."

Stupid boy doesn't even know the difference between a stiff back and good posture, Misfeata snarled again internally.

"I'm fine, but thank you for being worried," she toyed with a flattering smile. "Gotta go now." She said and walked away. She was relieved that Paul had finally left her alone.

I slammed myself against her again. My impact affected her next wobbled step as she went to clutch her head but hesitated. She slammed back into me, almost completely wiping me out of consciousness again.

"Don't try to play these little games with me girl," Misfeata lectured. Suddenly I had the sudden sensation that spiders were crawling all over my skin. No not my skin, my consciousness but in here it almost felt like the same thing. It was dark and cold and there was nowhere to go. The only glimmer of light I saw was through the eyes of my own body. But I had never felt so disconnected from it before. It felt as if every time Misfeata took over, I was getting further from ever gaining control again. I was screaming uncontrollably in fear into the darkness until she stopped her torturous game. *"I can make it very miserable for you in there so don't test me,"* she hissed.

I wanted to continue to fight her but I simply didn't have the strength and a small part of me feared what else she might do. I was so desperate to get my body back and yet the fear that now towered over me had an unbelievable grasp on me. Is this forever? Has Misfeata finally won? How had I not known she had taken over?

Paige was flipping her dagger in the air as she always did. She looked up and contemplated Misfeata for a while, who she would assume to have been me. Misfeata was taking particular interest in Paige. She continued to flip her knife in the air catching it with the handle with grace even if there was a small jolt of water beneath us.

"What do you want?" Paige said directly. I was used to Paige's harsh tone, but even now she had a slight edge to it that I wasn't so used to.

"Just wanted to come out and chat," Misfeata responded.

"I don't like 'chat'," Paige said now resting her chin on her palm in a bored manner.

Misfeata ignored the comment and still rested her elbows casually behind her as she leant her back against the boat. Paige didn't look at Misfeata and continued to watch her blade.

"What are you?" Misfeata asked. There was no hesitation in Paige's next flip of her blade. She did not answer until Misfeata repeated herself. "I said-"

"I heard you, I just didn't care much for what you had to say," Paige said sassily. With all of Misfeata's inner strength she contained her more barbaric nature and swallowed her pride.

"Please tell me," she said. "I have let you be a part of my group for quite some time. Don't you think it's time you trust me with your secret? I know you're not human."

"I'm as human as they come," she said tiredly. A jolt of the river sent a few specs of water onto my skin. I could both feel the sensation and not. I too, had been curious for a while as to what or who Paige really was.

"Don't mess with me," Misfeata hissed. She quickly regained herself, realizing she had let herself slip. "You feel surprisingly familiar to me." Misfeata said openly and gave Paige an inquisitive look. "I know you are not a Shielder but I feel as if we have met somewhere before. I don't know, it might be the whole Misfeata thing," she palmed off casually.

Paige looked at me dead on. The intensity of her gaze even struck curiosity into Misfeata.

"You and I have never met, no matter how long you have roamed the earth for Misfeata, and no matter how many times you have possessed your host's body. I am here for Karla and to only be here for Karla, not you," Paige snarled. *Paige knows its Misfeata?* Paige swung her legs over, jumping onto the wooden deck.

"How do-" Misfeata was cut off when Paige raised her knife to her throat. Misfeata could've deflected it very easily, but instead she let the edge stick to her throat.

"Don't you ever try to touch me," Paige snapped.

"What are you going to do little lamb? Slit Karla's throat?" Misfeata slowly rose her hand to Paige's and rested her fingers on hers for a moment. There was contemplation that danced in Paige's eyes. "I think not." Misfeata said with a twisted smile. She began to press on Paige's hand to lower the blade. "However I congratulate you. You've piqued my interest even more."

"Karla," one of the Shielders called out. Misfeata kept her gaze on Paige for a moment. Even though I was only slightly taller than Paige, there seemed to be a very large and superior difference between the two.

"What?" Misfeata snapped. She startled the young Shielder.

"Christopher wants to see you," he said dejected.

"Of course she does," Misfeata murmured. She removed her hand from Paige's and began to follow the young Shielder. She looked over her shoulder once in a triumphant glare against Paige. Paige's hands were scrunched into fists. Before I walked into the wooden door which was opened for me, Paige's blade made the tiniest of noises as it swooshed past my ear. It thudded into the wood right next to my face. The handle sprang lightly from impact. Misfeata only smiled, she had known the blade was directed her way but knew there was no threat. It was simply an intimidation tactic.

Misfeata smiled and pulled out the blade. She looked at Paige still with the triumphant gleam on her face and threw the blade to the ground disgustedly.

"Next time, aim not to miss," Misfeata wavered off and continued to follow the young man. There was a lot of tension in Misfeata when it came to Christopher. Most of the reason was because she wasn't in charge. There were only a few candles that lit inside. There was a large open room where everyone huddled awkwardly and close to one another. In the corner was my own group who had all noticed me and gave me a curious expression.

In the other corner sat Jennifer. She looked as if she hadn't slept for days. Her eyes were wide but looked dead. She looked gaunt and near death. A woman beside her told her to eat, but Jennifer was dazed in her own world. She seemed to be a broken remainder of the beautiful woman she once was. The thought of Kingsly's death weighed heavily on my mind. That was what had broken her, she now looked like a doll of sorts.

There was only two small rooms on the main deck which catered for two toilets and a small room which Christopher occupied upstairs. Upstairs was where the Shielders rotated on handling the ship. Other Shielders slept upstairs as well, because this room was already full.

We walked past the small corridor which had the two toilets in separate rooms. There wasn't even showers here. I was led up the wooden and frail stairs that creaked with every step. Around the staircase the young Shielder opened the door to Christopher's room.

When he opened it, the visual of her sitting behind her small wooden desk was only lightly seen by the singular candle. If it weren't for my keen eyesight I might have struggled seeing her.

In front of her was one tattered chair, of which Misfeata decided not to take. Instead she closed the door behind her and leant against it with arms folded. The young Shielder made his leave.

Christopher was writing in a book with a quill. The room was small and only fit the width of the desk and room to walk around. There were big windows behind her which had been covered by tattered sheets. I imagined if it weren't for those, she would have perfect lighting from the moonlight cascading around her.

"Please take a seat," she offered not looking up at me and continuing to write in what looked to be her journal.

"I'll stand," Misfeatea said. After finishing the sentence she wrote, Christopher closed her book with a timid smile.

"Of course you will."

"Why have you requested me?" Misfeata asked. The tension between the two was eerily thick and they were both aware of it.

"I found something interesting on that ghastly Starkorf which infected my daughter," she spat as she shuffled beneath her desk to grab something.

"You knew the father was Stakorf," Misfeata said, much to my surprise. I imagined that something like that would seem almost trivial to her. But my heart felt for Jennifer and what she now experienced. What if she did die while giving birth? Her greatest fears of having no one to look after her unborn child was present. She had to live. But remembering her already doll like state, it's as if her soul had already died and moved on. She appeared to be only an empty shell.

"Of course I knew," Christopher snapped. "I had tried on many occasions to abort that abomination without her knowing. It simply clung and now drains her of all life. No matter what poisons or herbs I put in her food without her knowing the damn beast survived and now my daughter will die at the hands of that creature and I will have to kill it myself."

I had shouted back in response, but it wasn't audible. I hated Christopher for the way she saw the unborn baby and wishing its death. Who could be so cruel? How could she do that to her own daughter and her own grandchild? Misfeata however was unflinching. She was curious as to what Christopher reached for under the desk.

"I don't care much for what you feel you have to do. What did you have to show me?" Misfeata prodded. She didn't much like suspense or waiting and had already scanned the presence of what it might be. What she detected before it was revealed made her snarl at Christopher.

Christopher pulled up the backpack which Kingsly once carried. I too recognised that back pack. It was the same one which carried the collars for Lucas and me so we could face one another. Confirming both of our suspicions Christopher raised an eyebrow.

"You've seen this before," she questioned. Misfeata backed further against the wall instinctually.

"It weakens me," she simply said. "But no I haven't seen those particularly but I know those gems," she lied. She cursed my name when I agreed to put the collar on. But she was aware of Christopher's curiosity and couldn't associate us with already having known Kingsly. Misfeata was also ashamed that she couldn't overbear the gems or rip out Lucas's throat when we spent that time together. She wasn't present during that time, she was too weak to come forth. What she knew happened between me and Lucas was a little hazy as she tried to recall my memories. But even in my weakened state as it had happened she could only find snippets. Something which irritated her greatly.

"I found these on that abominations father. It would appear that there is both one for you and the prince. Let's be honest, these are weapons purely built to weaken both of you. It wouldn't affect any other Shielder or Starkorf. So it had me thinking."

"Did this experience of 'thinking' hurt you," Misfeata poised. Christopher shot her an angered stare. Her Shield built within her in frustration and her grip tightened on the collars. Her lips pressed together tightly before she continued to speak. Misfeata only smiled. It was much like Paige, there was a superior presence around Misfeata. In this instance it was something, for once, Christopher didn't attempt to challenge.

"I don't know who you think you are child. But insolence is something that will not be tolerated here, even if you are the host of Misfeata. I actually was going to offer you a gift that I thought you might appreciate with consideration to your Uncle's beliefs, I think that this sort of tactic," she held up the collars with consideration. "Might work hand in hand with finding a way to exorcize Misfeata from you."

Misfeata scoffed. "It's not possible."

"Really?" Christopher questioned. "Because I have one of many journals from Elisabeth, the prior host to Misfeata, which would believe otherwise. I only carry this one around with me," she said as she opened a drawer and revealed a tattered and leather bound book. "But I know of a small library which holds all of Elisabeth's written word. She had contemplated and started sourcing the solution herself. Maybe this is something that could help you in finding that solution."

"Why are you telling me this?" Misfeata again attempted to sound like me. She almost scoffed at the idea again but was bothered by people fishing for information. From the sensation I felt well from within her, I could guess that this had been an old battle she once fought with Elisabeth. But Misfeata wanted to know what Christopher's ulterior motives were. She was sensing that if anything, she was hoping to gain Misfeata's strength. It surprised me that Misfeata hated me and had previously stated because I was born human and technically was that she was weaker because of it. Yet, she was also against the thought of being in another host.

"Don't think I am becoming attached. You are simply younger than this old witch," she snarled at me internally. Yet even when she said it I knew there must have been some form of personal attachment. We resented each other, yet there was an undeniable bond like no other. How could there not be after being within the same body for so long? We were now slipping into becoming one person and merging our voices together. In a sense sometimes it felt like we were back to back without ever asking or wanting it, it was just how our entirety was changing.

"Because I want the prince dead. You are bait, I've made this clear from the start. I will aid you in fighting Eden, because when the prince is dead then he will claim their throne." It was still odd to hear Lucas being revered as the 'prince', I had only ever known him as Lucas. "When Lucas is dead then so is Tyran. I want to banish them and lead my people into a new era where we will eradicate their race entirely. When killing a snake you go for the head."

"So why the journal?" Misfeata asked with arms crossed stubbornly.

"Because Karla, I want to offer you a proper human life that was taken away from you. I won't lie to you. I don't want you or your people to stay here. After this war is over I want you gone. For now you hold a significant power that I need, but I don't like you challenging my leadership or authority. Without that power of Misfeata within you my people won't feel mislead or astray. Let us make this very clear. I am in charge here and these are my people."

Misfeata twisted a sick smile. Christopher had finally confessed and confirmed her thoughts. It gave Misfeata a sick sense of pleasure to hear her admit it out loud. "I am the creator of your people." She said as she walked up to Christopher's table in a superior way. Christopher studied her intently. "Never forget that." Misfeata slipped her hand onto Elisabeth's journal and took it from the table. She looked hauntingly at Christopher who couldn't look away.

"Is it you right now Misfeata?" She asked. Her tone had instantly dropped to that of a sacred follower. Christopher was evidently confused. She both rose to her role but there was an aura around Misfeata which made people fall in line around her to what position she wanted them to be in.

Misfeata began to walk away and I could sense that Christopher's straightened posture relaxed slightly and she was confused by her sudden obedience.

"Thanks for the book," Misfeata said as she waved it in the air before leaving the room.

Chapter Eighteen- Possession

*M*isfeata walked out with a charming hum. She looked over the Shielders in front of her as if their existence were nothing. She looked to her left deciding what to do now. I had wondered how she had occupied herself over these past two days, having no recollection of the time spent. There was a part of Misfeata that wanted to throw the journal away leaving no evidence of her former host's thoughts. Misfeata found it only a form of evidence and possibly an entry of the things she once forced Elisabeth to do.

I couldn't sense an inclination or image of specific things she had forced her to do. Misfeata kept that well-hidden. I had heard stories and could gather assumptions for myself. I know that Misfeata used to force Elisabeth to drain so she could live longer. I didn't hear the specifics of whether it was animals or humans. Not that it mattered, it was a contradiction. She hated the race which drained and feasted off humans yet she began to practice the same.

Misfeata tapped on the leather spine of the journal lightly in contemplative thought. This was only one journal, one of many as Christopher indicated. Misfeata wanted to visit that library, only so she could eradicate any evidence. It surprised me that she had never thought of this sooner. Surely she was present for most of the journal entries that Elisabeth had written.

"Shut up," she snarled at me. It was then that I had the inclination that this was something Misfeata had been searching for, for some time. But over the seventeen years of being dormant in me until my abilities were awakened, Misfeata had lost where the Shielders had revered Elisabeth's death and placed her journals.

Misfeata walked down the stairs. She ignored the few who greeted us. Well me. Still none of them knew, no one could tell. Only Paige had figured it out and Christopher had an inclination. Misfeata hadn't confirmed with her like she had Paige.

She avoided looking into the room in case anyone I knew tried to approach her in conversation. She hated being stuck on this boat. She walked outside where the fresh breeze swept over her. She stretched out her arms lightly enjoying the breeze. She closed her eyes and took a deep breath.

"It's amazing to feel alive again and not trapped," she toyed. I was furious. I went to barge into her consciousness again but a choking sensation crept up on me. *"Ah ahh, none of that. Just go to sleep like a good girl."*

The fear terrorized me. I receded, scared that she would do something else to me.

"Karla," Paul said from behind us. Misfeata almost growled by his interruption as she turned to look at him.

"Yes," she responded. She took a few more steps back until she rested on the edge of the boat. Only a few others were outside. Most of them huddled inside and away from the cold.

"Do you love me?" He asked. Misfeata reacted exactly how I would have. Her burrowed eyebrows both confused and shocked. I had never told Paul that I had loved him. It was rather confronting even for Paul.

"Well of course I do," she said timidly but still keeping her distance. I contemplated it myself. Did I love Paul? I knew I did, with everything that we had been through and all that I felt for him. But I loved Mum, my Uncle, I would dare say I even loved Ashley. Paul was certainly special to me, but I had never gathered the courage or thought to think or tell him that I actually loved him. I was so terrified of the feelings that I had for him and clung to that I thought it was too selfish to ever confess such a thing. And never could I be so bold as to say it.

Paul smiled charmingly. "Then I know it's not you."

"Sorry?" Misfeata questioned as she dipped her head to the side slightly. Paul was putting her off, which was something that didn't too often happen to Misfeata.

"I know it's you Misfeata. You've been actively avoiding us all these last few days since we got on the boat. Karla doesn't say 'gotta', 'mmhmmm k' or walk with such a stiff posture. And lastly I know she wouldn't have responded to that question in such a casual way." He started walking towards Misfeata. She tried to keep her distance from him because he irritated her, but now she didn't see the point in keeping up the charade. A sharp edge of fear trailed over me.

"You think you've got it all figured out don't you child," she sneered back. "You with your beautiful dark hair and gorgeous green eyes. You have taken away too much of her time already. I don't much enjoy when my hosts hold attachments. It makes them weak and threatens their body."

"Return her right now," Paul said fiercely. His knuckles were turning white as he clenched his fists angrily.

"Are you sure you want her back? I can tell you everything that she has ever said and done with Lucas." Paul hesitated to take his next step but stayed focused. My heart wrenched as I saw that sudden insecurity on his face. I knew I had hurt him by my wavering feelings for the both of them.

"I'm not going to play games with you Misfeata," Paul said deeply, his voice was rough and domineering. Within seconds Misfeata had closed the distance between them and grabbed Paul by the throat. She lifted him into the air where his feet no longer touched the ground. I barged into her over and over again attempting to shatter the wall that came between us. She only pushed back just as hard to keep me away.

"Let him go!" I screamed at her. Misfeata studied him for a moment as he grasped around his throat. I continued to smash into her, unable to gather the upper hand. I so desperately wanted to control my body and make her stop.

"I will have so much pleasure when I snap your neck and throw you into the river," she smiled.

"Karla," my mother's voice rang out from behind Paul. Misfeata twisted her head in an inhumanly way.

"Maybe the mother next too," she smiled. "Paul, you wouldn't believe how many times I told Karla to keep her distance from you, well from everyone. I tried to tell her you would all die, but she just didn't push you away. That was a weakness and it will be the cause of your death."

I continued to slam into Misfeata for control. Paul began to smile. His face had begun to turn purple.

"No, the only thing we need to keep a distance from is you," Paul said with a smile. "You let your guard down Misfeata."

A jolt hit Misfeata which took her breath away. She instantly dropped Paul and placed her hand on her stomach from the nauseous feeling that came over her. I was all too familiar with this foreign presence. Scott was now within my body.

"Get out!" She snarled. She attempted to project her Shield but Scott prevented her from using it. Suddenly Misfeata could no longer move. Much like he had once done to me, he barred her from moving.

134

She fought voraciously within, but to no avail. Paul coughed as he massaged his throat. My mother came to his aid.

Behind us Ashley and Paige had crept up.

"Sorry Karlz this will hurt, but it's all you from here," Ashley said. He clamped the red gemmed collar around my throat. The burning sensation wasn't anywhere near as bad as physically feeling it. But oh how Misfeata burned from it. I felt myself fading out of consciousness, much like when I used it, Misfeata fell away.

But I clung tightly, knowing it affected her far more than me. She was unable to move or do anything. Her screams were only internal as she still tried to push Scott out. The collar was far more effective on Misfeata and I waited for that one weakened moment to hit Misfeata hard. It was like pushing against and falling back into my own body. As soon as I had, Scott released his grip of me and I fell to the floor in pain.

"Karla," Paul said desperately as he smoothed his hand over my face. I gave a weakened smile.

"Hey," I whispered dryly trying to ignore the burning sensation around my throat.

"Thank god, it worked," he said as he busted open the collar and threw it towards the others. I coughed coarsely now feeling the cool sweep of the breeze over my skin. I was in control of my body once again.

My mother held my face to her chest as she cried with glee. I realized then that the others had all different positioning. My Uncle had been hiding from the shadows behind the wooden door. When looking up I could see that Suzumiya, Chris and Helena were on the top floor watching and waiting for any action that might have broken out.

"How did you know that it wasn't me?" I asked Paul desperately. I thought no one had noticed. It was more than likely that Paige had told them.

"We all had our suspicions," Scott said casually beside me as if he were some gallant hero. In a sense, he was. None of this would have been possible without his element being involved. "Paul picked up on it first." Scott gave me a wink and a smile that had my cheeks burning from redness.

"How did you know that it would work?" I asked, thinking of the makeshift plan they had. "I could have killed you!"

Paul smiled and leant over to me. He pressed a kiss to my nose surprising me but making me angrier. "I am serious Paul, she could have killed you."

"But she didn't," he said with a smile.

"Martin ran a few suggestions with us," Scott began.

"Martin?" I questioned surprised by their association.

"Yes this one apparently had the best ratio outcome or something like that. I don't know how he works, but yea, this was his number one. Well that's nice it worked out after all," Scott cheered.

"But Misfeata will come back," I said desperately and almost in a panic. "I didn't even know, I only woke up tonight. I don't know what she did in those two days," I cried. My mother still held me into an embrace and Paul ushered me to calm.

"We will fix this Karla," he said soothingly.

"You can't fix this. You can't fix me," I snapped. I instantly regretted taking my frustration out on Paul. I could feel vomit rise in my stomach and tears begin to stream down my face. He gave me a pitied expression and rubbed his warm hand over my cheek.

Martin crept out from where my Uncle had been standing. He held his hands behind his back as he approached us.

"My suggestion is to pull part of the gem out from the collar and form it into a bracelet. It won't be to the same extent, but it will both hurt and drain you. However, it should also be so overpowering that it keeps Misfeata dormant for a while longer; or perhaps to the point where she won't have the strength to overpower you."

"How do you know all this?" Ashley asked him.

"It is just a theory," Martin shrugged. "But I've also read a few of Elisabeth's journals. She for a short period used the same sort of tactic."

"Did it work?" I asked desperately. I didn't care if I had to suffer in pain every day, as long as Misfeata vanished and was unable to possess my body.

"For a while. I haven't read all her entries. There were ones afterwards I read that stated she still struggled with Misfeata, making me believe that she no longer possessed or used that jewellery. It would've left her in a weakened and vulnerable state as well. So perhaps Elisabeth realized she needed that strength more to survive."

"Karla, it is only temporary," My Uncle said. "If we can find these other journals," he said pointing to the one that he had picked up from the ground beside me. "Then we might have an inclination or clue towards Sebastian's grave. Karla, we need to get rid of Misfeata."

"This bracelet will only be a temporary fix. If you were to have it on for too long for extended periods of time, I imagine that it would put your life at risk. You need energy and your Shield to survive. If that were completely drained and exhausted. . ." Martin said. "Christopher told me about the journals and that she can offer their location to you. I too wish to read more of those journals, so if you would like Karla, I can be your guide."

Everyone watched me intently. My mother still held me firmly making me want to cry even more into her arms. "I just want her gone," my voice came out in a small pitch.

"We will find a way," Paul said rubbing his thumb over my cheekbone. "Everything is going to be okay. We will find a cure for you." Tears streamed down my face. I curled myself into the arms of my mother and sobbed. Paul's hand trailed over my arm and held my hand firmly as I hid from him. I hid from them all. My mother couldn't do anything for me, we both knew this. And yet there was no comforting touch like that of your mother's arms.

Chapter Nineteen- Purpose

"You can't take anyone with you," Christopher said with arms crossed over her chest. It was only the two of us in her small office. It was now daytime and parts of sun streaked past the tattered sheets that covered the window. The burning sensation from the bracelet still rattled me. I felt tired but not to the extent when the collar was on me. The piece of jewellery still made me feel like a caged animal that had to be monitored.

"I can't exactly protect myself or fight with this," I said angrily and pointing to the bracelet. "And no offence but I don't think Martin is going to be my noble protector."

"You will have five of my men go with you, including Elijah. The others stay in the form of leverage," she said firmly.

"Leverage?" I questioned tiredly.

"To make sure you come back," she said simply. "It should only take you a few hours to walk there once on land. Which means I expect you back by the night. I can't very well let you all go at once and risk you not returning."

"And you think five men is going to protect me when I have an entire army after me? No offence but I would rather take my chances with the people who I have fought side by side with this entire time."

"My answer is final. It's the only way I will allow you to go. You forget Karla, I am doing this for your own sake. Don't be rude to my kind gesture." I took a shallow breath too exhausted to fight her. "Have Martin or Elijah collect me when we are leaving." I grabbed the door behind me. Before I left she had already announced the time of our departure.

"It will be soon. I've been travelling along this river the entire time to make sure we reach the closest point we can to it." I looked over my shoulder for a moment staring at Christopher. She was always calculating but it annoyed me to know that she had already presumed I would agree to this. But in the state I was in, I had to find something, anything to keep Misfeata away. I had to find clues in Elisabeth's journals. A part of me was hesitant to go ahead and read what some of those entries might say. I was terrified to know of the things that Misfeata forced Elisabeth to do and might possibly make me do. Was Elisabeth in control most of the time, being a pure descendant of Misfeata or did she struggle just as much as I did, even though I was originally human?

I left the room where Ashley, Paige and Paul waited. They filled the small corridor with arms crossed and leaning against the wall.

"When do we go?" Ashley asked.

"*We* don't," I said. "Only I go with a few of her men, Martin and Elijah," I replied.

"What?! No that's stupid. We go together," Ashley and Paul said in unison.

"Eww you guys make me sick. You both are like her pining brothers. Let her go she will be fine," Paige countered pushing them both out of her way as she approached me. "After all she is only going there to read some old books. You don't need much energy for that right." She grabbed my wrist assessing the bracelet. "Does it hurt?"

I looked at Paige for a moment as Paul and Ashley argued behind her. Paige was a little shorter than me, but was still a few years older. "How did you know it was Misfeata?" I asked. She didn't look at me only the bracelet as she rubbed her thumb over it, feeling its jarred texture.

"So you were in there after all listening in on our conversation," she mused. "Just a feeling. I would've thrown daggers at you even if it weren't her. I kind of have that reputation."

"Stop messing around Paige," Ashley said. "We need to go with her."

"We have to agree if it is the only way she is allowed to read these stupid books, which by the way," she turned to me seriously. "I think is a stupid waste of time. What if it isn't a real place or it's burnt to the ground already or something? I think we should be spending our time focusing on getting away from these people and back towards the fight where Eden is."

"You're always trigger happy aren't you," Paul said. "Going back to the place and person who wants Karla dead isn't exactly a smart move."

"I agree with Paul on this one," Ashley intervened. It seemed to surprise both of them that they agreed on something even though lately they had been getting along. "But I don't agree with you going by yourself to find these journals."

"It's the only way we can go directly to them. She won't let Martin lead the way unless I go by myself," I argued feeling faint as I stood in one spot for too long.

"Or we just find it ourselves," Ashley countered.

"We can't, it'll waste too much time," My Uncle interrupted from behind. We all turned to look at him. "We are already wasting too much time while she has that bracelet on. Her body can't hold out for long in that condition. She needs answers now. We need to find the resting place of Sebastian."

"You still believing in that fairy tale old man?" Paige chastised.

"I'm curious too," I admitted. "I didn't want to put much faith in it before. But I'm running out of ideas and options. I don't know how long I can keep my control of Misfeata and that terrifies me more than anything. I'm desperate."

Everyone fell silent. Paul lightly tugged my hand and pulled me into his embrace. I rested my head on his chest, comforted by his warmth. I was absolutely terrified. I had lost two entire days of my life. Two. What would it be next? Two weeks, a month, a year? I couldn't deny any makeshift fairy tale stories, I needed to believe in something or else I was already doomed. I already feared that it might have been too late.

"Just let me go. Trust me. I can handle this. If something happens I will have Elijah take the bracelet off and wait until I can properly protect myself." Paul went to argue but I raised my hand to the light stubble of his jawline.

"Hey, I'm practically immortal remember. No matter what damage I take during that time of rejuvenating I will still live. Have faith in me. I won't be gone for too long."

Paul's jaw clenched. He was about to argue but decided not to. "You make it so hard to argue with. I don't want you out there by yourself."

"I won't be. I will be okay. I will only be gone a few hours, Eden and his men couldn't have caught up yet. I will be fine. Now come, I only have a little while until I go, I want to check up on somebody."

I held his hand firmly and looked to Ashley who was about to start his argument again. "Don't," I said. "I can look after myself, this is something I need to do, even if it is on Christopher's conditions."

Weakly I walked towards the staircase. Paul pulled me back before I walked down them.

"What's wrong?" I asked. He gave me a smile and bent down in front of me offering his back to me.

"Hop on," he said, gesturing for a piggy back.

"Paul I am fine to walk," I said with a small smile.

"Come on. Some girls would think this is cute," he toyed with a sheepish smile.

"That's disgusting," Paige said as she pushed past us and down the staircase. I felt red streak across my cheeks. I instantly wanted to say no and thought it was stupid. But then, the occurring thought came to me that this may be the last time I ever got to do something so childish. I didn't know how long I had left. Misfeata proved that she could possess my body without my knowing. What if she erased me or my memories entirely?

I lounged over Paul as he collected my legs in his arms and comfortably sat me on his back.

"Where to my lady?" he toyed. I wrapped my arms around his chest with a smile. My smile slowly vanished as I thought of the person I wanted to visit.

"I want to see Jennifer." Paul kissed my knuckles and began to walk down the stairs. Only a few people looked at us in a confused manner as to why we were doing something childish. I imagined it was something that wasn't often done around here. Jennifer was in the same spot that she had been since I last saw her. She looked gaunt and malnourished. Her mouth looked parch and dry and her lips had begun to crack.

Paul propped me on my feet in front of her. The woman who was attending to her gave me a brief nod and handed over the bowl of food she had been trying to force her to eat. The meal was now cold and I wondered for how long she had been trying to force Jennifer to eat.

I fiddled in my leather jacket looking for the item I was after. Much to my joy it was still there. I left it in my pocket for a while longer.

"Jennifer," I said and knelt down in front of her. "Jennifer it's me." I was sitting directly in front of her but nothing registered. She just stared like a broken doll. If I didn't notice the small breaths she took I would've feared she was dead. "You should really eat." I said fiddling with the bowl in my hand. She only continued to stare and I knew there was no way that I would convince her to eat.

I placed the bowl on the floor and shuffled my hand into my jacket. I grabbed the necklace that once belonged to Kingsly. She was so shattered by his death, that all her instinct to live looked as if it had died alongside him. All her hopes for her child being looked after and taken to him had vanished right in front of her. I wondered how hard she had fought alongside him. I wondered if he had allowed her to fight at all. I had hoped that his death was quick. But having seen the wounds on his body I had the feeling that it wasn't.

I lifted my hand in front of her and opened it, the necklace dangled between my fingers and swung back and forth as if it were the object that hypnotised her.

"I got this for you, it was Kingsly's," I said. There was a slight motion in her eyes but then it faded again. She stared wide eyed still not really looking at the object in front of her. I wasn't sure what to do or say next. She had once been such a vibrant and strong young woman and by the death of her lover she was broken. So broken, she looked beyond repair. She had already been awaiting death, it was Kingsly who continued to fight to find a way to save her, but now she endangered her child too, didn't she see that? Did she forget how much she loved her child? But these were words I could never say out loud. She didn't need a lecture of all things right now. She just needed to know that she was cared for and I hoped that I would be witness to the glimmer in her eye when she came out of her current state.

"This belongs to you," I said. I grabbed her hand and opened it, dropping the silver into her hand. She was unflinching. Slowly her head dipped and she looked down at the piece. Tears welled in her eyes. Slowly her fingers curled around it and she rested it close to her chest as she looked away and silently cried. I reached out a hand to her but didn't dare to fully touch her. She was far away in a completely different world. She was mourning by herself and it was something that I felt I had no right to intrude on.

"Karla." Jennifer had flinched slightly under Elijah's summoning of me. He had kept his distance from us, staying near the doorway. He offered only a minor glace to Jennifer with pitied eyes. It was evident that Elijah's words still reached her, but for whatever reason he did not approach her, much to my surprise. I had seen the love in his eyes that he carried for her, when he spoke of her and fought for her. Then again, I wasn't present for the past two days, I don't know what had been said between the two. "We're going now," he said faintly and began to walk out. Paul leant me his hand to stand up. The red gem pulsed around my wrist sucking all the energy out of that arm more effectively than the rest of my body. It burned but I had become accustom to the pain. The first hour I whimpered with what felt to be torture. Eventually my entire wrist had become numb and accustomed to it.

Paul walked me out, followed by my mother and Helena. Elijah, Martin and another four Shielders waited for me. I recalled the face of the two closest to Elijah. They had been waiting for the Starkorf ambush with me before that entire town had been wiped out on that very memorable day.

The boat now slowly drifted and steered closer to the forestry woodland.

"Be safe," Paul said as he kissed me on the forehead.

"Always," I said. I gave my mother a hug as she watched me worriedly. I knew that my Uncle would've convinced them that this was the only way. Helena gave me a small smile and I couldn't help but wrap my arms around her too. Although Ashley's mother, she still held a motherly figure to me.

"Let's do this," Elijah commanded. He grabbed me in a clean sweep that startled me. Like the others before him, he built a slow run up and jumped over the edge, flawlessly jumping the boat and over the water of where we had not yet docked.

We jolted hard onto the ground, but he cushioned the fall slightly as he bent his knees.

"I can either carry you the entire way or we can walk. But you need to keep with our pace." He was already placing me down on my feet as I gave him a twisted smile.

"A walk is all you will get from me," I said raising the bracelet which limited any physical exertion I could perform. It was strange. I felt that in a way I had accepted my fate and no longer cared for how I spoke or what I did in front of others. I no longer considered what they would say or what they might think. I had changed so much over the past six months that I still didn't even know who I was. I looked behind me and waved to the others. All I knew was there were people who I loved and that I had to return to.

I followed Elijah and his men into the woodland. Martin took his place by my side keeping to my pace. The others lead us to the place we needed to go. Obviously Elijah had also been to this place, as he led us speedily through the trees.

Chapter Twenty- Elisabeth's Library

I leant against the thick tree trunk with my hand on my waist gathering my breath. I hated to admit it but I now wished that I had Scott to use as some kind of horse. I questioned if that was an insulting thought. The group didn't care much for my slower pace or lack of ability to walk fast.

I panted harshly ignoring the analytical look Martin gave me.

"I can confirm a twenty-two percent chance that you will pass out before we arrive," he said in his drone like voice.

"Really? You're really doing that thing now?" I asked in a heaped breath. I pushed myself off the tree trunk and continued to walk and catch up to the others, defying Martin deliberately.

Elijah halted the group and looked around the trees for an alarming few seconds. He indicated for the others to fan out and came to my side with his weapons poised. I hadn't yet taken Aeisha out. I would if I had to, but right now I considered that it might only be an animal making sounds in the forest. I inhaled deeply, with my head hunched over still gathering my breath. My legs began to feel numb as I walked. I even considered asking Elijah to carry me, but I felt too proud to bother.

The others returned and reported to him, finding nothing.

"Grab her, Thomas," Elijah said to the man who had once stood by my side ready to fight. "She is slowing us down and Christopher wants us to return by nightfall. Within seconds the bulky man had gathered me close to his chest. I considered arguing but gave up as my legs began to feel numb all over. If he had placed me down now I didn't know if I could walk at all.

The pace ultimately picked up. They now ran through the forest and within the hour we had arrived at our destination.

It looked like an old ruin that hadn't been entered in years. Vines and moss had scaled the rocky wall which hid any clear entrance. At first I thought they had stopped for a break until I realized they were satisfied with their timing. Thomas placed me on the ground lightly, but quickly as if the thought of still carrying me repulsed him. I wobbled slightly at the gain of my weight on my legs, but quickly strengthened, ignoring the fiery burn of my wrist. I held onto the part of my arm where the bracelet clung, as if it were blocking the flames that rose.

I followed Martin who no longer noticed me. He crept around to the side scaling his hand along the mossy rock before dipping into a crevasse. The hole in the wall was so minor that if I hadn't seen him walk in myself I would've been convinced that he vanished. I self-consciously assessed the wall. The others impatiently stood behind me. Elijah pointed for two to stay guard outside.

I knew that I couldn't turn back and felt childish for fearing the dark that was ahead of me. I placed my hand along the rocky wall to guide me. I held out both hands to make sure I didn't trip or run into the wall. It was only pitch black for a moment until light started shining through again and lightened the very unfriendly tunnel.

My pace hurried towards that light. Following it and wedging myself uncomfortably between the rocks again I walked out into a small open courtyard of sorts. There was no rocky terrain, only blue sky and clouds. The green grass looked like it had never been trimmed and was to my elbows. I saw the tips of white statues peak over the tops of the grass. Perhaps this had once been looked after and maintained.

Martin grabbed my attention, who was now on the other side of the abandoned courtyard. He slipped into another moss and vine covered wall and I hurried to catch up to him, scraping through all the sharp grass. It took all my effort to push through it until I had reached the same entry point that Martin slipped through. My eyes had to readjust to the darkness again as I slipped through the narrower pathway.

I continued walking, with both hands out to steady my walk. I had tripped over twice now. Thomas gave me a disgruntled sigh of impatience before I continued to walk. I shot him a filthy look but wasn't sure if he could see it when it was this dark.

I was led once again by the peeking of a little light. It wasn't as bright as outside and when I slipped through the crevasse I realized that the large room was mostly closed in. There were holes in the rocky walls and roofing which shot patches of light across the room. A loud pitch noise pierced my ears. Bats flew towards me and up into the roofing. I covered my face as their breeze swept past me from their closeness.

I retracted my hands and took a few steps down the stairs. Water swirled around my leather boots slightly higher than my ankles.

The entire room was flooded where it looked like it had rained and slipped through the holes in the ceiling. A light slimy moss covered the edge of the water around the room against the rock. I steadied my steps until I was fully standing in the water and stood to the side so the others could get through. I clung to the rocky wall as my breath was taken away by the room.

My vision wasn't as adaptable as it usually was but still there was enough lighting for me to see. On my left were three wooden tables. They were piled one after another with a wooden chair to each. The wood looked like it had deteriorated over time, the legs looked like they would snap if any large amount of weight was added. The others walked through the water as I still scanned the room. Martin was already across from me, fully engrossed as he scanned through entire bookshelves.

In the corner of the room on the further left, looked to be a long forgotten fireplace. Water swirled slightly at the rim of its cement framing. There was a wooden dining table and chairs there. A small olden style stove and benching was beside the fireplace. Elijah walked around into that room and vanished behind a wall. I could only imagine that perhaps there was some kind of bedroom there.

Directly across from me was four large bookshelves. The books had been brought up a few shelves so none were damaged by the rising water levels. On my right was an open space which had one wooden practice dummy. It looked as if it had taken some serious hits over time. I instinctually drifted over to it, feeling the need to touch its course exterior. I never knew what Elisabeth looked like. I hadn't ever much thought about the woman who was host to Misfeata before. I touched the harsh wood, which left a splinter in my finger.

I questioned if she used this training dummy. I wondered what she thought of the war and how she best handled Misfeata. She had after all lived for a very long time. I pulled the splinter out and allowed curiosity to swallow me entirety. I walked over to the bookshelf and towards the same row that Martin did. He already studied over the pages with such a rapid pace; that not even I could have kept up with. I had a sense that it had something to do with his Element.

I had read the journal that Christopher had leant me the day before but it gave me very little to go on and hardly any mention of Misfeata. It was an entry dated when Elisabeth was travelling. When she had no real destination, and the few encounters with groups and individuals she had. All of it seemed normal, like she was exploring the world. None of it really indicated who or what Elisabeth was doing. I found it odd that out of all the journals Christopher could've carried that it was that one.

Martin snapped the book shut and placed it back on the shelf, he then collected another one. "This entire shelving is of her time during the Great Wall. If you head down to the end it was before Misfeata had been passed down to her due to the death of her parents. When you trail up it will be up to the point of the breaking of the wall and when all Shielders, Starkorfs and Elemental Breathers escaped. The shelving behind is the years afterwards."

"There are a lot of books here," I sighed in disbelief. Martin didn't look up from his book as he responded.

"Yes but although she held the age of mid-thirties when she died. She was eighteen when Misfeatea first awoke in her. In that same year that wall had shattered. It's been one hundred years since then. She was one hundred and one when she died and these are rather thorough entries. No one knew Misfeata lived on until only recently when rumor of your existence changed everything." Still he continued to scan through his book and then snapped it closed. He grabbed another one and exchanged the books. He gave me a side glance which hurried me and reminded me of why we came here. I grabbed the first one on my right. In this part of her time line it was after Misfeata had woken within her, but before the Wall had fallen.

This wall is unbreakable. The Starkorfs broke into our schooling again today. Still, I struggle to get used to their mutations. I had only ever heard the stories of them until two months ago when I had my first encounter with them. Mother and father had always told me stories, but I guess I was too stubborn to heed their council. One of them was stronger than me and broke my Shield. I thought it was only a child, but since learnt that it is a young woman who goes by the name of Raven. If it weren't for Max, I think I would've been drained dry. It's odd I can sense Misfeata growing within me, but no matter what, I try to supress her. Now that others know that I am the host of Misfeata they look at me as if I am some kind of God. I don't know, I just know I shouldn't call her forth and ask for her strength. She's unsettling and I know she is watching. I can sense that she is always watching.

I flicked to the next page and next entry. I remembered my first encounter when meeting Max Jacket, Scott's father. He first thought that I was Elisabeth by recognizing the blood that I carried. He had fought alongside her for many years. I had also been told that the hunger which grew in Elisabeth to kill Starkorfs truly awoken when her lover was killed before the shattering of the great wall. My stomach churned at the thought. I took a step to the side, with the water still pooling around my ankles and leant against the bookshelf.

I didn't allow myself to be distracted as the others either whistled bored or lazily read themselves. Elijah stayed on guard and cautious. Every hour one of the guards would come back to him and report if they sighted anything suspicious.

I scanned through numerous books engulfing the different life that Elisabeth lived.

I miss him, more than words could ever describe. I wish he were here with me. Like he always had been. I miss him teasing me. I miss him ignoring me, which I found so annoying, but look at me when I look away. I miss the nickname he gave me, that at the time I hated. What I hate most is the relieving feeling that often washes over me when I think of him. It's not me that is relieved by his death, but Misfeata. She is more apparent now. I almost lost myself to her entirely with the battle against Praytar. I should've killed his youngest son while I had the chance but I choked. He was but a boy. I missed my chance, I should've killed Lucas. He was the bait that drew me in. His brother was waiting. How could I have been so stupid as to have let my guard down, why did I leave myself open? If I hadn't then. . . He would still be alive, he would still be here. I hate that she laughs when I cry out his name in my sleep. I feel like I am going crazy with her echoing words.

I had wrapped myself around another bookshelf and now held a stick with a flame trying to help my reading as I continued to read. Oddly enough I felt her pain. Her every word felt like it resided with me. But the more years I covered, selecting random books at a time, the harder she became and the more susceptible to Misfeata's influence. The worst part was she slowly started to sound like Misfeata. It was a mixture of both her and Misfeata. I wondered if she was conscious of it. Had she given up? Had Misfeata won?

I look at this fresh open book. I don't know where my other books went. This time, it was two months. I can't recall anything from that time. I feel stronger and leaner. I stared at my hands for hours when I claimed my body once more. For two months she had possessed my body without my knowing. I scrubbed myself, feeling dirty. I look slightly younger and I feel as if this power could have only been gathered one way. Perhaps it was best that I couldn't recall what she had done. I don't even know who I am anymore. I am fighting an endless battle both internally and externally. My hatred for them runs deep and I want to be the saviour of humanity, but I can't also doubt my wish for a quiet day. For a peaceful one where I wasn't killing. Fighting is something I had always enjoyed, especially training in the school. But now, it all seems wrong. Pointless. I am not fighting for me anymore, I have no loved ones to fight for. I don't want to fight for the Elders any longer. I have moments where I wished this time had come to my father instead of me. I miss them. I wondered how they would've fared in this lifetime. I wonder if I

149

would have better control if Max was still around to ground me. I don't even know what I am writing now. It looks like some long winded suicide note. I am an existence that can't really die and yet right now that makes me mortified. Two months I've lost of my long and never dying life. I think maybe, it might be easier to give in to Misfeata. But then I can't help but have the urge to still fight her. Everyone has demons, mine is just more boisterous than the rest. I want to find a way to get rid of her. I want her gone so I can die. My only joy is to know that I will never bear any children to lay this curse upon. The three elders shouldn't be revered as they are. Next time when I come in contact with Praytar and both he and Misfeata lose control perhaps I will not fight for control. Maybe I will let Misfeata turn into whatever beast she desires so I am set free. But my greatest fear is that I will never actually be free, that instead I will be trapped in beast form alongside her. I don't know. I don't know what I am writing. I just want to die.

I looked up from the passage that I was reading. I waited until Elisabeth's voice no longer ran through my thoughts and I had to remind myself that these were not my own thoughts and yet it felt so familiar and that it was my own fears and hatred. I looked to my right at all the books to follow. I was now on the second bookshelf and Martin was on the last. Yet despite the entry in this book she continued.

I placed that book back into the shelving and went to pull out another one.

"Karla," Martin called out to me. It was the first voice that had broken the room's tension for a while.

I tiredly dragged myself along the bookshelf and around it to the next one. The water now felt like it was racing through cement and the chill was starting to bother me even with my leather jacket on. But I knew these were the results of wearing the bracelet. I was glad to have it on now, I wondered how hard Misfeata might have fought me to get rid of these books and burn them down.

"This entry here talks about the chains. This here is the original idea and concept of the chains around the neck. Look," Martin pointed to a sketch in the book that was identical to the ones Lucas and I wore. "Which means that whoever created those chains had either read this exact same book or replicated the idea or they were the originals. But looking at the dates and studying the collars more closely I doubt that. The original ones would've deteriorated."

"But why would they have made that do you think?" I asked. I knew the reasons as to why Lucas had created them so we could speak. But I realized the more logical answer was so the Elders could weaken one another.

"Lucas must have been here," I whispered in astonishment realizing that he must have read these very same books.

"What did you say?" Martin said as he scanned through the book. "That's weird."

"What is?" I asked peering over his shoulder with the flame.

"The rest of the pages are ripped out," he said shuffling between the covers. He placed it back on the shelf and went to grab the one next to it until he realized there were a few empty spaces beside it. He picked up the closest one and studied the date. "This is missing almost an entire year of journals. Someone has taken these ones specifically.

"Well what does that book say?" I asked creeping closer and wanting to know at what point we were up to in Elisabeth's life. We still had so much more reading to do and already it was night.

"We need to go. Christopher will be annoyed if we miss our expected time," Elijah said.

"But we haven't read them all yet, we need to keep searching," Martin said with a hint of annoyance. It was very rare for him to show any sign of emotion past his normal monotone robot like voice.

"Stash as many books as you can into this bag and read them when we're back on the ship. It's dark now," Elijah said looking up through some of the holes.

"Just one more hour," I asked desperately. I hadn't yet found anything that were helpful to me. "Please," I begged.

"Let them go for one more hour," Thomas said lazily. "It's nice to be off the boat for a while longer anyway. Don't worry, Jennifer will be in the same state as you left her."

"You shut your mouth," Elijah spat. He quickly recovered himself ashamed of his vulnerable outburst. So he was worried about her. Of course he was.

"One more hour and that's it. I am going to go check on the others," Elijah said obviously needing to escape for a moment to cool down. He slipped through the dark crevasse, leaving two of the other Shielders with us and Thomas who watched us lazily.

Martin and I began crazily reading over the journal entries. I don't know if we were looking for the same thing. I only knew that Elemental Breathers loved knowledge and that Martin probably had no intention of helping me. With all the focus I could muster, I tried to scan over as much as I could with the limited time left.

Chapter Twenty-One- A Familiar Presence

*T*he air went chill and large sweeps of wind tampered with my flame. I looked behind me a couple of times self-conscious of the eerie sensation that the place gave off. Elijah had still not returned and I felt less protected than I had when he was here. As much as I argued with Christopher about wanting my own protectors, I felt reasonably safer with Elijah around. I just wished that I didn't need to rely on everyone else for my own safety.

Martin seemed unmoved by the eerie presence that swept through the room and continued to scan through the books. I tried to follow his lead, but clung to Aeisha as soon as I heard something drop. I swung around, far too quickly for my delicate sense of balance right now and stumbled into the bookshelf. I hated my weakened and vulnerable state. Thomas raised his hand apologetically, after having dropped the piece of wood he was holding. He balanced carefully on the rotting wooden table. I was surprised it hadn't yet given out under his weight.

There was a small scuffling noise coming from the entry passage. Still on edge I studied it wearily. I knew that it was Elijah, but my paranoia and sense of vulnerability was edging at me. I waited patiently for his face to emerge from the dark. Martin snapped another book shut, startling me as I jumped in fright. I hadn't been this edgy for as long as I could remember. When I returned my stare at the entrance, my heart felt like it had been reefed my chest.

Kurt's all too familiar face crept out of the darkness. He instantly focused on me holding his hands out in a peaceful manner. He stayed near the entrance where others followed him into the room. I couldn't sense whether they were Starkorfs or Shielder's because of my weakened state.

The Shielder's to my surprise hadn't yet responded. Instead they watched the ten foreigners walk in. It dawned on me then, they weren't followers to Christopher. They were traitors too.

"It would appear you've survived this long Karla," Kurt said soothingly, the way his tone had always sounded. "Please come along with me peacefully."

"You are all traitors," I hissed to Thomas who was smiling the boldest. The others seemed unsure of their alliance but followed Thomas anyway. "Elijah as well?"

"That loyal hound? Pffft please," Thomas said as he walked and stood behind Kurt. "We made this arrangement on our own accordance. After all thanks to that nice little bracelet of yours and without your guards you are perfect for the picking."

Two of them approached Martin and I. Martin didn't look fearful, he only studied them. He leant over my shoulder to whisper to me. There was noise coming from outside and the clutter of weapons began clashing. I could only assume that it might've been Elijah coming to our rescue, but even then I feared the chances of him getting through ten of them to help us were slim. Even in my state I had to fight my hardest, but I could hardly stand.

"Perhaps if you will let me," Martin said gentlemanly. His hand drifted down my arm and wrapped around Aeisha, there was a firm defensiveness I had against him for reaching for my blades. In a soothing tone he reapproached with more urgency as two surrounded us. "The truth is Karla, I've never needed protection because the one that I am running from is far more powerful than this group of protection could ever offer me. I only stayed with them because it would be unbelievable that I would travel with a group of Shielders. He was the same master who trained me. My chances of winning this battle is one hundred percent."

He tugged Aeisha out of my hand, surprising me with his sudden alternative demeanor. He pressed me to the bookshelves behind us and lunged at the first Shielder. His speed took me by surprise as he challenged them and slashed through their Shields with Aeisha. I stared in bewilderment and was dumfounded. How was he able to break through their Shields without being a Shielder himself? Was it because he used Aeisha? He stabbed Aeisha into the neck of one. He side kicked the other away, slamming him into the nearby bookshelf. He reefed Aeisha out of the neck of the other and collected his sword before he dropped to his knees. He spun into an elegant dance of sorts slashing the blade across the other's stomach. I was so weak that I couldn't detect Shields but I had seen those two use them before. He was somehow breaking their Shields.

He knocked away the third attacker's weapon in a clean sweep. The difference in their strength was evident in that one clean movement. He didn't go out to the others though he stayed close to me, blocking their path to reach me. He simply swayed back and forth taking the same few steps so no matter how many of them came he still blocked their path.

Kurt paced back and forth slowly looking past Martin and only at me like I was his prey. I looked at him only for a moment before I was drawn back to Martin. The water in the dark night sloshed around as they attacked. Streaks of red poisoned the water that wavered at our ankles. He still had the same elegant frame that I judged him for when we first met. But I now realized that Martin was not weak at all despite his exterior impression. He killed them with such precision and lack of mercy that even I wanted to look away. Yet there was a part of me, the warrior that learnt to grow within, that thought his moves were beautiful.

"Retreat," Kurt said in frustration as he made his leave. I frowned in confusion as to why he would try to corner me here and not go as far as he could. Martin removed Aeisha from the ribcage of the man he had just stabbed.

"What?!" Thomas exclaimed. "But she is right here and vulnerable."

"Then bring her to me," Kurt simply replied in a superior way. It was still the same Kurt I had once known yet different. I didn't understand where he had gained the power nor these new followers. I was even more surprised that he still didn't try to cascade over Martin with force.

Thomas growled in agitation. "If you want something done, you have to do it yourself around here!" He took out both of his swords from his sheaths strapped to his back. He glided them through the air in a rotary motion as he approached Martin. The others had already begun to leave.

"Don't worry about them you fowl Breather," Thomas said. "I really hate your kind."

"Your kind is beneath me and yet you personally appeal to me as vermin," Martin retorted back. He seemed distracted as he said it. His eyes lit up as he reached out for a book across him on the bookshelf.

"Ah, this was the year I was looking for." He collected it with the same hand that he held Aeisha.

Thomas lunged toward him. Martin scraped his sword alongside the two of Thomas's that came over him in a cross figure. Thomas swung back one to hack at him but Martin was too quick. The water swished around his movement as he kicked Thomas back. Within seconds he had kneed him in the stomach and grabbed his head to his knee. His speed was near incomprehensible. He slashed at the tops of Thomas's legs and his towering scream shattered through.

"Never rely only on one defence," Martin said as Thomas dropped. As he did, Martin hacked upwards, decapitating Thomas. His head flew towards the wooden dummy and sploshed in the water. I held my hand over my mouth in horror. "Shielders become too dependent on their Shields."

Martin flickered the blood off his sword. His back was still to me as he opened the book and began to scan. I choked on a tear and vomit rose in my throat. I vomited into the water. I had fought so many battles and seen many things. But somehow in this very moment, Martin seemed to be the greatest monster I had seen.

It was as if Martin had forgotten I was there or he was so entranced in his reading. He snapped the book shut and looked over his shoulder at me.

"Who are you?" I choked out in disbelief.

"I am my master's prodigy. Besides him I stand a twelve percent chance of winning and that is with sporadic odds on my side."

"Who is your master?" I asked mortified at what strength this master of his was. I could only assume he was an Elemental Breather. "And how could you break their Shields?"

"Because I am my master's prodigy," he repeated as if it answered all my questions. "Some secrets cannot be shared Karla. You tell no one of this night. I cannot allow my identity to be found or be traced back to this place. If you were anyone else I would've killed you myself for being a witness. I entrust that you will keep this a secret so I am not forced to use such methods."

He walked towards me in a haunting gesture. It looked as if his size now towered over mine. He was tall but not lean muscled like I expected him to look after challenging so many and being victor so easily. "Some secrets and identities are best hidden."

He offered Aeisha back to me, the handle pointed politely to me. Slowly I took it. Martin threw away the sword creating a splash in the water nearby. Elijah came bursting through the doorway.

"What happened?!" He roared looking over the many bodies. He had a few cuts bleeding on his arms and face but he was still alive and well. "I heard the weapons outside clashing and then when I got here there was half a field of dead Starkorfs."

I countered a confused expression, I had thought that it was Elijah who was fighting outside. "Who?" I began to say but Martin cut me off.

"Well it would appear bracelet or no bracelet, this young Shielder still knows how to fight. I am indebted to her for saving me. I think we should take a few books and make our leave in case more come back. I predict a twenty-two percent chance that they will."

Elijah and I exchanged an uncertain glance. He looked down at Thomas and his other two men who had fallen. I didn't have the heart to tell him that they had betrayed him.

"They fought gallantly," I said. Elijah seemed to accept that and offered a small prayer to them. In the moments that it took Martin and I to stuff a backpack with books, Elijah had dragged the bodies out through the crevasse to burn them. I couldn't wait to leave this enclosed room which streaked with blood covered water. I couldn't take my eyes off the complacent Martin who dropped certain books into the bag.

"You never mention this night again," he said as he dropped the last book into his backpack. He zipped it up and threw it over his shoulder. It was odd to see a well-groomed Elemental Breather, still in suit, holding a bag over his shoulder. He trailed through the water and through the entrance. I didn't even look back at the room which held so much knowledge. I never wanted to remember this night again.

Elijah waited for us to reach him on the other side to the first entrance. I looked at the hands and legs which slipped out of the tall grass on my sides. I could smell the blood that surrounded me. There were so many dead bodies around me. Who had killed them all? I stood by Elijah's side as he held his lit stick. He gave another prayer. There was a small pile of his fallen comrades, in there were also the two scouts who had guarded the outskirts. I wondered if they too were traitors.

He threw the flamed stick onto the grass, hurriedly ushering for us to walk into the entrance and away from the grass fed circle of bodies. The grass instantly lit up. By the time we had exited, the smell of smoke had already begun to rise into the sky. The books inside would stay undamaged. The flames couldn't reach them and because of the cemented walls the flames could never escape.

I just felt sorry for the next group of Shielders who walked in and would be surrounded by burnt grass and the remains of corpses. Then a thought struck me. How did I not know that I had walked into the same thing and that the long grass had been burnt off and grown back covering any remains? A cold chill ran down my spine. I no longer wanted to think about it and tried to leave that imagery in the back of my mind. The pain that my bracelet was causing me started to become a relief and a reminder that I was still alive.

Chapter Twenty-Two- Memories

I couldn't look at Martin the same. I viewed him differently and now focused on his grace as he walked while Elijah carried me. I studied him for hours upon our return. He had the subtle grace that all Elemental Breathers had yet I never had considered that he were a fighter. I thought he was the nerd version of an Elemental Breather. I recalled him denying that he had killed any of them back there, claiming that it was me instead. I wondered if anyone within the Shielders he stayed with knew of his skill.

His speed I feared matched that even of the Elders. I had battled with Taskatae and thought her Element was to be feared, even Scott's. If he were an enemy I wasn't sure how I could challenge his Element. But Martin- he was both analytical, fast and lean. He was the ultimate weapon. The elders exemplified the same grace, but in comparison, I even thought of Misfeata as more merciful than Martin. He killed them without flinching or hesitation.

I jolted as Elijah still carried me. He had a few cuts and bruises to his face and arms from the fight but seemed like he didn't face a huge amount of opposition. An hour after leaving Elisabeth's library I couldn't hold myself up anymore. I dabbled in and out of consciousness, but stayed awake, just in case Misfeata was waiting for me. I couldn't feel her stir within me but knew that was never a true indication.

Suddenly I jolted and my eyes flashed open. We were now on the deck of the ship. I looked around hazed for a moment realizing that against all my efforts I had passed out. Elijah was trading me over to Paul who tucked me into his arms and close to his chest.

"Paul," I croaked, my voice came out dry and I was still seemingly delirious. I was so exhausted and fought my eyelids not to close. But instead they did. I could feel myself retreating into myself. I tried my hardest not to let myself go, but the darkness consumed me far too quickly and pulled me under. The last thing I felt was the warmth of Paul's tender kiss on my lips as I fell back to sleep.

I was back at Elisabeth's library. My mind was slightly off in this dream state Misfeata took me on. It was as if my mental exhaustion carried through to this other place as well. It was different however, the room was bright and beautiful. It didn't fill with water or have rotten wooden furniture. The fireplace was already lit and keeping the room warm.

I was amongst the bookshelves, where the binaries weren't so damaged and the shelving were only half filled. I heard a bang, and then another. Heavy panting followed. I walked out from between the shelves. A beautiful young woman with dusty looking brown hair punched into the wooden dummy. She continued to do circuits of six and then sometimes added kicks. The cloth that was wrapped around her knuckles didn't do much as she continued to bleed through them from too much practice.

"So this is where you've been?" A familiar but younger voice said. Max Jacket walked in. This was a vision of him before he was paralyzed and his wife murdered. I watched intently, confused as to whether this was some sort of memory or a creation of Misfeata's. Yet I couldn't sense Misfeata in the dream.

"It's always a pleasure to see you old friend," the woman said as she continued practice. "How did you find me? This was meant to be my secret home."

"I could detect you from afar Elisabeth and if you hadn't welcomed me in you would've detected and prevented my arrival long before I walked in," he replied. Elisabeth? I looked back to the woman which everyone revered to so much. She turned around taking a few simple breaths to ease herself. She grabbed a nearby cloth and wiped her face with it. Sweat dripped from her arms and face as she assessed Max.

"You haven't aged a bit my friend," she smiled.

"Nor have you, though I don't wish to ask why," he responded. She looked away ashamed and threw the cloth at the far away wooden chair. It had elegantly landed. She began to unwind the cloth around her knuckles. The busted knuckles that she once had while punching was now gone. Much like me she healed instantly.

"Why did you come?" She asked. It wasn't in an unfriendly manner although she was hostile. She reminded me of a woman who hadn't much contact with outsiders in a while. I had heard stories of all the fights and wars she lead and yet this felt like a pivotal moment in her being. For how long was she here? For how long did she hide away from the war? There was only one table and chair for studying here, unlike

160

the three that I had seen when we were there earlier today. Obviously at a later date they were added.

"I wanted you to know that I have to stop my search for Sebastian's grave for some time. My darling wife is pregnant you see," Max said with a glint of pride in his eyes. He was very different to the man that I had met. There was even a promiscuous youthful gleam to him. Still that gave me no indication of what time period we were in because Elemental Breathers far outlived humans with double if not more years than they did. I didn't exactly know how old Scott or Trish was. "A boy." He pressed with a smile. "I can just feel it."

"Really?" Elisabeth smiled. She sat down against the rocky wall with her hands rested on her knees. Max searched the room and decided that the wooden chair was more befitting for him. He sat down with his legs crossed. "Congratulations are in order. I had never considered the day when children would surround our future."

"You only choose it not to in yours," Max said cautiously. Obviously it was a sensitive topic. "I understand your reasoning not to, but my old friend, this isn't the only way you should live. You've locked your way for years now. I have been searching for you for some time now and I-"

"Two years I have lost of my life," she interrupted him. "It has only been three months now since I have been back. I do not know what I have done in that time. Or what she has done in my place. How could I possibly consider raising a child or family with that? How could I possibly attempt to open my heart to anyone when she will only kill them?"

I had read a journal entry of Elisabeth's which mentioned the time Misfeata had possessed her for two years. My heart sunk as I considered if I had the same fate. I had the sensation that Elisabeth never spoke to anyone so openly like she had Max.

Max looked to the floor and didn't reapproach her on the subject again.

"You know what I had done, don't you. You always have a way to find something," she confronted him. She was rather distressed thinking about what she might have done.

"My old friend, some things are best left unsaid," he simply replied. "I cannot go on my long journeys like I used to, searching for Sebastian's grave but I will continue to circulate with the resources I have." This was now the second time Max had spoken about Sebastian's grave. It almost seemed to be irrelevant when they spoke about these other subjects. Elisabeth was also looking for Sebastian's grave? Had she believed in it?

"Misfeata says it doesn't exist," she replied rubbing her face.

"I never knew you to be the type of woman to give up. On anything," Max responded seriously. I wondered what she was like within her more youthful reign. She was still young here, but I wanted to see her when she was eighteen or before Misfeata awoke within her. What kind of attitude and spirit did she have? Was she prepared for Misfeata because her father was the previous host or had it made no difference whatsoever?

"I have given up many times," she said in a slow depleted way. "The evidence of my near immortality prevails once again," she sneered. Max stayed quiet. Her exhausted self-reminded me much of myself. To the point of where I no longer wanted to fight when I was most tired. But I had my loved ones surround me. Elisabeth for a time hid herself from the world and lived with Misfeata inside for a far greater time. "The only way I can ever find peace is by the death of either Misfeata or Tyran and both are seemingly impossible no matter how many times we fight."

"Which is why I think you should find Sebastian's grave. There was so much power in that Elder too, Elisabeth. That much power could have not simply vanished," Max lectured.

"Or so the stories say. Nobody really knows if he was as strong as those two, because he has been dead for more than one lifetime now. You are clinging to a rumour. You Elemental Breathers often are led by such tips, and not all lead to results."

"I promised you that I would help you since the wall had fallen," Max said seriously. "Do not mock my intention to help you." He stood up, sweeping his hand over the wooden chair and assessing its dirt.

"My old friend, I wish things hadn't turned out like this," she said honestly. I saw a gleam of pity in Max's eyes, something I had never seen before. It made me sad to know that he was dead. I had hated him for all that he had done to me and my loved ones and the secrets that he kept. But in this moment, it was obvious that maybe after the death of his wife that he had changed too.

"I wish I could offer you another solution, one that you could believe in. Never be a stranger, you know where we are," he said. He leaned over her and pressed a kiss to her head. My eyebrows furrowed in confusion. There was so much tension between Elemental Breathers, Shielders and Starkorfs. But amongst them there were still friendships like this. I recalled the stories that once Elemental Breathers and Shielder's trained and fought alongside one another against the Starkorfs. When had that changed?

Elisabeth shut her eyes, reminiscing the touch. "You are lucky Max," she said as he began to walk away. "I too wish I could've started my own family and returned to my lover every day. You look after them." It was more like a command, letting a part of her old self shine through. I imagined that she would've been a very strong and confident woman.

"With my life," he said with a smile. He slipped through the cracks and disappeared. Elisabeth stayed there and then she began to cry.

"Go away!" she said grabbing her head. I could hear the whisper of Misfeata but couldn't hear what she was saying exactly. "Go away!" Elisabeth screamed again. She grabbed the foot of the dummy and flung it across the room. It smashed against the empty book shelf with inhumanly force. She continued to sob into her hands.

I looked over my shoulder as an all too familiar presence crept forward. Misfeata's long green dress dragged along the dusty floor, both her hands poised in front of her lady like. Her long red hair and amber eyes were always breathtaking. She stood beside me in a non-threatening manner and watched Elisabeth as she ran into turmoil.

"Why did you show me this?" I asked her.

"You were curious about Elisabeth were you not?" she said in a passive tone. "She became broken. I tried to help her and let her disappear but she continued to come back. Well for certain periods of time."

I looked over to Elisabeth who no longer cried. I looked to the ground not wanting to witness it. It was no longer Elisabeth, I could just somehow tell. Misfeata was now in control of her body.

"I want you to take two things from this," she began in her well poised way. "One. Although your bracelet temporarily locks me out, it can't hold forever. Two. That not even Elisabeth believed in Sebastian's grave. It is not real."

I smiled in a haunting manner, one that I hoped unsettled her. "Are you just ashamed to find him and be a disappointment? You've carried on a war for centuries, how could you possibly show your face with pride to your angelic brother? I think that it is not me or Elisabeth that is in denial, but you Misfeata. Perhaps you are the broken and dysfunctional one here?"

Her face was hard. Her eyes screamed at me in rage. However, her mouth never opened to say a word. Instead the world around me spun and that blackness turned into a quiet and well longed for slumber.

Chapter Twenty-Three- The Unexpected

I stirred at the lighting which now shone in my eyes. I was huddled in the corner on the uncomfortable floor with a light blanket thrown over me. Everyone busily hurried around me. It was crowded and everyone spoke amongst themselves. I shuffled the blanket off still squinting at the sun which shone through the wooden door. The boat still glided smoothly over the water.

I yawned and stretched lazily happy with the rest I had. I rubbed my wrists in a waking manner and was startled when I found the bracelet wasn't there. I flicked my blankets off in a dramatic throw searching near my ankles.

"Karla what's wrong." My mother's voice startled me as I looked up at her and realized she had been sitting next to me the whole time.

"Where's the bracelet?" I panicked and searched for it.

"Sweetie, it's okay. We had to take it off for a little while just so you can gain a little of your strength back," my mother ushered.

"No we can't, Misfeata will come back," I grabbed her hands in a desperate plea.

"Nor will you if you keep relying on it," Scott's voice interrupted. He and Helena were sitting across from me. Helena gave me those sad eyes which she too often held for me. "You were out cold for an entire day. We took that bracelet off hours ago but you didn't budge. Your mother was fretting you went into a coma or something."

I looked between her and Scott unsure what to say. "But I *need* that." I thought about the memory of Elisabeth and how Misfeata so easily possessed her. If Elisabeth couldn't keep her away, what chance did I now have? I searched the room. There were less Shielders than before. The Shielder who often attended Jennifer had changed into an older woman. Jennifer was seated awkwardly in the same position across from me.

"Where is everyone?" I asked. I couldn't see any of the others.

"They ran out for a while to get some food and supplies," Helena said. "Being on this boat is only temporary until Christopher has mastered a new plan of attack. We can't survive on here for too long. There are too many and supplies are short."

"Not to forget to mention that you all haven't showered in days. You all repulse me," Scott said in disgust.

"Did Paul go?" I asked unsettled that they let him onto the land when he couldn't shield himself like the others. My mind was at ease if Ashley was with him. But still, I couldn't rest assured unless I was the one protecting him.

"Lover boy is gone. My gosh I am going to buy both of you a dog leash for one another," he sighed dramatically. I ignored his comment. I looked around the boat again and edged closer to Scott in a whisper.

"And Martin?"

"Martin?" His head snapped up in confusion. "Well he is on the boat of course. Why would you want to know where Martin is?"

I dipped my hand and looked at my bear wrist again. For a moment I felt I was in either denial or hiding secrets. Did I really witness what Martin was capable of? He told me not to tell anyone and somehow with his analytical skill I thought he would know if I had.

"We took some books from Elisabeth library. I need to read those," I said in a quiet tone hoping that no one would detect my lie.

"Oh those old books," Scott said as he flicked his hand through his white hair superiorly. "Martin like read those like a super whizz within hours. He just like looks at the thing and he's done. I wish I had that Element where I could absorb that much knowledge at once," he whined. "I suppose I couldn't be beautiful and smart as well."

"You've certainly come out of your shell since I last saw you," Helena said in a motherly tone. It must have been a shock to everyone when they found out about Scott's true identity. He considered this for a moment and gave her a very bold and childish smile. He flicked his head slightly in a prestige way and stood up.

"I will find these dusty old books for you to read," he said.

"Hey Scott," I grabbed him before he had left. I was thinking back to his father's search of Sebastian's grave. Scott also wanted to search and believed in it. "Your father, he had searched for Sebastian's grave as well, hadn't he?"

Scott offered a sad smile. Although his father showed so much hostility towards him, I could still see the pain and mourning in Scott's expression. "He had. With no luck," Scott said. "The thing with

166

Sebastian's grave is. It's near impossible. So to speak it doesn't exist, but only because it hasn't been found. My father wrote theories down in books, which I had found and read over. But no matter what parts of the world he ventured to, nothing offered him an answer to his resting place. He tried Karla, he tried so hard. My mother told me all the time the amount of years he put into that research for Elisabeth, but in the end it was all futile."

"But you believe in it?" I asked sceptically.

"Yes. That amount of power doesn't just vanish into thin air. His weapon must still be out there somewhere. " His words reminded me so much of his father in his younger days when he spoke to Elisabeth.

"What do you think about their theory on removing Misfeata?" I asked. Scott was abrupt and honest in his opinion. I prepared myself for his answer.

"I don't know how you could possibly do that or where that theory came from. But I think if we were to find his grave and weapon then they might be a nicely written bound notepad that states, 'Please read this if wanting to remove an Elder'." He moved his fingers along as if writing the title in bold. His mockery only seemed to make me angry. "Karla, I am not sure. But I think we will find some sort of way. That cheap bracelet you wear can't stay on for too long. So we're just going to have to make another way. I'll go find these books."

"Seth hadn't ever mentioned anything about it before. Since finding out about Kurt," Helena choked on her words. Seth and Kurt were extremely close. I pitied the depth of treachery Helena must've felt when it was announced. As well as Suzumiya and Chris. When I looked around I noticed they weren't on this ship either. They would've been itching to hunt for food. "Since finding out about Kurt I realized there was probably a lot that he hadn't spoken about with us. I am hopeful that we will find something. Although Kurt betrayed us, he wasn't a silly man. He led us safely all these years because he was clued on. I think if he is pursuing this to the degree where he would betray his own people; that there must be some proof or evidence there."

My mother watched between Helena and me. She had never met Kurt. She seemed most lost amongst everyone. I wished that she didn't know of this world but couldn't deny the comfort I had by having her here.

"Kurt was there," I admitted. "At the library. He had come for me with others."

"Martin had mentioned that. I am glad you had the strength to hold them off and come back to us safely. It's unlike Kurt to fall back from an opportunity unless he knows he's wasting resources. Neither he nor Seth ever went in rash. I don't know who Ashley got that trait from," she said with a coy smile.

Scott had returned with Martin trailing not far behind him. He carried the bag which held the books in it. Still it was odd to see a well-dressed Elemental Breather hold a bag over his shoulder. He didn't wear a suit like Scott did, but he still wore a nice dress shirt and pants with the Elemental Breathers swirls. The white shirt was evidently white amongst all odds. Surely one smudge of dirt or something would've spoiled it.

Martin dumped the bag beside me and watched me as he always did with his analytical expression. It made me uncomfortable. It was as if he were trying to see through me, see if I had yet told anyone about what I saw.

I pulled the bag closer and opened it looking inside. We had gathered a few. A knock to the boat pushed everyone to the side as the boat moaned in pain. I jumped out of my make-do bed on wobbly feet. Much like the others on the ship we ran outside onto the deck where flames had started blazing. Shielders began bucketing water on it and others went outside to challenge the enemy.

"Scott come out here!" The enemy yelled. I pressed through the Shielders who busily flooded the fire with water. Martin and Scott stood side by side. I stood next to Scott and looked down at his sister, Trish who was shouting out his name in anger. She fought off the Shielder's wavering her flames around. Her dress looked tattered and dirty which was so unlike her kind; and especially unlike Trish. She shot a powerful flame at one of the Shielders knocking into their Shield with so much force that they flew over the edge and splashed into the river.

"Like annoying ants!" She snarled.

"Is that your sister?" Martin asked as he continued to watch the performance. He had his arms crossed over his chest as he watched what seemed to be some kind of bland amusement for him.

Scott stared at Trish somewhat embarrassed by her behaviour. "Yep. That's the baby sis. I'm coming, I'm coming. Don't get your knickers in a twist." He changed into a white dove and flew over the edge and swooped down. No one listened to him as they continued to fight off Trish.

"Stand down," Christopher roared from the second level. I looked up at her in bewilderment. I was surprised she hadn't come out sooner and attacked. "Deal with her, she's not welcome," she said to Scott. She watched on as if she were assessing him and his loyalty. Of course he had none. He just looked at her in a stupid way. Trish stopped throwing flames. Although she requested for Scott it appeared she was more furious when confronted by him.

A loud cry from inside broke my attention and I pushed back through the crowd to the howling of a woman. Helena, my mother and a few others followed. It was Jennifer who was crying seated beside the older woman who was caring for her. A lot of the Shielders in the room watched on with little interest. Jennifer clutched at her pelvis screaming. Her face looked gaunt and exhausted.

The woman beside her held her hand and looked up at my mother and Helena with need of some kind of reassurance. "I think she has started contractions," she said. "But she hasn't eaten or drunk in days. She won't have the strength to deliver this child safely."

My mother shifted her jacket off and walked over with Helena hurriedly. I followed them slowly and dazed. Both of them knew how to help Jennifer. I stood afar unsure of how I could help. Jennifer screamed out in jolts of pain. But still it appeared she wasn't really there. It seemed only a reflex of what her body was going through. There was a moment where life sparked in her life. She looked at me directly with so much pain it broke my heart.

"Protect him," she said with a knowing gleam in her eye. I spun around and saw that Christopher was watching from the doorway with arms crossed. She made eye contact with me and turned her back to me walking back up the stairs. I looked back at Jennifer who continued to cry out in pain, but she had vanished. She again hid behind the numb doll like mask she had been behind since the death of Kingsly. Unsure of what to do I dropped to my knees beside her and grabbed her other hand. She had to survive and face her child in the world to come.

*

I wasn't exactly sure what was happening, but I knew that my hand hurt from her strong grasp. A lot of the others had shifted upstairs to give her more privacy. My mother had thrown a sheet over her legs so she didn't seem as exposed when she had to take off her pants.

The others had still not yet returned and we were docked waiting for their arrival. The longer the process went the gaunter Jennifer seemed to be. I slapped her on the face slightly when her grip loosened and scared me. Now with my bracelet off I could feel her strength fading in and out. The child was draining her.

Christopher now and then checked up on Jennifer's progress around the corner of the doorway. I was wary of her and her positioning. I was glad to feel my strength slowly grow back after being supressed for so long.

My mother and Helena had long ago began to instruct her to push. But Jennifer simply hadn't the strength. For all the mighty woman she once was and how much she had cared for this child and wanted it to enter the world safely, she was too weakened to do so.

I grabbed the back of her neck and forced her head to look at me. I rattled her slightly with desperation until I could see that she was actually looking at me and not in that doll like frame of hers. "Come on. This is your baby. You have to bring it into the world safely."

Her eyes began to tear up and then suddenly she was forced over by a wave of determination. She screamed out loudly as she contracted a large push. My mother and Helena encouraged her to get her breath before pushing again. Jennifer flopped back into my arms exhausted. As I held her hand I could feel that her pulse was slowing. This child was draining her of everything.

I desperately tried to find a way to put my energy into her. I imagined reversing what I would do draining, but nothing worked. I couldn't do anything. I desperately tried. I looked up, startled to find that the others had returned.

Elijah burst through the doors, dropping the four birds he had bound over his back. He took my place grabbing her hand and pushing back her hair.

"You have to stay with me," he said desperately. "Come on you can do this." Another loud scream came from her as she pushed hard again. I looked away at the amount of blood beneath the sheet I saw.

I curled into Paul's arms for a moment of relief and continued to watch. "I can't help her," I said near to tears. I so desperately wanted to help her and Scott hadn't yet returned. I asked him if he could try to enter her body while she gave birth. If he could replenish her while she was being drained. But he said that was impossible even for him because then he would be susceptible to the child draining him. He also said that it was against Mother Nature. I thought there were greater things in the world that went against Mother Nature.

I could feel that she was fading. Jennifer was dying and there was nothing that I could do. I leant over to Ashley. "Prepare everything we need, we will be going soon." He gave me a confused look but nodded his head and began packing a few of the blankets. Paige followed his lead. Suzumiya and Chris looked at one another and followed suit. I didn't even need to mention it and they knew. Few of the Shielders remained in this room. It consisted of only my group, the supportive older woman and Elijah. Elijah desperately pleaded Jennifer to stay with him.

Jennifer gave out a high pitch cry. It dulled as did her pulse. I took a step forward but retreated and coward into Paul's neck. He held me tightly. Elijah began to tap on her and then jolt her body.

My mother screamed wildly as she went to hold the baby. I ran over to them straight away forgetting that I should've been there sooner. On reflexes my mother had almost dropped the baby which was coming out. I pushed my mother aside and projected my Shield so I didn't touch its skin. I gently nestled the rest of it out. A baby's scream began to encircle the room.

"I need-" I had begun to shout over my shoulder but Paul was already on his knees beside me offering me his jacket. I wrapped the child up feverishly.

"You can't touch this child's skin," I lectured my mother. My mother seemed confused but understanding instantly struck Helena. At first she drifted away from it but then refocused and her maternal instinct kicked in.

"Pass him here Karla," Helena said. I could hear the footsteps coming from behind me and made sure to act quickly. I slid out Aeisha and quickly cut the umbilical cord. I hoped there was no special way to do it because it only gave me enough time to slice the cord and lunge behind me at Christopher who brought her sword over us.

I scraped the sword away with enough force to make her take a step back.

"This is my right! That creature killed my daughter!" Christopher screamed.

"Leave!" I yelled at the others behind me. "I will catch up." I lunged at Christopher. My strength had returned. I felt the slither of Misfeata within but nothing that I thought threatened her to try and possess my body right now.

"That creature killed my child!" She spat disgusted. She looked over my shoulder in rage as the others fled the boat with the baby. I held her off and slammed her into the wall.

"It's a baby!" I spat back disgusted in her. "No matter what it was born, it had no choice! It is innocent!" Other Shielders had burst into the room now unsure of what was happening. Christopher flung me off but I allowed her. I was only wasting time with her. I didn't want to kill her. I glanced down quickly at the very pale Jennifer. Elijah held her in his arms crying. She looked ghostly white and gaunt. Yet, when I looked at her face there seemed to be a glimmer of peace. I hoped that in the afterlife she would find the life that she had always wanted with Kingsly.

A white pigeon flew into the room and then disappeared. Suddenly Jennifer dropped to the ground asleep. Scott left her body and reappeared in front of me.

"Time to go!" He said and grabbed my hand to pull me out. The other Shielders had begun to lunge at us after their leader was struck down in front of them. A lot of them stayed back unsure as to whether they should challenge me or not. I ran outside onto the deck and built up a slight run up and jumped over the edge lunging myself over the water.

I hit the ground and ran immediately into the bushes and towards where I felt the others presence. Much to my surprise Martin was waiting patiently beside a tree with his hands poised together.

"You both took long enough," he said. "I've already pointed the others into the direction of the car." He pointed into a direction for us to follow.

I wanted to ask him why he was helping and following us but decided there was a time and a place. After all we now had a lot of Shielders chasing us. I ran faster, pelting towards where I could hear in the near distance the baby screaming. I had to keep to my promise and make sure that I protected Jennifer's baby with my life. I couldn't save her, but I could save her baby boy.

Chapter Twenty-Four- Hiding

$\mathcal{W}$e didn't have much time to think about or next plan. Ashley, Paul, Helena, my mother, and I piled into our car while the others squished into the other. Much to my despair Trish was one of those members. I didn't have time argue because we had to leave and distance ourselves before Christopher tried to follow us. And she would follow. To her, I was the solution she was looking for. Now she had a greater reason to hunt us down.

I couldn't understand how heavy her hatred for this baby was, would she seek it out purely for revenge? How could anyone possibly plan that for a newborn baby, especially their grandson? The baby hadn't stopped crying since we escaped. He was still wrapped in Paul's jacket and we added a few more cloth's to keep him warm. My mother who rocked him back and forth tried her hardest to settle him down, but to no success.

"We need to buy some formula and proper blankets," my mother said. Ashley looked in his rear view mirror keeping an eye on the roads behind us to make sure that no one followed. Paul kept a lookout on the sides, but for a moment looked over his shoulder at us. He reached out his hand to me and I took it in comfort. He gave me a small reassuring smile and let go. He continued his watch.

I wished he had held on for a moment longer. I was becoming accustomed to his affection and comfort, and he filled me with such relief and support that I only wanted more. I looked down at the wailing child which was covered completely so no one could make skin to skin contact with it. Although Helena was disgusted at first when she discovered it was a Starkorf she sat beside my mother trying to comfort the baby and coo it to sleep.

The baby continued to wail. I wondered if it cried because somehow, even being a newborn, he had sensed that his parents were dead. I wondered if he was scared and felt alone. I knew it was a silly thought to have for a newborn, but what if they instinctually knew. What is the future for this child? Who would raise and look after him and teach him the things that it needed to be taught? This wasn't a normal baby.

I remembered what Kingsly and Jennifer begged me to do. To make sure that this child was safe. I projected my shield around my index finger and placed it in his little palm. The size difference was startling. My mother had tried to clean him up as best she could but this baby needed a proper bath, food and a place to properly sleep. It saddened me to know that besides the small touch my mother had placed on his skin when born, that this was the closest thing to a singular touch he had. This was the closest anyone could get to him.

I had hoped that I would have some magical touch, but he continued to wail. He didn't press down on my finger or anything of the sort. He continued to wail with his red scrunched up face, his cry deafening.

"Martin knows where he is going," I said hoping it would be some reassurance to the two mothers who had decided to take this baby under their wing. I was grateful for that because although I intended to flee with the child, I had no understanding of how to look after one and I never thought about the aftermath of that either. I just couldn't stand witness to watch a baby murdered.

I couldn't pull away, I kept my finger there for the next two hours that we drove. The baby wailed the entire time. Eventually the others pulled over. My mother and Helena stayed in the car with the baby. It was colder outside in the night. I walked around the car and met them in the middle of the road. It had for too long been only a dirt road but we now had gravel and a few street lights could be seen in the distance.

Suzumiya and Chris were exchanging a hateful glance at Trish. She pointed her nose in the air and looked down on them. Chris held back Suzumiya as she took flight for action. My uncle went and checked on my mother to make sure she and the baby were okay. Martin and Scott walked up to us scrunching their face with an annoyed expression as the sound of the baby's wailing rang through when my Uncle opened the car door.

"I can't proceed any further," Martin said. "I need to avoid being in public places and my identity being seen. I have organized protection in a city another hour from here. I have channels but Scott has booked them. They are Elemental Breathers who act as security. They are of the most elite."

"We will protect them," I said with haste.

"That's a stupid plan," Paige spat. She leant against the side of the car with her hands across her chest.

"I agree with Paige for once," Ashley said. She gave him a demonic look at the comment 'for once'. "Karla you have both Christopher and Eden after you. We need to pull away from the baby and our mothers to protect them."

"Even if it is in a city I doubt it will stop them from pursuing," Suzumiya said.

"But we can't trust some hired security guards that we don't know to watch over them," I said horridly.

"They will in a sense be living a normal human life," Martin said. "The positioning I've created means they will be staying in a small apartment. The guards are situated both beside and frontal. If that concerns you then you could have some of your own go with them, although I would suggest against that. This is only a minor event in the grand scheme of things. If you stay close to them I predict a seventy-eight percent chance that they will be pursued within the next two weeks. If you stay away from than that drops to twenty-one percent."

"Keep in mind that you should be keeping as many troops as you can," Scott said as he realigned the edge of his jacket.

"I would rather the protection go to my mother then me," I said. Scott looked up at me with a charming smile.

"Dear child, you have four different enemies after you. You need all the brute force you can get. You have Eden who will stop at nothing and who has half an army behind him; Christopher who requires you for her own ambitions to kill off Lucas and to absorb your power; Kurt who although doesn't have many behind him is somehow still keeping track of your progress and Lucas who-"

"Lucas isn't an enemy," I cut him off. Paul gave me a saddened expression. Ashley only became furious.

"He is. He is the biggest. Did you forget that he is literally the Elder who wants to kill you," Ashley flushed.

"That's Tyran who wants to kill me, not Lucas. He helped us back there with Eden," I said pointing in that direction.

"No matter who you think is friend or foe I have given you the facts and my offer," Martin said. "I don't so kindly treat others or extend my resources, so either take it or you have nothing to fall back on. Either way, I don't like keeping to the roads," Martin said looking around sceptically. He didn't like being in the open not because he thought that the others who hunted me were close; but because he was paranoid of those who searched for him. I wondered what sort of group it was that pursued him and who he really was.

"Karla," Ashley said. "I don't like leaving them as much as you do. But I think right now it's our only choice." It surprised me that Ashley supported this considering he was leaving the security of his mother into unknown hands. Helena wasn't weak by any means, but she also wasn't the strongest of Shielders and like him she didn't have the ability to shield.

I looked to Chris and Suzumiya. Suzumiya shook her head at me. "Karla, we have been locked up for months, we need to fight."

Chris flopped his arm around Suzumiya lazily. "Come on Suzu, it will only be temporary. After they sort out their own troubles we will go out in force. We owe this to Seth."

She gave him an angry look before dumping her shoulders. "Fine," she said. "We will go with them. But I am not changing that baby's nappy."

"What are you doing with the baby?" Trish asked disgustedly. I gave her a harsh glare, one that she smugly regarded. I wouldn't have answered, but everyone else looked at me questionably.

"I promised Jennifer I would keep him safe, and that I will. He is a baby. He had no choice as to how he was born. Surely none of you could agree that killing him was the right thing to do," I said firmly. No one disagreed.

"You did the right thing," Paul said. I looked into his beautiful green eyes and grabbed his hand.

"I want you and my Uncle to go with them too," I said.

"No," he said firmly.

"I can't protect you from the things that are about to happen if you come. I want to keep you safe and away from all of this."

"We've gone this far together, we will do the rest together. I am not letting that Elder take possess you again. I can't lose you again," he said. Paige scoffed at us and wavered away what she thought to be theatrics.

"Decide what you will do and who goes where," Martin said. He threw a small bag at me. I opened it revealing gold inside. "Give that to whoever is going. That is payment for the apartment and security. It's all been organized. That small note in the bottom of the bag has the address of where to meet them. Go to that address and drop them off, they will take them through a secret passage in case anyone has followed you. They won't see them disappear into the city and then you can come back and meet us, we will give you twelve hours."

Martin turned and grabbed two backpacks from the car. One was filled with the journals of Elisabeth and the other I wasn't too sure of. Scott wavered me a coy look and followed him as did Trish. The rest of us walked over to the car. My Uncle had his head dipped into the car as he spoke to my mother and Helena. Ashley threw him the keys and he caught them. He looked at them curious.

"You are going to a city, you will be staying in an apartment and you will have Elemental Breathers act as your security there just in case someone searches for you. We will take you to the address we've been given and someone will take you secretly to a new location. We will have to split up then so there is no further association between us in case someone has been tailing us. I would rather you go with them. Suzumiya and Chris will also be going."

"But what about Sebastian's grave?" My Uncle asked.

"Right now I am prioritizing the safety of the baby, Helena and Mom. We will figure out our next plan and where to go from there, but we need to look after them first. I need to trust their safety with you. The rest of us will return here and think of a plan. We need to remove the danger before we can take them out of hiding."

Uncle Kyle, much like Suzumiya and Chris looked hesitant.

"Karla, I don't want you out there in the open," my mother said worriedly. Helena placed a hand on her arm with a comforting smile.

"I don't like sending out my boy either, but you must have faith in them," Helena said. My mother went to argue but said nothing. It was evident a bond had formed between the two of which filled me with fondness. They were exactly what one another needed to help in the healing process of losing their husbands. An image of my father came to mind and I looked away from my mother ashamed. I tried so much not to think of that horrible act I had done and the death of my father. Still, I couldn't handle the loss or even heal. I shoved it down and away from my mind.

"Take the other two with you," Uncle Kyle said. Suzumiya perked up with anticipation. "I can look after them. We are only babysitting after all. I want you to have as many people surrounding you as possible and please don't give up on Sebastian's grave. It has to be real," my Uncle pleaded.

Scott still watched us from the trees waiting to see our departure. It was odd to see him so quickly flock to Martin and Trish.

Despite everything we had been through he had still always been by our side. Trish stood not far away from him and gave us all an impatient glare. Martin had already disappeared. I flushed with anger that Trish had now joined us, for what reason I didn't know. She hated her brother.

A flash of the memory between Elisabeth and Max Jacket came to mind. He had once cared deeply about Elisabeth and was joyful to learn of his wife's pregnancy, I was curious to know if it was her death that made him into the twisted dark man he became. Looking at Trish, I wondered if like any child, she was lost not having anyone or anything familiar. Elemental Breathers were stubborn and independent, but I wondered if maybe she simply missed having some form of family by her side. I didn't trust her as she stated she wanted to kill Lucas. But I had the confidence that between Lucas and her, Lucas would win. Right now I just had to focus on the protection of my mother and then leaving as much distance between us. I had to protect her and the baby, and distance was the best solution I had- no matter how much I wanted to protect them myself. I would go to the city with them and make sure they arrived there safely. I didn't trust the hours' drive between here and the city, anything could happen within that time frame.

"We will trail you in the other car," Ashley said. "From now on we can't speak with one another or show association, we will only follow you to make sure you get there safely. So say your Goodbyes now."

"Look after them," I said to my Uncle as I gave him a hug. I reached my hand into the car to my mother and squeezed her hand tightly. "I love you Mom, please look after him."

I could tell she didn't want me to leave. Worry flashed through her eyes but instead she gave me a reassuring smile. "I will look after him. Please only worry about and look after yourself. Paul, look after her."

Paul nodded his head in respect.

"Ashley be safe," Helena said. Ashley pressed a kiss to his mother's cheek.

"I will," he said. Paige began to mock Ashley as we walked away from the car.

"Momma's boy," she teased.

"Shut up," he said barging in to her slightly. She took the bump with ease, not trying to dodge it but not taking much impact from it either.

We quickly gathered into the car, squeezing in tightly and followed the car which my Uncle drove. I just had to make sure they arrived there safely before we dealt with whatever war was waiting for us.

Chapter Twenty-Five- Confessions

$\mathcal{W}$e followed them closely from behind until we started to see lights in the near distance. We backed off slightly. Street lights started to streak by our sides with perfectly cemented roads. We had gone into a city once since the awakening of Misfeata. Each time I now entered one it was like an entirely different world. We had once gone with Scott when we needed to shop for Elemental Breather clothing. Back then I stared at the bright lights mesmerized. Like then there were people who were everywhere as if the world we fought in and saw never existed.

This time I only focused on one thing and that was watching very closely the surroundings of the vehicle my Uncle drove. I looked at every passer-by sceptically. My hand was tapping lightly on my leg as we waited at a set of lights behind them. I was ready for an attack at any time. Paul intertwined his fingers with mine. I looked at him startled by the touch.

"It's okay," he said. My tapping softened and he squeezed tighter for it to come to a complete stop. Chris was watching us from the corner of his eyes. He gave me a cheesy grin and popped a large bubble of gum which exploded on his face. Everyone flinched because of the noise.

"Relax guys," he said. Obviously everyone was on edge. We indicated right following my Uncle. He took another couple of turns before stopping in front of a small corner shop. I looked at it with suspicion.

"This isn't the address," Ashley said. My heart jumped out of my chest as I went to jump out of the car.

"They would have to get formula and something for the baby to wear before going into a public place," Paige said obviously. "Idiots." She added. Helena got out of the car and walked across the street to the convenience store.

"Follow her," I said to Suzumiya and Chris. They slipped out of the car expectantly.

"I love role play, let's act like a lovey dovey couple," Chris said boldly. I still didn't know if they had made progress on their "friendship" or not.

Suzumiya streaked a slight red. "Don't touch me," she snapped. They followed Helena in casually.

"I am going to stay by the car to make sure no one suspicious comes close," Paige said. She jumped out of the car in her heavy boots and wandered over and leant on the post beside their car. My Uncle didn't look twice at her. A passer-by walked past and she gave them a terrifying expression. I focused my hearing in her direction so I could listen in to anything that might be said. My body had fully replenished now and with it I felt the stir of Misfeata awakening. I made sure that we still had the bracelet which would keep her at bay. I felt that soon I would need to put it on again, not wanting to take the risk of her possessing me again for days if not more.

A man walked past Paige and she slipped her hands in her pockets casually. He looked at her sceptically. She posed oddly with one leg up against the pole.

"What is she doing," Ashley began to shake his head. The man stopped and looked at Paige.

"Got a smoke," she said in a rough ground voice. The man smiled at her, he looked to be ten years older than her. He stopped and pulled out a packet offering her one. Ashley's knuckles were turning white over the steering wheel.

"She is meant to be a ghost not bringing attention to herself," he growled. Helena was walking towards the car across the road. Behind her Chris and Suzumiya walked, looking left and right to avoid cars. Chris had his arm lazily around her shoulder which she flushed red over.

I focused again on Paige and the foreign man. I sensed that he was human. She pulled out the smoke and snapped it in half. Her once reasonable youthful expression turning hard.

"Quit. It's disgusting," she snapped.

"Did you just snap my smoke," the man growled. Paige pushed herself off the pole with a smile satisfied by her work. She began to walk away and the man grabbed her shoulder demanding an answer. With heightened speed Paige swung around and kneed the man in the stomach winding him. He dropped to his knees and then the side when he hit the ground.

Paige smugly dusted her hands as she practically skipped to the car. Paul and I exchanged a glance. He lightly laughed at my opened jaw. Paige would pick a fight with anyone for any reason.

She opened the door and slid into the passenger seat.

"Are you out of your mind?" Ashley said. "Which part of keeping a low profile don't you understand?" It occurred to me then that Ashley and Paige had a weird relationship. They had from the start. I didn't think it was romantic, but in a way since becoming a part of our group Ashley closely monitored and constantly lectured Paige. I think in a way it was the closest thing she had to a friend.

"Don't be such a granny. I am so over these long days of no fighting. So I had a little fun," she threw her boots up against the front glass. "You are totally sucking at your job right now." She pointed to my Uncle's car which was now driving off. Ashley pursued still giving her an angry expression. She was smiling as if his disapproving reaction was exactly why she had done it.

"She grabbed some formula, nappies and clothing," Suzumiya reported.

"Hubba Bubba?" Chris offered us some gum with excitement. "Suzu was so kind to let me buy two packets this time." It always surprised me how goofy Chris acted and that he was a fighter. But I had seen him fight and knew the skill was there. Still his attitude outside of that was. . . unusual.

More lights flashed around us as night became more apparent. Drunks were now evident as a few stumbled and laughed on the side streets. We were now within what looked to be the center of the city. My Uncle had found a parking space for the car and we stopped and parked a few up from him. They stopped in front of a pop culture looking Japanese shop.

Most of the customers in there were teenagers hanging out with their friends. "Is it about time we started acting our age?" I asked Paul, Paige and Ashley.

"She is not getting out, not after how she acted before," Ashley said angrily.

"Stop being such a cry baby," she teased, satisfied that he was still annoyed.

Paul slipped out of the car and I followed him. "We will be back, if anything happens one of us will flag you down. If you see anything suspicious walk past the store twice, I will keep a visual on the windows," I said. Suzumiya and Chris nodded.

I closed the door behind me and walked onto the side walk. We looked like a group of rebellious teens. I tried to comb through my hair slightly with my fingers, when was the last time I had the chance to brush it?

My mother, Uncle and Helena walked into the shop. I could still hear the baby wailing. People walked around us casually. My eyes flickered back and forth. I wasn't used to so many people around me at once. Paul interlaced his fingers with mine. I looked up at him again startled. I was so caught up in my speculative eye that I didn't notice it was me who stood out.

"It's okay. They are all human. No one is going to hurt them," he said reassuringly. Misfeata stirred within me. I didn't know if it were her or a swirl of anxiety. How long had I been out of civilization for? I was so used to being on edge and ready for an attack that I now realized even if I ever had the chance to escape this world, how would I go with placing myself back into the human world?

Ashley and Paige walked behind us casually, both relaxed. Ashley refused to look at Paige, still angry at her previous actions. She held her hands behind her neck stretching, she was most pleased with herself. Paul opened the door for me. Chatter flooded my ears as we walked in. I was hesitant to walk in as I watched all the customers. I thought that they all stopped and stared at me, as if knowing there was something different about me.

Paul tightened his grip on my hand. My eyes scanned over the people, searching for the enemy. I felt as if the room were getting smaller. The loud noise of people chattering annoyed me. So many people. So many people living a leisurely life unsuspecting of the dangers outside these walls. One person looked at me and I began to reach for my weapon. They knew who I was, they were here to attack my people.

Suddenly, Paul's warm lips were on mine, snapping me out of my paranoid haze. I closed my eyes melting into him for that moment. All thought vanished from me. His gentle lips left mine and I looked into his steady green eyes.

"Karla," he said adoringly. "Come back to me. This is okay. No one here is going to hurt them." I looked back at the person who was once staring at me. They were now laughing at a joke the person across from them had made. I no longer focused on all the noise and faces but the pop cultured restaurant which had red booths along the sides and dining tables on the right. The wailing baby broke my intake of the room as I looked towards where my mother, Helena and Uncle had sat.

Ashley and Paige waited for us patiently, sliding into a booth on the side. Ashley was looking at me worriedly. I felt sick in the stomach. I had become so paranoid that I couldn't immerse myself into the human world so easily like the rest of them. I was so fearful of everyone being the enemy that I had begun to be paranoid.

"I-" I began to explain to Paul but he pressed another sweet kiss to my lips taking my words away.

"You don't have to explain yourself," he said adoringly. Paul knew, he just understood me even when I didn't know myself. How had he not been effected like I had? How could he and the others so easily adapt with normal humans, while I struggled and began to fear them. "We will work on it." He smiled and pressed a kiss to my temple. He walked me over to the booth where we sat and pretended to look over the menu.

It was nostalgic looking over a menu. I never ate out much but doing such a normal thing reminded me of how far from the normal world we were.

"Buy me that one," Paige said expectantly to Ashley as she pointed to a meal.

"No," Ashley responded firmly. He continued to look over the edge of the menu through the window.

"Hi, how are you all this evening," a waitress greeted with pen to notepad. She was very pretty and looked at both Ashley and Paul approvingly.

"Could you give us a little longer to decide please," Paul asked with a smile. The blonde waitress seemed to melt under his gentleman like response and smiled beautifully. She walked away to her fellow colleagues. One of the girls looked over her shoulder to look at Paul. I had forgotten how popular he once was at our school in our home town. I looked over my shoulder at him, he gave me a small smile and continued to watch my mother.

"Someone has approached them," he said casually as he leant his arm over my shoulder. I grabbed his hand and looked past our intertwined fingers and to my mother's table. There were two slender males who greeted them. Both wore suits with the swirls of Elemental Breathers. A lot of the nearby girls admired them from afar. I supposed in the human world many of them thought they were unbelievable good looking men. My Uncle briefly revealed the bag which held the gold in it.

One of them nodded and pointed for them to go through the kitchen. The baby was still wailing as they followed them. They all slipped through the kitchen doors as a waitress came out with three plates. Once the doors were closed, I could no longer see them. They were gone. Had vanished.

I waited for another minute in silence before deciding to leave. We had accomplished our task here. They had been escorted safely and it was now time for us to return to the real fight which was about to break. It was like a heaviness had suddenly dawned on us once our parentals had left. We now had a war to face.

We left and walked on the main street again. Everyone playfully laughed and fluttered about. The beautiful lights that ornamentally were positioned in trees took my interest. I so badly wanted to be human again and live in a perfect human world. But I now realized that it had been a long time since I was a part of it and maybe I was too broken to be around so many people. Was it better for me to stay in this world that I had adjusted to?

We piled in the car and took our leave through the streets until we headed out to meet in the woodlands where the others waited for us.

"Going back isn't all you thought it would be. It's difficult to return to what was long ago buried for you," Misfeata mused.

At the tone of her voice I clamped down on Paul's hand. She was back, her voice was clear. I needed my bracelet. I didn't want to hear her tease me or reveal what it was I was avoiding to say out loud.

Knowingly, Paul wrapped his arm around me and pulled me into his chest. I buried my face into him. I had been doing this now far too often. I was too dependent on the comfort Paul gave me. How ironic that I was viewed as one of the most powerful Shielders to currently exist and yet the source of my power and strength was in the embrace of Paul. It was the thing which reassured me and pressured me to keep fighting on.

Misfeata growled at the contact. She tried to wrap her tentacles around my consciousness to pull me back, but I fought her. I fought against her so I could hold on to this gentle embrace. After moments of struggling against one another I pressed my lips to Paul. My mind went blank and only focused on the warmth that he provided me with. The escapism that he too often provided. My tongue mixed with his, desperate to hold me to this earth.

Slowly Misfeata's strength depleted and the struggle was no more. Finally her voice had stopped and she had vanished.

"Thank you," I whispered in a shaky breath to Paul as I leant my forehead to his.

"For what?" He asked. I looked into his gorgeous green eyes which I adored so much. I trailed my fingers over his muscled arms which bound me so tightly to his. He was so strong.

"For keeping me sane and not giving up on me," I said honestly. He might not know the extent of my fight, but somehow he knew when I needed comfort. No matter how much I fought against it at the start, Paul was exactly what I needed.

"Karla I would do anything for you," he said. He rubbed his thumb over my cheek bone as he looked at me adoringly. "Because I love you."

A stray tear glided down my cheek. I hadn't even noticed that it was there. I felt undeserving of those words and its meaning. But I couldn't deny the overflow of happiness and relief it offered me. I placed my hand over his and a few more tears spilled over my eyes.

"I love you too," I said. My voice was now shaky. "So much." I tried to contain my tears that overflowed but I couldn't escape how much I depended on Paul. I loved him so much. He stayed by my side even in my ugliest of times. He had seen me at my worst and I felt he sometimes knew my demons even more than me.

Paul pressed another light kiss to my lips with a smile.

"That makes me very happy to hear," he said with a smile that made me feel foolish that I was crying. I laughed lightly as I began to wipe away the few stray tears.

"Ewww, get a room," Paige said. I looked over my shoulder and realized that her, Suzumiya and Chris were looking at us. Ashley was peering in his rear-view mirror. I laughed to myself and buried my head into Paul's chest embarrassed.

I really did love Paul.

Chapter Twenty-Six- Hindrance

$\mathcal{W}$e walked into the woods for about an hour until we found Martin, Scott, and Trish's make-shift camp. Everyone gave Trish an expected look when referring to the unlit firewood. Much to my surprise she submitted. She clicked her fingers and started a fire instantly. Most of us curled around the fire with very little protection from the cold night. We had a few blankets which aided in breaking the icy wind. Suzumiya and Chris shared one. Although their teeth didn't chatter and they didn't complain they seemed to be taking a blue tinge. We were lucky that because of our Shielder blood we all had a higher tolerance than humans. I found comfort around the fire.

Paul sat beside me reading over the journals with me. Ashley and Paige were first on watch as they scouted in two different areas. A blanket was thrown over Paul and I keeping us closely together. Trish looked over her nails and filed them in a manner that was far too similar to Scott. Martin was quiet and stared into the flames without looking away. Scott often teased him looking between the fire and Martin and questioning him as to what the flames ever did to him. He only received a scowl.

I flicked into another page of the journal I was currently reading. We had thrown in random books and because of that it seemed I was only getting random flashes of her life and world. This time the journal revolved around her after she left her library which back then was a home to her. This was two years after. In that time I gathered that Misfeata had possessed her for four months. She retreated back to her home, but only for a while before deciding to leave.

I have been travelling now in search of Praytar for one month now. Usually he leaves himself more open, leading me to him. He wants the fight just as much as I do. I want to kill him. I hope when I do it will all be over, but I know I must then fight his two sons who will then inherit Tyran. I know if I source Praytar's location I should find his sons too. I think I will kill Nathanial and Lucas first. That way Tyran has nowhere to go. I have a score to settle with Nathanial. And the youngest, Lucas, is very young. He should be easy to kill off. I hesitated once, I won't hesitate again. Still even with my search, I've been confronted with his first in command Eden and his daughter Raven. Eden handles a lot of Praytar's army. Only for one purpose, to find me. I've confronted them so many times in the past that I've decided it is best to avoid them. If I don't rely on Misfeata's strength they are surprisingly strong. I also couldn't be bothered to confront their army. I just want to go straight for the kill with Praytar and his sons. I will have to go back to my library soon. My bag weighs down heavily from journals alone. I don't even know if these journals make sense. Who else would read them? I just need somewhere to vent, to scream, to cry. It has been years since the death of my loved ones, but I still miss them. Not that I would expose that weakness to anyone. And besides what does it matter, they are already dead. I failed to protect them. I wonder if or when I die, and I hope that I will escape this prison soon. . . . Will I have the chance to be greeted by them in the afterlife or will I go to a darker place? Will even my soul be interlaced with Misfeata forever, when does this nightmare end?

I looked up from my book and over at Paul who tiredly still read. Elisabeth had lost her loved ones already. I wonder what gave her the strength to continue to fight. I only found the pursuit to do so because I had them to protect.

"Found anything yet?" Paul asked. His voice was exhausted and he began to sound a bit hazily from the cold. I shook my head.

"Why don't you rest for a bit," I said taking the book from him. "I will be awake for a little longer so I would rather one of us sleep." Martin watched us closely. It made me feel uncomfortable. Paul went to argue, but let me take the book from his hand. We were sitting on the hard ground in front of the warm fire. He rested his head on my shoulder and wrapped the blanket around him tighter.

"Wake me when it is my turn to be on watch," he said. He rested his head on my shoulder and I absentmindedly brushed my fingers through his hair as I scanned through other pages. Much of them were the same. I felt intrusive reading her greatest thoughts but could relate. I placed that journal down and collected the next one.

I don't even know what year I am in. I think it is winter here. I don't know, the weather doesn't even affect me. I've set myself aflame so many times that although it burns and hurts, I recover within minutes. The same with the cold, no matter how cold the temperature my body always heals. It makes me question if the third Elder, Sebastian could really be dead. If he was in his original form and burnt alive, yet I am only a host and can't die from the flames then how could he? Misfeata challenges any thought I have of her brother, but I feel like I am onto something. I think Misfeata is in denial the most about her brother's disappearance. I have the feeling she is ashamed of the things she has done. I woke up three days ago finding myself in a camp amongst others. This was the first entry I have been able to write since then. I don't know how long she had taken over my body. I feel like I slept for a while but it might've only been a few days. These Shielder's look up to me, like I am their saint or something. I despise how much Misfeata is revered amongst my kind. If only they knew what she was really like and about. I am possessive of Aeisha, but I wonder how Misfeata would cope without them. I have thought about hiding them once, but know it is pointless. I can't handle the idea of losing my blades either. It's odd I don't know who Misfeata's identity is anymore or my own. I fear still we are simply becoming one. It has now almost been forty years since Misfeata possessed me and the wall has been broken. I don't look a day older than the moment I became her host. I fear who she has drained and killed to survive. I wonder if others knew that secret if she would still be seen in such a way. There is a young man here, of what I've seen he is one of the strongest. He has an infatuation for me it would appear. Considering I have never met him and only Misfeata I wonder if it is Misfeata he is infatuated with. Misfeata doesn't have emotions or think of things as love. But I can feel her stirring and watching him intently. A sick feeling comes to mind.

Paul slightly snored as I was still stroking my hand through his hair. He had since changed positions, lying down curled in a ball against the wind. He had his head rested on my lap. I flicked through and continued to read Elisabeth's entries.

He watches me more now, not me. I again was pushed back into myself. Misfeata is mimicking me, acting as I would. No one can tell the difference. No one even knows who I am. I've tried to escape twice now, but she takes control. It's getting harder to fight against her. Last time I was fully made dormant, I watched as she approached the young man and was what appeared to be flirting. I hate her. I now know what she is doing. She is trying to create another heir. She holds no personal attachment to him. He is young, but leader to his group. He is strong. That is all she cares for. I hate the way he touches my skin and she responds to him. I slam into her every time but I can't break through to claim my body once again. It's cold where I am now. I have vowed to only love one and share my body with one- and I buried him long ago. Misfeata is using me and trying to create a new heir. . . I don't want to have a child. I don't want to put this curse onto anyone else. But she has a will of her own. I don't know how much time I have. This world is twisted. I have run far away from that place of Shielders, I can't be their leader. I can't allow Misfeata to have contact with any others. I need to find a place to rid of her. I need to look for Sebastian's grave. I thought it was a hallucination and I haven't heard from Max for years. But I need to find a way, I need to find a place where it can be true. I need to rid myself of Misfeata so I can let my old age catch up to me quickly and die. I have once met one other Elemental Breather who spoke of Sebastian's grave. He was fully covered and I couldn't identify his face. He wore a black mask and black clothing. I don't know who he is, but I would recognise the voice. I need to find him again and find what else he knows of this Sebastian's grave. He told me once that if I wanted to know to find him again. Back then it was Misfeata in control. She had fought him viciously, but despite her strength he countered her and could break through her Shield. I need to find this man and make him my ally.

I looked up from the journal across at Martin who was still watching me intensely. Martin was able to break through the shields. Elisabeth had made contact with someone just like that. I thought of the time difference however. There was one hundred years between Elisabeth's time and my own, then another seventeen until my curse was triggered. Elemental Breathers lived longer but weren't immortal. Martin would be far too young to be that very same person. I flicked to the next page which had been torn out at the center. The next few after that had been as well. It continued on with Elisabeth's return of her library to put away some of her books.

I looked at Martin again almost in accusation.

"Some of the pages have been ripped out like the others we found in the library," Martin said. "It appears someone else holds this information and doesn't want us to read it."

"How many people know of Elisabeth's library?" I asked him accusingly. I had the impression that Martin knew more then he lead on. That his identity was someone important, or at least the 'Master' he spoke about was.

"Not many, but some could've stumbled upon it. My question to you would be if you think the Prince has ventured upon it. He did after all create the collars which were exemplified in the journals. Either him or someone who he has made contact with has been to the library."

I considered this although I wanted to defend Lucas instantly. But the truth was, he had created those collars. And he had promised me he would find a way. He was also looking for Sebastian's grave. It sounded as if Sebastian's grave was spoken about a lot more now, then it was in Elisabeth's time. It was only a theory, but now it felt like everyone was searching for it. What, or who was that interlacing factor that was spreading that theory? Was it a real place?

My body froze disjointedly and I cried in pain. Paul shot up instantly and looked over me. Martin assessed me interested. Sharp stabbing pains began from my stomach and crawled up to my chest. I pushed Paul away knowing what was to come. He tried to step closer but I warned him off.

Martin stood up and watched me closer. I screamed in pain as my entire body froze. My body was again dying. It was taking me longer to muster my strength, it now felt harder to project my Shield.

"Hurry you stupid girl," Misfeata supported me internally. I felt her aiding me in projecting my Shield. I thought she might've tried to take advantage of the situation but instead I felt her force behind me. Together we projected my Shield and it combusted. It shot adrenalin through my blood and I took a heavy breath and coughed into the dirt. Patches of blood sprayed under me from where I had been choking. Misfeata swirled within me, relieved and weakened like I had been.

"If you keep using that bracelet we won't be able to combust our Shield," she quickly assessed.

"Are you okay?" Paul lifted me from the ground. He helped me up and wiped away the blood which was on my lips. My eyesight was shaky as I focused on Martin.

"Absolutely fascinating," he said. He was holding up a vial of blood. He looked between it and me.

"What is that?" I asked disgusted. My stomach churned from what I thought he might say.

"This is a vial of your blood. I've been studying it. Just now, did you know that your blood within this small vial reacts exactly the same way to which it would within you. Misfeata's blood stirs as if a parasite and when you release that adrenalin it creates a sort of bubbling effect throughout your blood cell's to kill of the parasite effect."

"When did you get my blood?" I snapped, taking a step towards him.

"Well, when you were unconscious for two days of course. I have to study it if I am to create a long term solution for you against Misfeata," Martin said. We eyed one another. I wanted to attack him and knock the blood from his hand but I knew that if we were to fight, that I might not be able to win. I hadn't fought for a long time. I thought no matter what, with Misfeata's strength I could win in any battle. And right now, as I leaned heavily against Paul, I couldn't involve him.

"I told him to do it," Scott said waving around his hand. "Get upset with me if you must," he said dramatically. "But how crazy is this, you don't even have to like chill your blood or anything. It just never changes." He pointed at it like it was some cool toy.

"Did you know about this?" I asked Paul feeling betrayed. When had they taken my blood? I felt oddly violated. Paul gave me a saddened expression.

"I did. When you didn't wake up we were all worried. We wanted to find a solution," he said. My heart turned at his confession. I knew this wasn't a decision only he made but he was the only one here that I could accuse or had admitted the truth to me. I pushed him away slowly so I could stand on my own two feet. He gave me that space although I knew he was hurt.

"If anyone is to be your solution, it's me," Martin said factually. "As it so happens to be, blood is also a specialty of mine."

I stood up straight wanting to be on my own. I didn't trust Martin and felt so violated to know he was studying me in such a way, as if I were an interesting experiment to him.

"I don't even know you," I said. "I'm going on watch."

"Karla-" Paul reached out to me but I avoided his touch. I walked out to the trees where I found Ashley.

"Hey what's up with you?" He asked curiously.

"I don't want to talk about it. Let's swap watch," I said. He didn't ask any further questions.

"I'm not tired so I will stay on watch. I'll clear this area," he said pointing into the direction which was closer to Paige.

"I will scout further out," I said striding further out. I tapped my fingers lightly on the handle of Aeisha. My blood was pumping from the adrenalin that pumped through my veins. I was fired up and angry. I willed for someone to come and challenge me. Misfeata stirred within me again. I could no longer tell if the comfort and joy of fighting was Misfeata's sick pleasure or my own. I didn't know whose thoughts were whose. But I wanted to fight.

Chapter Twenty-Seven- The Real Enemy

$\mathcal{I}$continued to walk into the bushes, slashing Aeisha along certain trees. My anger only building. I felt like I was losing my mind and no longer able to contain my anger. I felt like I was splitting into two and breaking from the seams. I just wanted to scream and for everything to fade away. My breaking point had come. I no longer knew who I was or which world I belonged to. I no longer wanted to fight but I felt like I didn't deserve a normal life any longer. There was a part of me that did want to fight, when I was at this breaking point I only wanted to vent physically. I began running hoping that exertion would be the same outlet.

.   After minutes of running with tears down my face I slashed Aeisha's blades across a tree and then the other, effortlessly I hacked into the tree with tears streaming down my face. They were precise cuts but still sloppy. I just hacked and cut. I began punching into the trunk hastily. My knuckles bleeding as I tried to find a way to release the inner pain that I contained. I didn't want to live a life like this, where I had no choice or a place I felt like I could go to. I felt like this was no longer my life and I feared what could happen in the future.

I slashed at the tree again. "Why couldn't I be normal?!" I punched into it again. "Why did it have to be me?" I began to break into hysterics. "Why can't I trust anyone, why do they all betray me?!" I stabbed Aeisha into the tree and reefed it out with another tear. "What am I doing?" I began pounding into the tree with kicks and punches. "Why does it have to be me?" I sobbed. I began to cry. I weakly punched into the tree again and buckled at my knees. I clung to the tree as my tears that for so long built up now streamed down my face.

My breaths were short and quick and I had to steady myself so I could properly breathe. But the wailing and crying did not stop. I was having a meltdown. Everything that had happened until this point finally broke me. Lucas's betrayal; Scott's betrayal; Kurt's betrayal; the death of Seth and my father; the countless times that Paul's life was endangered because of me; Lucas's death; almost everyone around me had lost their lives for being involved with me. I was cursed and selfish for letting them stay close to me. What was I fighting for? Wouldn't it be easier if I just went away and never existed? Wouldn't it be easier if I let Tyran kill me?

"Excuse me," a gentle voice from behind me said. I whipped around to see a foreign old lady. She wore a long black dress which had the Elemental Breathers swirls on it. "I have a message for you." The woman held out her hands and lights beamed out of them. I raised Aeisha ready for the attack. Instead a projection of her hand manifested a figure in front of me. The image was crystal clear.

"Lucas?" I asked. Lucas stood in front of me. He looked down at me and crouched extending his hand.

"What happened?" He asked. The Elemental Breather behind him stayed very still. I reached out for his hand, but my hand fell through. He looked at his own hand disappointed that it fell through and we couldn't touch.

"Is this real?" I asked sceptically. I began tidying myself up and wiping away at my eyes. I was embarrassed that he now saw me like this.

"As real as it can be." He sat down on the floor in front of me at eye level. What happened, why are you crying?"

"How do I know it's really you?" I asked suspiciously. I had been tricked so many times I no longer knew what and who to believe.

Lucas gave a cocky smile and looked to the sky as he thought for a while. "Okay I have one. You couldn't control your Shield when learning with Kurt. So you and I once sat in a meadow near the institute. I told you to put pressure on my hands and squeeze when the pressure of your Shield became too much. It was the first time I had seen your fascinated and beautiful smile. It was the first time you had control of your Shield."

A tear slid down my face as I remembered it perfectly. It was only the two of us there.

"You remembered that?" I asked with a small voice.

"Of course I remembered that," he said with a grin. "It was a breathtaking sight I couldn't forget."

"You treated me horribly after that," I said with a small laugh.

"You were chucking a tantrum about not wanting to pick a weapon," he toyed back. I began to laugh a little amongst tears. The sound of my own laughter brought me relief. "Why are you crying?"

I crossed my legs as I sat and wiped at my face with the edge of my leather jacket. My lip began to quiver as I no longer had the strength to act tough. Misfeata was disgruntled by my ability to communicate with Lucas. She couldn't sense Tyran this way and so she didn't act uncontrollably.

"I don't know who I am anymore Lucas. It's just constant fighting. I don't even know what world I want to be a part of anymore. I don't know if I belong in the human world or this world anymore," I admitted out loud.

"You know you always have a place in this world. When we figure out how, you and I can debate which part of that world we are in together," he said reassuringly. My eyes fogged up with tears once again. My heart felt like it split. I was so relieved to hear that but was still so torn with Paul. I loved Paul. But I still fretted for my future. I felt like I was not only choosing between who I wanted to be with but also the different futures I could have. I was so tired of this war that I didn't even know if a future was what I wanted. I was so tired.

"I'm just so tired of the fighting Lucas, I don't know where I want to be anymore," I admitted with tears streaming down my face. My shoulders sagged and I let the tears flow. I didn't care if I looked pathetic in front of Lucas. I so badly wanted him to hold me but also had reservations because of the love I shared for Paul. Both of them looked after me in their own way. Both of them had supported me in different steps of my journey.

The thing I once ran away from most, and that was love from either of them, was what I now needed most.

"I am hoping to end it soon," he said. He again reached out his hand to touch my face but it vanished through my skin. It was only a projection of him, it wasn't really Lucas. It made me feel colder and lonelier. "I had to pay a pretty penny for this Elemental Breather. Her duplicate is with you now. I assume because I haven't been reported back to by Kingsly, that. . ."

"He is dead," I said stiffly. "So is Jennifer. We fled with their baby." I wiped away a tear and focused on my breathing again. I tried to push away the depressing memories so I wouldn't be overwhelmed once again. I had to pull myself together. No one else could do it for me. Misfeata slithered within me and I knew if I let my guard down and continue breakdown that she would try to take advantage.

"He was a good man," Lucas said with consideration. "That is why I had this Elemental Breather search for you. She can find anyone and project communication. I needed to speak with you. I had to see you."

"I miss you too," I said in a small sob. The truth was, that no matter what betrayal had happened between Lucas and me and no matter how much everyone hated him; I still remembered his tender touch and protection that he offered me. Even now when we were enemies, he still looked out for me. He gave me a saddened smile. His brown eyes were almost transparent.

"Karla, I've been searching through my father's journals. He used to keep handy notes of things he found vital or important to him. I found amongst them a few torn out notes. He linked them with some of his own findings. I think they might've been Elisabeth's. I've been putting the two together and of those passages I think it describes Sebastian's grave." He was flicking through a journal and a few notes which he had collected from his flooring. He looked up at me with a smile. "However with that gleam in your eye, I assume you've done some research of your own."

I wiped away my last tear. "I found Elisabeth's journals. There were some with torn pages. I was wondering who might've taken them. I haven't found any further information. Only that a man in an all-black attire which hid his face was the person who informed her of Sebastian's grave."

Lucas went quiet and looked down at his notes for a while. "My father mentioned the same thing. The notes which were taken, these were brought back by Raven. They are Elisabeth's research. She started backtracking to their origin where they originally were awoken by the humans which found them. She had a theory that maybe there might be answers there."

"Do you think she was onto something? Does it say anything about how to get rid of the Elders?" I asked know creeping up to my knees. I was consumed by the ideal. Maybe we were finally getting somewhere, we were finally finding that maybe this wasn't a fairy-tale after all.

"No they don't. But this was brought in after the theory of the collars. I think that, maybe when it is found it might have something to do with the blades. All of them have to be brought together. But that's just my theory. I think maybe the collars weren't just made to weaken one another. Maybe they both needed to be there for something to happen. In this I can see that Elisabeth didn't think that Sebastian had completely vanished, my father thought the same."

"So they were both trying to find Sebastian's grave. What did they find?" I asked, I was now creeping closer to Lucas. I was so hopeful that this could be real.

"Nothing. My father kept coming back to the unknown man who informed him of it in the first place. My father loved the power he had from Tyran. I think it wasn't so he could get rid of Tyran, but find a way to get rid of Misfeata who was his only challenger. Elisabeth's was to free herself and rid of Tyran the same time."

"What do you want Lucas?" I asked. The question came out so direct and serious that I felt uncomfortable with the silence that followed. I hadn't meant to ask it so directly.

"I want to help you in whatever choice you make. But I don't want to live in a world where I want to hurt you. And if the power from Tyran is what will force me to do that, then I don't want it. I want to restore my people and make them see the world differently. I don't want this war anymore. I've watched too many die in all my years of living. If the greatest gift I can offer you is freedom Karla, then I would lay my life down for that. It was me who brought you into this mess. I never knew who you were, and if I had I wouldn't have triggered your curse. For that I will always be sorry."

"You don't have to be sorry," I said. I went to put my hand on his but remembered that I couldn't. "If it wasn't you it would've been someone else. You came at the right time remember, others were following me as well."

"I just want to protect you." He placed the journals down. "I am telling you all of this because tomorrow I am confronting Eden. Although he is not as powerful as Tyran I want to rely on my own strength. Eden was my mentor and trained me since I was a child. He is the leader of half of my father's army. On top of that he has the remains of Taskatae's creatures. I am certain I can't die," he said closing and opening his leather gloved hand. "I don't think either of us can, unless we destroy one another. I don't want to hurt my people, but he won't stop until he has found you."

"You can't continue to fight my battles for me Lucas," I said desperately. I worried for him going into this war. I had seen him die once before. Tyran wasn't within his blood then, but still surely there was a limit. There must've been some weakness even for us.

"You know it's been reported to me that they have some of your blood. I didn't doubt you for a moment. I know you didn't supply it."

"My blood?" I asked sceptically and curiously. "Why would they have my blood? How?" I thought of Martin instantly. Had he supplied the enemy with my blood, but why, that didn't make any sense? Then again, I didn't fully trust him either.

"Remember when Harmony used to shoot arrows and they used to break your Shield," he said with a sad smile. "I never knew who she really was. And I never realized she was in contact with my brother. She used to dip her arrows with his blood. Oddly enough our blood can penetrate one another's Shields. My source told me this and that I should be wary. I believe in my people who I am fighting alongside tomorrow. I just thought you should know. Whoever you are with you shouldn't trust. Someone has been using you."

"I want to fight by your side tomorrow," I said hastily. "It's not your fight alone. Eden is after me, I should be there."

"You know we can't get close to one another. Let me do this for you, Karla. If protection is all I can offer you then let me do that much," he said with a warm smile.

A branch snapped close by and I armed myself with Aeisha.

"What is-" Lucas's projected figure cut out. The Elemental Breather in front of me was now bleeding out. Martin stood behind her. He kicked her to the ground, her form sprinkled into pixels and vanished.

"Are you crazy?" he said. "That was only a duplicate now I will have to find the true form of her."

"Why did you do that?!" I jumped into standing with my weapons poised. He was still his usual cold, calculating self. He straightened his well-groomed shirt.

"Let me assure you that there are greater dangers out there then Eden. You have opened a link between my positioning and those who are chasing me. Why do you think that I hide in the shadows? You've basically lead them straight to me. We need to leave now."

A rattle in the nearby treetops hastily came towards us. I used my keen eyesight and hearing to focus on what it was that charged towards us.

"Go back to the camp. Make sure everyone runs and gets away from here and me," Martin said. He walked between the enemy that approached us. "Don't look back."

A figure all in black with a covered black masked balanced lightly on the tops of one of the trees. Their head bopped from side to side eerily. It made a clicking noise.

"You left yourself open. It didn't take me long to find you," the voice said. It was female. Her form was slender.

"I've been on the run now for a year, and you only find me now," Martin said picking up a thick log which evidently held no weight for him.

"Oh Marteno," the way she pronounced his name was different to how we called him, it sounded older. "You and I both know that one year is nothing in our lifetime." Her black mask looked directly at me. There were light swirls on her material which forced me to believe that she was an Elemental Breather, it reminded me much of the description that Elisabeth once wrote in her journals. "Ohhhh," her voice was haunting and seemed to echo around us. "You are with one of the Elder's. What an interesting choice of companionship. I wonder what master will do when he finds out."

She lunged off the treetops and towards Martin, with striking speed he threw the log at her. It collided and threw her into a tree. The log snapped another two in its path.

"Run now!" Martin said to me. Hastily I ran into the trees, fearing what this fight's outcome might be. Both their speeds and strengths far out matched mine. I had no idea who these Elemental Breathers were and who it was that branded them, by the name of Master.

Chapter Twenty-Eight- Shock

$\mathcal{I}$ ran as fast I could towards the rest of the group. The fire in the distance grew closer and I began to yell. "Run! Run!" I wasn't sure what we were up against, but I knew it was something far beyond what we had handled before. Instinct. It was the one thing I relied upon most now. There is always a knowingness when danger is near. Knowing when you are no longer the predator but now the prey.

"Karla, what's-" I grabbed Paul by the sleeve and tugged him towards the others.

"We have to leave! Martin is up against some super Elemental Breather or something, we need to go!"

"Martin?" Scott said seriously. He looked behind and changed into an owl within seconds.

"No wait!" I called out after Scott but he had already vanished towards where I had left Martin behind. Ashley ran out of the trees as the others now gathered their weapons. Trish removed her lace gloves ready to attack Ashley until she realized it was him.

"What happened?" Ashley asked. "I heard you screaming."

"We need to leave now!" I said. I began to pull Paul towards the direction of the car. I know that they wanted to abandon it, but it was the fastest thing to escape. First we had to make it there alive.

"Wait, Paige is still on watch!" Ashley said. We all stopped for a moment in what felt like the longest moment of silence.

"She would've chased the fight," I said with realization. Paige always followed the fight.

"I will get her, you guys go now," I said running back towards where I had left Martin.

"Wait no Karla," Paul grabbed my arm. I pulled away from him.

"None of you understand! You cannot match this Elemental Breather!" Paul looked wounded at first and Ashley seemed offended. I looked at the others- Trish, Suzumiya and Chris. They all considered themselves skilled fighters, which I wouldn't deny. But this, this enemy was far greater than any battle we had experienced before.

"Bring her back safely," Ashley said with belief in me.

"I am coming," Trish said arrogantly. "If my brother is in there and it's an Elemental fight, then I should showcase my superiority." Her pupils were consumed into blackness. "I hate my brother, but won't let him embarrass me by being killed by a lesser Elemental Breather."

"Be safe," Paul said. I was grateful that my word was final and that they believed in my urgency and judgement of the battle. Paul kissed me passionately before letting go and following the others. Trish and I ran towards the clashes of noise. The ground beneath us shook from some form of impact. It sounded like explosives were hitting the ground.

Rapid speed flashed across my sight. I stopped where Scott had. He watched on trying to trace the speed between Martin and the foreign Elemental Breather as well. A hand reached out and grabbed me. It was Paige.

"I thought you were here. We need to run!" She said. It was the first time I had ever seen such urgency in Paige's eyes. I had never seen her run away from a fight. It wasn't in her nature. Martin was thrown against a tree. He shattered the first one he was thrown into and then he stopped at the second behind it. The ground beneath us shook. I realized it wasn't bombs but the impact of their fighting that shook the ground.

Paige began to tug on me. As we turned, we were greeted by the completely covered black Elemental Breather. She dipped her head to the side. "Master will be intrigued to know he was with you. I can only think of one reason."

Flames swirled around Paige and me as Trish held off the foreign Elemental Breather. Suddenly Martin was by my side and attacking the woman again. He now had a sword that duplicated the same as the attacker. I assumed she must have had two and he stole one. Their blades collided and they flicked one another off easily.

Paige tugged at me to leave. Scott still watched Martin and the woman as they fought. Much to my surprise he seemed to be worried about him.

"What are you doing?" I said. Scott was unpredictable. He often fled from fights or became an almighty ally to be reckoned with.

"Trust me when I say, he is the only way you can get rid of Misfeata. If he is killed you have no chance," he said not taking his sight from them. "I am trying to pinpoint her so I can enter her body and knock her unconscious. I just can't match her speed."

I looked at his side profile for a moment. The only chance to get rid of Misfeata? I looked back towards the fight that was destroying trees in front of me. The cracking of their roots pulling from the ground and pushing over was the only thing I could hear besides their weapons clashing.

"If that is the case then I will help you pin her," I said with determination.

"No!" Paige said. I looked back at her desperation. Why was she acting so weird, what did she know? If this was the only person who could help me get rid of Misfeata I wasn't going to watch him die before my eyes. I had already seen far too much of that. I shrugged Paige off.

Misfeata swirled within me, ready and excited for the fight. As I took my first step I still couldn't identify if it were her or me taking that step. We were merging into one. Our intention was the same and the thrill of bloodshed now conquered us.

I traced their fighting. My keen sight hardly matched their speed. Misfeata revelled in the challenge. Although she still didn't believe in Sebastian's grave, she felt relieved to finally have an opponent which might challenge her. *"Let me,"* Misfeata slithered within me. I didn't have time to put defences against her or fight against it. Misfeata happily took claim to my body. I no longer had my bracelet to keep her away.

She traced the Elemental Breathers footing and within seconds lunged. She jumped towards her striking at the woman. The Elemental Breather countered Aeisha with her own. She kicked towards us making us jump back. She had created enough space between us so she could counter Martin who plunged his sword towards her. She deflected it and elbowed it out of his hand. She struck at his chest with her knee but he jumped back.

Misfeata clattered both of Aeisha's blades into one hand and collected the sword which was flung in the air. She balanced it quickly and threw it towards the Elemental Breather like a spear. The woman curved around it so it didn't hit her. Behind her, Martin moved to the side from the blade and collected the handle as it passed him, he spun with its force rounding it into a protective position before she lunged for him again.

Misfeata projected her Shield into her right fist. She crept up on the Elemental Breather and struck at her from behind. Her Shield shattered much to Misfeata's surprise when it came close to impacting the woman. The woman struck around with lightning speed and kicked us into the closest tree. The impact left Misfeata winded. She waited for a moment, staggering to stand until she could breath.

As soon as she took that breath she jumped straight into the battle, fully recovered. She now knew that like Martin, her Shield would do nothing. It was something she didn't understand, her Shield worked against everyone but something she quickly factored into the fight. This time Trish was taking educated guesses as to where she thought the other Elemental Breather was jumping to. If anything it became a distraction to both Martin and Misfeata as they avoided the flames.

Misfeata crossed over her blades, hoping to slice at the woman's back but she jumped in time, avoiding me. Martin pounced on her and glided his blade across her stomach. It only touched her faintly as she was able to dig her blade underneath his and deflect it. Taking advantage of the moment, Misfeata sliced at her ankle and kicked her into the tree. Her kick wasn't as powerful as Martin's or the Elemental Breathers but it still left her with a moment of hesitation before getting up.

She stood back up rattling off the bits of tree which shattered on her. The way she moved was inhumanly as she swayed her head back and forth lazily.

"I am not allowed to kill you. But I can hurt you severely," she mused beneath her mask. She lunged for me but Martin countered her, they danced for moments with their weapons. Both collided and shattered into pieces under the force. They both threw away the damaged weapons and went into hand to hand combat. Both Martin and she continuously tried to lock one another in grips I hadn't yet learned. Neither could get the hold on the other. A flame shot towards them breaking them apart.

The Elemental Breather lunged for me and Misfeata readied herself with a smile. She was aiming for a clean strike to her chest. The sudden streak of a shadow formed in front of us and Paige was there. The Elemental Breather punched her in the face and paused for a moment. A shattering noise came from Paige's face and the impact of the hit forced Paige to twist her face towards me.

Blue shards protruded from Paige's face. Misfeata gasped recognizing the gems. She instantly retreated within me. I staggered into the control of my body. Everything seemed as if it had paused in that moment, although hardly any time was wasted. Part of Paige's face was a brilliant blue gem, it reminded me much of the red and green of Tyran and Misfeata's. It moulded around the Elemental Breathers fist like the gems that protruded from my own skin once did. When Misfeata lost control and began turning into a beast.

Paige growled at the woman and suddenly vanished. The form of shadows spun around the Elemental Breather who went to jump away, but something grabbed her from beneath and pulled her feet into the ground. She was trapped for a moment, I watched on in confusion.

Scott behind me vanished and I could sense that he had entered the Elemental Breather. It took him longer than usual as the Elemental Breather continued to struggle against the shadow like figure that held her now and Scott who was within her body. Was Paige the shadowed creature?

Her rigid body tensed and finally gave up. She collapsed unconscious onto the dirt. Martin walked over casually and looked at Scott with what I assumed to be surprise.

"I never thought of that," Martin said. He seemed disheartened by his own work.

"Not every answer is in numbers, boy genius," Scott teased. From the shadows that once held down the Elemental Breather came Paige. She formed into her normal human self. Her cheek was still fractured in beautiful blue.

"Who are you?" I asked. My voice was distant, I don't know if I was shocked, frightened or mesmerized. I had fought alongside Paige for so long. Never had I considered her to somehow be linked to. . . Sebastian. I looked at the blue gem, still unsure of why I assumed that. But the way that Misfeata retreated, I thought she would only ever react in such a scared and ashamed manner if she were confronted by her youngest brother. Paige raised her hand to her face.

"Can you fix this?" She asked Scott with a monotone.

"If they have found me already it means I have to gather all the pieces into one now," Martin said.

"What are you all talking about, who are you people?" I demanded angrily. What was everyone talking about, none of it made sense to me.

"To put simply," Martin began. "Paige is one key of two to Sebastian's grave. However I have the feeling she knows already where the other is. We need both of them to enter the gravesite. We leave now, we have to gather the other pieces. Tomorrow we will be a part of this war. Time is running out, we have to act now before the others are upon us." He looked down at the Elemental Breather woman who laid unconscious.

I looked at Paige in shock. I thought I might have even choked back a tear. Who was she? Why was she a part of Sebastian's grave? How? A part of me still believed it was a myth, but now I couldn't comprehend anything.

"I am Shadow," Paige said formerly. "My sister and I are the gatekeepers of Sebastian's grave. Essentially we are the creatures that he formed. Like when Tyran and Misfeata lose control and turn into beasts. My sister and I are the remains of his soul. We are the protectors of Sebastian's and Princess Carla's grave. We are both the light and darkness of his remains. We've been watching your progress for some time now."

I opened my mouth to say something, but my words were inaudible. I made an odd noise which was more of a shocked and disbelieving sigh.

"We don't have time for this right now. We need to head towards the war. If you want to make it to Sebastian's grave we need all the pawns I've put into place," Martin said.

"How do you know of all this?!" I demanded from him. He looked back at me in his calculating manner.

"Because I am the very person who has been organizing the defeat of the Elders for the past one hundred years. It is a way to weaken my master. Who do you think was the one that told the likes of Christopher and Kurt? I needed to gather the right pawns at the right time. All so I could pick up the pieces at once. This war tomorrow, it will have all the pieces I need."

"You knew about all of this?" I asked Scott desperately. He had betrayed Paul and me once, but even this felt grander.

"I had my suspicions, but I wasn't sure until everything has been verified now." He looked to Martin. "My father once mentioned to me the theory of your Master and his five followers. It was revered more as a haunted nightmare to make our kind scared of something in the world. How did you free yourself from him?"

"I didn't," Martin said with hesitation. "Another one of my kindred did. She and I are the only ones that escaped. I haven't seen her since. Three of his followers remain now." He looked down at the Elemental Breather who was still unconscious, indicating she was one of them. "We need to do this before the other two find us and she catches up. We don't have time for these answers. I will explain it to you all shortly. Just know that my end goal, resides with yours Karla. I can take Misfeata away. For now that's all you need to know. If you know anymore it will only put you in greater danger. But I am your only chance of ridding her. If I die or if you or the Prince die, there is no second chance."

"We need to find the others," Paige said. Scott walked over to her and began to heal over her cheek.

"It only needs to be temporary," she said. "Not perfect as long as it covers it with skin so the others don't see. They can't know of my true form."

They began walking into the direction that the others had fled in. I reached out for Misfeata, looking for answers but she had hid in the pits of the darkest parts within me. I had never felt so alone. What was happening around me? Who was who? Who did I believe? Where did I go? Strangely enough my first thought was the war that Martin spoke about and Lucas who would be left to fight by himself.

"How do you know where this fight will break out?" I called out after him. He looked over his shoulder calculatingly. Like always.

"Because I was the one who motioned it."

Chapter Twenty-Nine- Preparations

*W*e raced towards the others with heightened pace. I didn't even know how to absorb all of this new information. Nothing made sense to me. If Martin, or Marteno or whatever his true identity was claimed to have once been a follower like the Elemental Breather we had just fought, then doesn't that mean that he too once wore an entire black suit with black mask? Was Martin the link between informing Elisabeth and Praytar long ago about Sebsastian's grave? He claimed to have told Christopher and Kurt, who both sought it for their own purpose. They both tried to use me for their own gain.

Even if he were an Elemental Breather he still looked too young to have been plotting this over one hundred years ago. Who was he really, and who was his master that he continued to talk about? I wanted to ask so many questions and to stop for a moment so that someone could explain what was happening to me, but the rush was upon us. In every step we took there was an intense sense of urgency. The others were waiting beside the car. They were armed and ready in case an enemy confronted them instead of us.

"What happened?" Ashley asked as he walked towards us with urgency. Paige's face was healed, it looked jarred beneath, but a light layer of skin had formed over. Ashley looked at her oddly but didn't ask any further questions.

"Now we fight," Martin said. He indicated his finger in a circular motion. "Let's wrap this up. Follow Scott, we will lead you to the fight. Today is the day all of you have been training for. Don't hesitate for a moment. There will be a lot of bloodshed. But this is something that has to happen. We are confronting Eden and his army."

The others fell into silence. I wanted to tell them that we had all been tricked, that this wasn't something we had to do. Yet, it was. If we didn't erase this enemy, my mother would never be safe. We would all still be on the run. Even if this war was to Martin's advantage this was something that we had to confront. I despised that we had been played and were a part of a larger scheme then any of us had ever realized.

"Karla," Scott grabbed my attention. I was too far in a daze to pull away from him. I didn't know what to think about any of them anymore. Were they still my ally or enemy? Were they a friend or a stranger who had tricked and used me? "Remember when you once asked me if I could turn into a dragon," he said giddily. "I've never tried it but I think today I will pull out all the flash bling. A lot of Taskatae's creatures survived and have been taken over by Eden. I am going to light them up like sheep." He gave me the most flamboyant smile. I couldn't help but return the small smile. Even if he had tricked me. Surely there was some bond of friendship formed after all that we had been through together.

"Trish, you can't attack Lucas," I said to her sternly. Her eyes flickered black, her pupils flicking back and forth. She didn't like being told what to do. "We are there to fight Eden and his people."

"I go for blood and revenge," Trish spat. "I don't fight for you and you can't tell me where I can and can't be."

Martin held back my arms as I threatened to end this here so she wouldn't become a threat when we got there. "Look at your numbers, you need all the help you can get."

"She's not fighting for the same reasons as us," I said angrily.

"No one here is fighting for the same reasons. Everyone has their own purpose and reasoning of being here. Everyone is fighting for something or someone different," Martin said. I looked at the others. They all shuffled uncomfortably. "Trish might openly say that she is here for revenge but you cannot claim that one of the others here today don't have a particular purpose or person in mind to avenge. This war isn't just yours Karla, we all have our own reason to fight it."

"I hate Lucas," Ashley said openly. "You know I do after what happened with my father. I'm not there to fight Lucas. But I am there to kill as many Starkorfs as I can. For all those disgusting creatures that were there that day that tied my mother and used her as bait. I despise those who were watching as my father was killed. I want to kill every single one of them so I know my mother will never be threatened again."

"They killed my father long ago," Suzumiya spoke up. Chris rubbed her shoulders behind her, comforting her. It was the first time she had ever said it out loud to me. "They took what was precious to me. It was a member of Eden's army which did that. I want to find that man. I don't even have a name, so I can only hope as I slice through them, that one of them is him."

"I hate that they've hurt those I've loved," Chris said simply. "And I will always have Suzumiya's back. Until death." She placed her hand on his with a weak reassuring smile.

"I want to protect you no matter what," Paul said as he stepped forward. "If this will help you and possibly get us closer to the place we need to be so you can be rid of this curse then I will take that step with you hand in hand. I don't care about the risks Karla. I've never asked for your protection. I've always only wanted to be your equal and make sure you are safe."

"And sane," Paige added harshly. I looked at her but she flashed me a twisted smile. Although I now knew who she was, she didn't act differently.

"As touching as this moment is we need to leave," Martin said. "Shift or do whatever you do," he said to Scott who looked offended. He placed his hand to his chest with a baffled expression.

"What do you think I am some sort of pet?" He looked away from Martin upset with his bottom lip quivering in dramatics. Suddenly he changed into a horse.

"Thata' boy," Martin said as he patted his back. Scott kicked out a back leg in agitation. His silky black coat glistened in the moonlight which slowly began to hide behind clouds. Martin and Trish jumped on Scott as the rest of us piled in the car.

"Half a tank, I hope that it lasts," Ashley added as he started the car. Paige sat in the passenger seat as the rest of us squashed in the back. Paul grabbed my knuckles and gently brushed a kiss to them.

"I am sorry," he whispered. I twisted a sad expression. Something so small really seemed insignificant now. We were about to face a battle where the numbers were against us.

"I shouldn't have reacted how I did," I said pressing a kiss to his lips. He had never betrayed me. Out of everyone here, Paul was the one who had been most honest with me this entire time. He would have only done it when he thought it was in my best interest. It would've been a group decision as well, who knew, it might've been my mother who asked Martin to sample my blood and test it.

Ashley began driving and following the others. Scott's beautiful black coat wavered in the moonlight as he galloped on the road. Soon the cemented roads turned into dirt. We were heading into the same direction we previously ran from. I didn't know if we would be confronted by Christopher's group or even Kurt's. I didn't know what the numbers were that we faced or what would be the outcome. I

211

hoped that Lucas and I didn't get too close to one another where we couldn't control the Elders within.

I didn't know what to expect from Martin. What was he up to and how would his plan play out. He made it very obvious that he had alternative plans. And who knew if the group which followed him would find us?

A loud crunch broke my concentration on the many thoughts that preoccupied me. I looked over to Ashley who was biting into a red apple.

"Are you serious?" Paige accused. "We are about to head into a war and you are munching down on an apple."

Ashley gave a cheesy smile. "I'm sorry but I am starving. What, you want me to go into the fight on an empty stomach. I don't exactly see anyone cooking a roast here."

"Twenty dollars says that you will get a stich from it," Paige threatened. Her black boots were up on the dashboard pressed against the glass.

"I am pretty sure you don't even have one dollar to your name," Ashley said with a smile and took another bite.

"I will steal one of Scott's gold pieces to lay down that bet," she said seriously.

"I would love to see Scott's expression when he hears that you are comparing twenty dollars to one gold piece," Paul said with a laugh. Ashley looked in the rear-view mirror with a smile.

I let the small moment of jokes fill me. It seemed like it was the last breaking of the ice before we confronted what was to come.

"So this is it guys," Ashley said. We must have all been thinking the same because we all fell into a silence. Ashley threw the core of his apple out the window. "In case I don't get to say it to you all afterwards. It's been a pleasure fighting alongside you."

"We are all going to come back in one piece," Suzumiya said firmly.

"Yea don't think you can get out of kitchen cleaning duties that easily," Chris said to Ashley with a smile. He popped a piece of gum with a cheesy smile.

"Thank you for helping me with all of this," I said in a small voice. "I couldn't have survived without any of you." I looked them all dead in the eye. No matter what our background or reasons for fighting today, the truth was that all of them had played a large part in my journey. My survival rate from the very start was near to nothing and yet because of all of them and so many others, including Lucas, I had survived. It was time to give back that gift, I had to fight for all of them and make sure they all returned alive. Paul pressed a small kiss to my cheek.

I gave him a small smile and a kiss to the lips. "I can't tell you to stay in the car can I?" I asked seriously. I placed both of my hands on his face, memorizing the touch.

"You know the answer to that already," he said. He pressed a kiss to my nose. "You know I will be there with you until the end. We will both make it out okay."

I pressed my lips to Paul's and his kiss burned through me so passionately I feared that he thought it was our last. His tongue led mine as I let myself fall into him as easily as I always did. I had to fight my hardest. I saw Paul as an equal, but against some of those that we might have to challenge I would have to make sure I always had a visual on him.

Paul protected me from losing my sanity. I wanted to protect him from the weakness he held of not being able to project a Shield in this unworldly battle. I had to avoid Lucas but find a way to still protect him from Eden. I knew he was strong but there was a part of me that felt like I mostly had to protect Lucas from himself. Tyran had only been within him for a small time now, I was certain that Lucas still didn't understand the extent of the power he had and the control he could have if possessed by him. I had to help, somehow. I had to find a way to protect all those that I loved, without losing myself to Misfeata.

Chapter Thirty- Battle Cry

$\mathscr{D}$awn had broken out over the hill we ventured towards. Behind us it was still dark. There was a certain suspenseful atmosphere in the car. We all had our weapons, we had all trained, and we had all fought. But nothing felt as life changing as now. This was going to be the greatest battle any of us had faced and all we had was a few hours notice. I had much respect for all of them. They never doubted anyone within our group, no one questioned if anyone wanted to flee. We could all rely on one another because we were all here for our own reasons.

Only a few minutes later Scott had halted. Trish and Martin jumped off him and he shifted into his normal form. He stroked through his white hair, straightening it. We pulled over and jumped out of the car. After being cramped in the back seat, it was nice to stretch. Scott was now polishing his shoes with concentration. "Eww, I got them dirty."

"Please brother, we are about to enter a battle for goodness sake," Trish said angrily. She had her arms crossed over her chest with impatience.

"Exactly, what if rumor spreads amongst other Elemental Breathers that I went in such a raggedy state."

"Follow that path," Martin pointed to a small manmade trail amongst trees. "Just follow it until you feel as if you should stop and wait, you will know where."

"You're not joining us?" I asked surprised. Martin and I had pulled away from the group so no one else could overhear our conversation.

"I told you, I can't be seen so publicly. I can't risk my exposure. I will find you. Everything will come into play, don't worry about that child."

"That is exactly what I am worried about," I hissed feverishly. "I don't know what your plan is and I don't know if you are risking our lives for your own intentions."

"I'm not risking anyone's life, they are here because they want to. I've just simply been orchestrating my own scheme behind the scenes. I told you, my plan benefits you. It's too soon to reveal anything to you. If I do now you won't act of your own accord in the battle. You focus on your own desire and let me worry about mine. Just know, that I am no threat to you."

Ashley walked over looking between the two of us. "Is everything okay?"

"Good luck Karla," Martin said. He patted me on the shoulder. "I hope that everything works out for the both of us."

"So typical of the weaker Elemental Breathers to escape while they can," Ashley said as he shook his head in annoyance. I had forgotten that no one else knew of Martin's strength or ability except for Paige, Trish, Scott and me. I watched Martin as he left. He quickly disappeared into the shadows. I looked at the manmade trail which had scattered leaves and branches on it. Everyone stretched enjoying the freedom of no longer being trapped in the car.

They quickly reassessed their weapons. Chris practiced with his nunchucks. I still found it odd that it was his choice of weapon, but remembered how easily he could use them. Suzumiya was stretching in her cat like poses. I saw the hilts of small knives and daggers sticking out of her boots, jacket and well almost everywhere. She always had hidden weapons. She had a large sword strapped to her back in a beautiful bronze sheath.

Ashley cracked his neck back and forth and rolled his shoulder blades. He had one large sword strapped to his back. I looked at Paul who also held a sword but what grabbed my attention was his studded leather gloves. Studs protruded from each knuckle.

"Those are new," I said with consideration. I had never seen him use them before.

"They were a gift from Mom," Ashley said. "I asked if we could give him a pair considering he does better with his hand to hand combat with his experience in boxing and what not."

"Do I look like a bad ass?" Paul said with a cheeky grin.

"I wouldn't mess with you," I said with a smile. I pulled his leather jacket and kissed him on the lips. "But I still think I could beat you to a pulp." He arched an eyebrow in challenge.

"Well then, after all this we will just have to see."

"Can we just get this over and done with?!" Trish growled from behind us. Scott and her began to walk into the woodland. The sun still broke out making the air feel colder. We walked for half an hour before the trail stopped. It ended on a hill and overlooked a large valley. My stomach felt as if it had sunk as I looked upon the dead looking grass. Only part of it had lightened in the sun. The sun was breaking out over the hill on the other side and was still stretching towards us.

"I think this is the place," I said. It was a steep hill. If we had to descend it, we would be sliding. Unlike the dead and dirt-like arena before us the hill we stood on was very luscious and green.

Misfeata began to swirl in my stomach. I clutched at the nauseous sensation. She only reacted when a certain Elder was close by. I could slowly feel the presence of Lucas creep closer. He wouldn't have known that we planned to join him in this fight. I wondered if he now knew, did he feel and react how I did?

Something on the hill opposing us on the left grabbed my attention. Much to my surprise, I recognized the group. Friend or foe, I wasn't yet sure. Christopher and Elijah stood at the focal point of her group. Their numbers were still large. She eyed my small group. I could see her expression with my heightened eyesight. She was not happy to see me, but I suspected she wasn't surprised. I wondered how much of this gathering was because of Martin's plan. I looked around trying to find him but to no avail.

A large horn bellowed from across us. My heart skipped a beat. I grabbed Paul's hand nervous as to what would reveal itself. I found courage and strength remembering my mother and father. I had to fight for them today. I had to do this or there would be no end. I would constantly be hunted.

The horn bellowed out again and I could hear the march of footsteps in the near distance. In the outline of the rising sun, small shadows streaked across the dirt-like arena. Eden, creatures of Taskatae, and his army marched to the top of the hill. He was on top of some horse like creature which had snake heads for ears and tails. The twisted creature sickly reminded me too much of the death of my father. It brought back memories of the battle we had already faced against Taskatae.

The horn rung out again. My first battle had been with Raven, she was the one who opened my eyes to this sick and twisted world. She was the first being I had killed. And now I stand here, reminiscent her death, thinking if I could have done anything differently. Could I have ever avoided this?

Misfeata still swirled within me. I tensed knowing that Lucas was also close by. How close was too close, what were our limits until we turned on one another? I pushed Misfeata down with a frightful pressure. She fought against me.

"I want to oversee and end this battle," she snarled within me. *"Today will be the day that I claim my victory and defeat my brother."*

The horn sounded again. To my right an army that matched the size of Eden's crept from the shadowed tree tops. With the same strengthened sight Lucas and I stared at one another despite the distance. He pulled a painful expression. His eyes closed for a moment as he pressed his palm to his head. I could sense that Tyran was stirring within him as much as Misfeata were in me. I didn't know if we had restraint to be so close. I had been used to Misfeata within me for longer, but he was a Starkorf by birth and already knew of Tyran. We had to fight for control so we wouldn't hurt each other. Both of us had to be here today for this battle. It was inevitable.

How ironic that we both wanted to protect one another more than anything, yet we were the most poisonous source to one another's demise. Everyone stood in their respected groups. The wind passed through us like a swirl of our very last thoughts.

"Until the end," I said to my group. Paul flexed his studded leather gloves in preparation. The others pulled out their weapons.

"Little sister," Scott said passively. "A thought just occurred to me. I think I could shift into a dragon, but I don't think that I can create fire." This snapped Trish's attention from Lucas's direction. The horn sounded and the wolf like creatures that snarled beside Eden sprinted towards the center.

Trish huffed in annoyance. She dropped both of her lace gloves to the ground. Scott's and her eyes both engulfed with the black, hiding their pupils. "Than just this once let me be your fire."

Scott smiled and suddenly grabbed his sister's hand. He threw her into the air and lunged towards the drop of the hill. Spectacularly he changed into a brown scaled dragon. It was the ordinary type I had seen in movies and children's books. One tail, a slender figure with four legs and a pointed nose. Trish landed gracefully on his back. So boldly and easily that it looked as if they had rehearsed it numerous times before.

The creatures continued to pour over the hill. Scott's reptile scream filled the air of battle. Trish began shooting flames towards the creatures while keeping her balance. All at once, the four sides of the hills began to fill with their respected parties. The time for war was now.

I took the lead of my group sliding down the slippery hill. I held Aeisha against the ground just in case I had to use it to anchor my balance. I hit the ground running and towards the waves of creatures. One by one their screams echoed through the hills as they were set alight by Trish. Christopher's group countered Eden's men first. Their weapons clattered against one another in a forceful blow. Fortunately, Christopher sided with us this time.

Lucas stayed on the hill with a few of his men. I ignored the swirls of Misfeata. It felt as if she were pacing back and forth eyeing Lucas off. Like Christopher who hit the left side of Eden's army, Lucas's people struck at his right.

Loud noises from above startled me as bird like creatures began to attack from high up. They swooped at Scott and Trish. She shot flames at them as they continued to swipe at her. One of them caught her off guard and knocked her off. She was thrown over Scott who quickly realized and dived for his sister. But the gravity was too fast.

I didn't like Trish, often I wanted to kill her. But today she fought with me. I ran at her descending figure. I pulsated my Shield beneath me and jumped to catch her before she crashed into the ground. I broke our fall as we landed, not so gracefully. Scott maintained his form in the sky fighting off the creatures in the air. I heaved myself from the gravelled ground after taking cuts to the face from my fall. A Starkorf lunged for me and flames tore at it, backing it away from me as I stood up.

Trish gracefully swept a flame around me giving me time to recoup myself and prepare myself against the next attacker. She lowered her flames and focused on the wolf creatures which snarled around her. I spotted Paul's positioning which was close to the others. It appeared that they had banded with some of Christopher's group. They used them as the shield's and attacked from behind when they had broken the Starkorfs shield. It seemed that without creating a strategy, everyone protected one another. It was strange, but my own words echoed through my thoughts. *No matter what our background or past, we all have something here today that we are fighting for.*

I shattered the Starkorfs shield who attacked me, slicing at his arm and kicking him away. A whip wrapped around my arm. Instead of being taken away with it I reefed back on it pulling that Starkorf towards me. I had never been a killer, but a part of me realized that sometimes I had to. I plunged my blade into their chest. My eyes surveyed between three people.

The positioning of Paul to make sure he was protected by the others. Eden, who walked across the battle field and sliced through Starkorfs and Shilders with eyes only for me. And Lucas who watched from the hills. I felt bad for taking away his claim and right to this fight. He had planned to be the one to take down Eden. But we were both wary that if he came closer, we were the greatest threat to one another.

My leg buckled as Misfeata swarmed me. I pushed her down with a loud gasp. She scratched at my insides painfully trying to get out. *No!* I had control. I had to defeat her today. I couldn't let her have control.

I raised my sight, just in time from my inner struggle. I rolled myself to the side avoiding Eden's sword which had come down over my head. I balanced with grace only to stagger with my next step. Misfeata choked me. I looked over my shoulder, knowing why. Lucas had begun to descend the hill.

I didn't know if it was because he was concerned that Eden advanced on me or if Tyran had already taken over. But Misfeata screamed with blood filled hatred. I choked on her suffocating effects. I had to cling on, I couldn't lose to her. I had to face Eden myself.

Her shadow like claws reached out for me and she consumed my consciousness. I was again trapped. I banged against the glass wall which kept me in. Misfeata knew where Tyran was, and now I was certain that it was him. It had to be.

Eden struck at our back. Misfeata spun in hatred and snarled at him.

"You annoy me!" She snapped. She gently balanced Aeisha on her open palm and pulsated her Shield towards him. Aeisha shot out towards his chest like a spear. He deflected it but Misfeata had already jumped towards him with her partnered blade. He countered her attack with a wobbled step. He was shocked by the sudden turnaround in strength. Misfeata collected her second blade from the ground. Her mind frenzied over only one person, and he was approaching. She knew exactly where Tyran was.

"You think because you lead an army, you can defeat me, an Elder!" Misfeata snapped. She lunged for him again, hacking her two blades towards Eden with such grace that he struggled to keep up. For all the rumors of his greatness, it did him no justice now. There was an opening. Misfeata plunged Aeisha into his chest. At the same time Borac pierced through his stomach from behind. Eden's mouth opened in shock as he looked down at the blades. Lucas stood behind him and it was Tyran's voice that rang through.

"Actually sister, this is my army," he said with a twisted smile. Both of them retracted their blades. Eden dropped to the ground dead. He was nothing but an object in their way. I clawed at Misfeata trying to reach the surface and claim my body once again. I didn't want to fight Lucas or hurt him. This was everything we tried to avoid. I so desperately wished that I had my bracelet or the collars which weakened us both.

There was no sign of desperation or struggle in Lucas's eyes. They were once the eyes I so long ago fell in love with and now they reflected a sick and twisted anger. It was Tyran. The war around us carried on. It only filled their hatred of one another more.

Tyran struck first aiming for Misfeata's face. She dodged it striking at his stomach. Aeisha pulsed in my hand. She screamed for the touch and spill of Tyran's blood. Misfeata continued to push against me, trying to snuff me out completely so I wouldn't be conscious for any of this. I clung on by what felt like a mere thread. I couldn't let her erase me.

Aeisha scraped against Tyran's chin but it was almost as if he allowed it to happen. He smiled as it further provoked him. "I've missed this," he mused. He brought Borac down as a distraction, we countered his blades but then he kicked us. We made enough room to avoid his foot, if it hadn't been for the red shards that protruded from them. Three red shards extended out of his knee towards us. Misfeata was able to cut through two that came towards us but didn't make it in time for the third which pierced her arm. She pulsated her shield within to break the shards away before it absorbed too much of her strength.

"Are we playing the petty strategies already," Misfeata taunted. Blood spilled over my arm. The three red gems which had protruded from Lucas's knee had been chiselled down from her cutting through them, but still the edges of them protruded sharply.

"Please sister, I think we've tried every tactic in all the books," he smiled with satisfaction. He lunged for us again. He pulsated his Shield into his feet and jumped down on us. He intended to use his spiked knee over us, but Misfeata had already predicted his move. She jumped to the side avoiding him. She pulsated Aeisha towards the back of his head. He swung around in time deflecting it with ease.

"Stop! Please Misfeata!" I begged. A Shielder had bumped into Lucas accidently and he slit her throat without mercy. She was a mere object in his pathway. Red gems began to slide out from beneath his left wrist as he still held Borac with his right hand. It seemed to replicate the same shape as Borac. *"Make him stop!"* I screamed, he was destroying Lucas's body. His father, Praytar was never able to come back to human form after Tyran had so carelessly destroyed him into a creature the first time that we had battled. *"Make him stop!"*

"Shut up!" Misfeata screamed out frustrated as she deflected Borac. She dodged the makeshift gem blade. My arm felt as if it were set alight. It contorted for an odd moment into a painful piercing sensation. I screamed from within where no one could hear my scream. My entire left arm crystalized and protruded with green shards. The makeshift weapon clashed into it as my arm only continued to tear and grow into something inhuman.

I screamed silently in so much pain. The crystals formed perfectly into a well-rounded Shield. It was attached to my arm which was now covered in a rough green surface.

"Be grateful I have more control than him. He will most certainly lose his entirety. You will only have to deal with the loss of your arm," she snarled.

Misfeata deflected Borac with her shielded arm. She came out from beneath it, twisting my shoulder awkwardly and plunging into Lucas's chest. I screamed in horror internally as I knew the strike was clean. Misfeata growled in frustration, pulling back Aeisha before it was taken in by the red gem that grew over Lucas's chest. There were tiny droplets of blood which tipped the gems and fell to the dirt ground.

Tyran looked down at his chest with a sick smile. "Phew, that was close. Going for the kill so soon sister, I thought we could dance a little longer." The fight surrounding us seemed to be invisible. I so desperately wished that there was someone that could help us. That could offer us the strength that we needed to claim our bodies for ourselves.

"I wonder what you would do if I were fully protected by my gem," Tyran twisted with pleasure. I wasn't sure if he only spoke to Misfeata or me as well. "I am sure destroying your lover here might cut you deeper, such emotion might even affect Misfeata. Shall I tell you about how much he is screaming inside?!" Tyran said. The red gem of his chest began to slowly creep over his body.

"Stop it!" I screamed. *"Let me out!"* I wanted to protect Lucas more than anything. Misfeata stumbled back slightly in pain as I affected her. Tyran smiled victorious as he went to jump. Instead he

couldn't. He looked down to find that he was being held down by shadows. This was Paige. I would know this anywhere. A woman that looked exactly like Paige but with white hair, long white dress, and fairer skin stood behind him. Misfeata snarled at the intrusion. The girl held her hands in front of her and opened her palms, a blinding light distracted everyone across the battlefield. Misfeata heard an arrow nearby, although she couldn't see as she was blinded by such light, she protected herself with both her gem armour and her Shield. She slashed at three arrows which shot towards her. One pierced me in the side of the stomach. One which she hadn't countered.

The arrow burned and she screamed at the pain it inflicted. I recalled this tactic. This had Lucas's blood. While distracted with the pain of the arrow, a heavy metal clambered down on Misfeata. She slashed at the person who had crept up behind her. Her neck burned as the red gems absorbed her strength. The blinding light which came from the girl's palms swept away.

Misfeata retreated without control. The shackles around my neck was too much for her to handle. I choked my breath of air, heavily breathing from all the pain. I both wanted to hack my own arm off and try to rip away the collar. They were replicas of the collars which Lucas and I had once worn but so much worse. Someone had lifted me up and began to carry me away with unmatched speed. Slowly my vision came to from the blinding light. I was being carried up the hill of which Lucas once stood up on.

Behind me the others who were fighting, slowly regained their sight also. They looked at one another uncertain of what just happened. I jolted beneath whoever it was that carried me. I looked down recognising the shirt. "Martin?" My voice rasped. I looked over to my right, frightful at what I saw.

A black horse, which I presumed to be Scott carried the unconscious Lucas which had three arrows protruding from his back. Like me he had been shackled with the collar. The difference was that although my arm still glamored with a green shield. Half of his body had been taken over by the red gem. I feared that he would not come back to me.

"It's time for us to create a family reunion young one," Martin said as he ran from the woodland. I drifted into the pain of the gems that were wrapped around my throat. I couldn't hold on to anything anymore. I fell into a certain and familiar darkness. Every time I fell into this pit, I didn't know if it was the final place to rest. I felt that every time I reached this place, I was closer to my true death. How many times could someone defy death?

Chapter Thirty-One- Shadow and Light

*M*y body ached as I drowned in darkness. Every cell of my body wanted to give up. Misfeata wasn't here, I was again alone. I found it ironic that I despised her, and yet I had gotten used to her being with me. Someone spoke my name but I didn't want to wake to it. I knew the pain that was to come. I knew how my body would swell in pain. I didn't want to go to that place. I felt bliss here, my thoughts echoed and repeated one another.

"Karla." It was my name again being called out. How cruel of them to expect me to wake up. It was too much. I couldn't handle the suffering anymore. I simply wanted to slip away. "Karla." My body was jolted slightly in desperation. I recognized the voice. I noted the desperation in his tone. Drops of water dropped on my face, no not water it must have been tears. "Karla, please." Paul's tone begged. "You promised not to leave me." Had I made that promise? If I had I would've meant it when I said it. "We are so close," he whispered. I felt a warmness fill me. I wanted to pinpoint that sensation. When I did, I had realized it had already started pulling me out from my darkness. He pressed fluttering kisses to my face. My body began to feel heavy again and I ached. No I burnt. I tried to go back to that bliss darkness but I was rousing. I was already there. I was still alive.

My eyes fluttered open and I spluttered blood onto Paul's face in greeting. I was in so much pain, it was so excruciating. My head flopped over his arm as I saw Lucas still unconscious beside me. Weakly I tried to hold myself up but couldn't.

Paul looked at Lucas over his shoulder and then me. "He's been unconscious this entire time. Here, let me. This might help," Paul lifted me uncomfortably and I tried to hold in my painful screams. He lightly lifted me, my head bobbled weakly. He perched me against a rock of sorts beside Lucas. I hovered my hand over his face, not wanting to touch because he would drain me.

He was so pale and half of him was covered in the gemmed red. I noticed that his collar was no longer on. I tried lifting my own hand to my throat but weakly gave up.

"You don't have it on either," Paul said already knowing what I was attempting to do. He was crouched in front of me. My head bobbled back and forth, still fighting consciousness. The remains of my body felt shattered. It pained Paul to know how much I cared about Lucas, but he still brought me to him.

"Thank you," My voice rasped. He gave me a small smile before moving to the side to reveal where we were. Behind him the others stood. We were in some kind of ruins. The rocks around us had been broken, there were purple flowers which covered the ground. In the middle of the enclosed ruins was a statue of a woman holding her hands together. The image of her reminded me of someone.

"It is Princess Carla," Paige interrupted my daze with consideration. The way she spoke her name was with such fondness and admiration I wasn't sure if it were the same Paige. "Well in memory of her. She was Sebastian's wife. Here he rests in her memory."

Martin and the woman who looked identical to Paige, but with white hair and in a white dress came out from the ruins' entrance. I presumed that she was 'light' and the sister of Paige.

"They are still fighting in the nearby woods," Scott said casually to Martin. "The victor will be here within minutes I imagine," Scott said assessing his nails.

"Then fight them off. They cannot enter these grounds."

"We will protect these ruins, it is our duty," Paige and Light said at the same time.

"But we cannot proceed to do this without you two," Martin said. "Or him unconscious." He pointed to Lucas.

"We will hold them off," Suzumiya and Chris said. "We can lay out a few traps quickly."

"Who?" My voice was almost inaudible. Martin dipped down to my level.

"Kurt and Christopher's groups are now fighting to reach here. Karla, they want to source your power. The reason why I told both of them about this possibility was because I needed a lot of Starkorfs and Shielders to surround the ruins while we performed this, I needed that power. You need to wake him up or we can't do it."

I looked at Lucas, only slightly conscious.

"I don't understand," I squeaked. It was much easier to fade back into the darkness.

"No, no, no," Paul tapped on my cheek, waking me back up before I hid within myself again. "Karla, Martin can take Misfeata away."

I burrowed my eyebrows in confusion.

"It is as he says, but we only have a small amount of time," Martin confirmed. I could feel my strength ever so slightly regaining but I didn't think it was enough to feed Lucas to consciousness. The arrows which were once protruding from his back had been pulled out, he still bled slightly. Obviously his healing had dropped significantly as well. The only way I knew how to bring him to consciousness was to provide him with my own strength. I lightly reached my hand over my knee to try and touch his face.

"No," Paul said catching my hand. "You're too weak,"

"It's the only way I know how," I gasped. Tears began to break over my eyes. I didn't know how else to help Lucas other than to feed him my strength. Paul gave me a firm look before looking away.

"Ashley, I don't want to sound like a sook or anything but I need your help," Paul said. He ripped off his glove with his teeth and looked at Lucas with a disgruntled measure.

"It's going to burn man," Ashley said with consideration. Hatred filled his eyes as he looked upon Lucas. I wondered if he had even thought about killing him while he laid there so weakly.

"I know that," Paul growled. "Why do you think that I need you to hold me down?!"

"Done," Ashley said as he flashed an arrogant smile. He pushed down on Paul's hand to Lucas's face. Paul began grunting and scrunching up his face in pain. Swear words continued to pour out of his mouth as he tried to pull his hand back but Ashley held it firm. I watched Lucas as color began to slowly creep into his face again.

"That should be enough," Ashley said flinging his hand off Paul's. Paul leapt from his spot and away from Lucas. He scampered to the wall holding his hand to his mouth.

"Damn, that hurts," his voice was croaky. My eyes filled with tears due to the fact that he had to do that to himself. I knew all too well how torturous the feeling of being drained was. Lucas' eyes began to roll back and forth.

"Good, lift him," Martin instructed Ashley. He scoffed in arrogance.

"I am not touching him," he said with hatred.

226

"I will," Paul said. He struggled to stand. He pressed his hand against one of the rocks for a moment as he gathered his focus. "You grab Karla."

"She's probably heavier anyway," Ashley teased as he delicately lifted me.

"Like you are one to talk you great big ape," Paige snapped back in my defence.

"Whatever little miss Shadow or whatever you are," Ashley toyed back.

"You have become friends with these people?" She who was known as Light asked.

"No," Paige snapped dignified. "This is why I didn't want to go out and find them. You should've gone."

"We don't have much longer Shadow. Perhaps you should say how you really feel," Light responded. Paige gave her consideration and looked at Ashley again. She raised her nose in the air and followed Martin into the ruins. Ashley walked with me delicately to make sure not to put me in more discomfort. I still wanted to rest and hide in that place of darkness. I had no fight left in me Misfeata wasn't here, she was silent. I could finally be at peace.

Paul struggled under Lucas's weight as he walked in behind us. Trish and Scott followed. Flames were pre-lit on the wall. Not much made sense to me at this point. In the small circular room there were two cemented coffins. I didn't have to guess whose they were, I presumed that they were Sebastian's and Carla's. In the center was a cemented pedestal with a bowl. Further back in the room were three openings.

Memories seemed to flood me as soon as I looked at them. I knew this place. No not me, but Misfeata. This was the very same ruins of where they were awoken.

"This place," I said. A beautiful gemmed blue weapon grabbed my attention. The blade was firmly speared into the ground. "Sheliste." I said. The word felt so comforting to me. It was Sebastian's Immortal Blade. It had never vanished.

"It was here this entire time," Lucas said quietly. I looked over to him. He looked like he was only a few steps away from death.

"What is this place?" I asked, looking at all the spider webs and patches of dust that filled it.

"This is Sebastian's grave. But also where the three Elders first awoke," Martin explained. Misfeata stirred lightly within me, yet I felt as if she was trying to creep further down. She was avoiding being a part of this. She didn't want to acknowledge that her brother's existence might still be a part of this world. Anticipation filled me. No not me, it was her emotions that were welling inside of me.

"How do you know this?" I asked. Paige and her sister stood beside the coffins protectively. They stood so still that they looked as if they were a part of the cemented furniture.

"Because I was here the day that my Master created them. I witnessed fifty years after when they were found and awoken," Martin said. Scott and Trish brought Borac and Aeisha forward to Martin who stood in front of the bowl. Both Lucas and I froze with the desperation to have our blades back. A chill filled the room the closer the blades got together.

"How is that possible?" Ashley spoke up. He still held me firmly to his chest. Lucas was still sloppily laid over Paul's shoulder.

"Because I am Marteno, one of the five followers of my Master. My Master is the first Elemental Breather in existence, he is the first Immortal being."

The room swirled with a colder chill.

"Surely you didn't believe that your race was far superior," Trish scoffed.

"This isn't general knowledge," Martin chastised her. "Only few know. But your entire race was only created as a mere trial to please my Master. By getting rid of the three Elders and their Immortal Blades I am weakening him slightly. I ran away from him a year ago. But I and another have been plotting against him since the time he rose the Great Wall. It was a trial really. For all those years that Elemental Breathers, Shielders, and Starkorfs were trapped, he watched on in entertainment. Like them, his five followers were created by him. I myself was once his favourite. My expertise and Element were his favourite to use. When the wall shattered by the aid of myself and the second follower who escaped, he no longer wanted to contain the races, he simply wanted to see how they would act over time in the human world instead. He has no care for the humans and what might happen to them."

I couldn't believe all that he had said. I knew that Elemental Breathers thought they were superior but not to that extent. The others around me looked like statues as they absorbed this. Their entire life they had been raised on beliefs, culture, and sacrifices, to now learn that they were only some experiment.

"Why are you doing all this?" I asked in a small voice.

"Because, I need to weaken my Master. The Elders are one way to do that. Being created from him, it will take a toll on his strength. And for that I had to gather all the right pieces into this place here. The only way any of this would tie all of this together was his blood. It's the only way that the Elders can be released. But of course they have their own consciousness so they need to agree to surrender and depart from their hosts."

Lucas and I looked at one another with anticipation, we knew how much the siblings hated one another more than anyone could fathom.

"How did you get your Master's blood?" Ashley asked. We all looked up at Martin in anticipation.

"That was the easiest ingredient to gather. It runs through my veins of course."

"They are getting closer," Paige said hastily. "We need to begin."

"The rest is up to you," Martin said to Paige. "You are Sebastian's only channel."

Paige and Light looked at one another. "Well sister," light said to Paige and grabbed her hand. "We've been guarding this place for a very long time now. I think it's time to say our farewells too." Paige gave her a knowing nod and held her hand.

A sickness swirled within me and I coughed up blood. Ashley tried to make my fall a little more delicate as I dropped to my knees with nausea and pain. The room felt as if it spun around me and Misfeata buried further into my consciousness.

Suddenly everything was bright and I didn't feel sick anymore. I looked around and found myself at the same tree Misfeata once shared a memory with me. It was on a hill which once looked down at Sebastian when he was burned alive. The sky was blue with near to no clouds. The wind rattled slightly in the wind. I looked beside me where Lucas stood warily as well. There was no tension between us. No desire to kill one another.

I reached my hand out to his and held his hand. A touch I had desired for so long, a form of closure that we could once again be brought together without trying to hurt one another. Across from us Paige and Light still held hands. Suddenly in between us stood three figures.

Misfeata showcased her beautiful green gown, her beautiful red hair flowed over her shoulders. Tyran was handsome, much to my surprise. He had tan skin and an opened shirt with black pants. The third, who I could only assume to be Sebastian because of his similar features to Tyran.

Neither Misfeata nor Tyran looked him in the eye. They were astonished by what was happening.

"My family," Sebastian said. His voice was so smooth and nurturing. I remembered when they had identified the three Elders with three different qualities. Misfeata the wise. Tyran the strong. Sebastian the compassionate. It was fitting for him. "Please end this. This has gone on for too long."

"You've been alive this whole time?" Misfeata exasperated angrily. Although she sounded bitter there was bewilderment in her tone. She choked back her tears.

"Everything we've done, we have done in your name!" Tyran said angrily.

"No, you can't claim that," Sebastian said. "Every sin you have done up to this point has been of your own doing in your own name. Both of you became greedy for strength and power. We were never like that. We have all loved and lost loved ones. But this was never what we were created for."

Misfeata and Tyran fell silent. I still felt that slight anxiety which connected Misfeata and me.

"This world, this human place is a cruel existence to be in," Misfeata choked back. It was alarming to see her spill with so many emotions. I didn't even recognize her.

"They killed my wife!" Tyran said hatefully.

"And mine too," Sebastian said calmly. "But when I found the tombs which we awoke in and decided to make it our resting place, I divided myself into my two parts. My light and shadow," he indicated between the two sisters behind him. "My consciousness had since drifted freely and you would not believe what I discovered when I freed myself. I never jumped into Shielder's bodies or anything of the sort. I simply floated."

Sebastian's name was called out from the distance. Misfeata and Tyran looked ahead expectantly. I don't know what they saw, but both of their eyes filled with painful tears. Misfeata's hands reached her mouth.

"Is it really them?" She gasped in tears. "Are we deserving to still be able to see them?"

Tyran dropped to his knees in shock. "My wife," he cried. The anxious sensation that once coursed through me filled with such love and lightness that tears began to drop from my own eyes. I didn't have to see what it was that they witnessed. I knew that their loved ones were there in the afterlife, whatever that meant.

"Karla," the familiar voice spoke out to me. I spun around so quickly I almost fell into him. My father stood in front of me wearing his usual sweatpants and sleeveless shirt. Tears spilled over my eyes and my vision of him gone. I reached out and hugged him.

"Dad," I cried out unable to believe that he was real. "Dad." I choked on tears as I hugged him firmly. "I am so sorry. I am so sorry. I didn't know. I am so sorry." My words became a babbling mess.

"Ssshhh," he said as he brushed back my hair. "Hey kiddo it's okay."

"No it's not," I choked. I held him tighter so ashamed of what I had done to him. I had killed my own father.

"Hey," he said rattling me slightly and forcing me to look up at him. His red hair was feverishly bright in the light. "I was trapped before you did that. You released me Karla. You gave me the one gift no one else could've. You are so strong."

"No," I said holding onto him tightly. He laughed slightly and pushed me back. He began wiping away my tears.

"Hey listen to me, I want you to know that I love you and your mother so much. I want you to look after her okay." I felt my father's presence leaving me and I clung to him tighter. I opened my eyes to not let his image escape me.

"Please don't go. Please Daddy!"

"I love you Karla. You have always been my proudest joy. Look after yourself." He vanished into nothingness. I searched moments longer but he was gone. I looked over to Lucas who also had tears spilling over his eyes. I wondered who it was that he saw.

I looked behind where the Elders still stood. Misfeata looked at me with so much remorse. I found there to be a similar expression on Tyran as he looked at Lucas.

"We're ready now," they both said at the same time. A light took away my eyesight and when I reopened them, I had to readjust to the darkness of the tombed room. It was an odd sensation. It wasn't me who picked myself up. It was Misfeata she was within me still. She didn't possess me as she normally did. It was different, it felt light. Loving even.

"*I am sorry for everything I have ever done to you,*" she said. She took small steps towards where Martin was and collected Aeisha. Lucas had a similar glaze over his eyes as he picked up Borac. "*Nothing I do can ever repair what I have broken of yours. I hate myself for the pain and suffering I have caused you. I am sorry.*" She sliced Aeisha against my palm and watched as droplets of my blood went into the bowl. Lucas had done the same. Paige and Light did the same across from us. The small layer of skin that had covered Paige's blue gemmed cheekbone now hung over her lip. "*Please look after yourself,*" Misfeata said. Martin cut his own hand and watched as his own blood dropped into the bowl. The blood started to mix strangely and in it I felt a swelling and nauseous point reach the pit of my stomach.

"You have to shatter the gems in your blades now," Martin said. "They are the last remains of your soul to this place. They were what kept you Immortal." Paige smiled for a second before letting go of Light's hand. She didn't seem to mind as she waited. Paige walked over to Ashley. He seemed sceptical of her at first.

She grabbed the sheath that was wrapped around her neck with her small blade. She pulled it out and chipped away a part of her cheek. A thick shard of blue gem broke off.

"You know that's not like sexy and stuff right," Ashley said mockingly. She smiled and began to awkwardly tie the rock into the string which held it around her chest. "That is the worst knot job I've ever seen."

"Shut up!" Paige exploded. "Do it yourself then." She threw it at Ashley who caught it against his chest. She held out her hand to him. He smiled at her and shook it. "Thank you for showing me this world."

"No, 'thank you for being my best friend or anything cool like that'," Ashley said with a smile.

"You're deluded if you ever thought we were friends," she mocked with a smile. "Don't get yourself killed without me being there to cover your back."

She walked back to Light and held her hand. "I'm ready now," she said with a smile. They both delicately placed Sheliste on the ground. "Look after yourself Karla." Paige gave me an expression filled with such fondness that I almost didn't recognise her. Paige stomped on the blade and instantly they vanished alongside its shattering noise.

Misfeata was still in control of my body as she rested her own blades on the ground. She only hesitated for a moment before shattering the first. *"Thank you for believing in this place and letting me find peace."* Before I could respond she shattered the second.

My body felt suddenly heavy as I looked around. *"Misfeata?"* I said in alarm. There was no response. I knew she was gone, I could just feel it. I looked up at Lucas who was as wide eyed as me.

"You only have a few more minutes until the withdrawal will affect you," Martin said to both Lucas and me. You will both pass out for about a week. That's a lot of strength to be taken from you. It was a pleasure knowing you both."

My entire body had fully restored and felt fine. Lucas also looked healed and no longer had red gems protruding from his skin. I looked at the ground and collected a thick piece of the broken gem. Its beautiful green was the symbol of my journey. I felt foolish for being sentimental about it. But I curled my fingers collecting the piece. Like I had, so did Lucas. He held a clump of his own red gem. I don't know if it was the form of closure for us, to know it had now ended.

"They retreated!" Suzumiya yelled as she ran into the room. "It seems like something took all their energy. They've both gone their separate ways."

Scott walked over to me with a flamboyant smile. "Don't you just feel like we've like taken on the world," he said dramatically with a smile. "Well now that you are going to be restored into your normal life and what not, I doubt we will meet again."

I rolled the green gem in my fingers anxiously. I had become so accustomed to having Scott around. For the last sense of judgement I tried to project my Shield. But it wasn't there. I was now once again, human.

"Come here," Scott said. He gave me an awkward hug and then pulled away. He dusted down his jacket. "Okay, that was more unsettling than I thought it would be." He dusted his hands and walked out with Trish following suit. Ashley walked out behind them. Paul came to my side.

"Do you feel okay?" He asked me pushing back parts of my hair. I nodded my head still confused by the sudden change of things. I looked at Lucas, wondering if he felt the same. Paul looked between the two of us and dropped his hands. "I will be outside when you are ready. Say what you have to Karla. You might not have the chance to see him again."

My heart pained at the expression Paul gave me. He knew how much I cared for both Lucas and him. It was as if both of them already knew my decision. Lucas yelled out to Paul before he left the room.

"Hey, look after her okay," Lucas said. Paul nodded and walked out.

"But I-" I began. Lucas cupped my face with his leather gloved hand.

"I know Karla," Lucas said. He rubbed my cheek as his pained eyes searched mine. "This was never meant to be your world. It was selfish of me to ever hope that you would choose me. My war won't end just here. But yours can, you are finally free and can live a normal life."

"But I love you," I sobbed pathetically. He smiled very arrogantly. Like he always did with his cocky expression.

"I know you do and I love you too. But I can't offer you the same things that Paul can. I want to, more than ever. But I have to restore my people now. I only ever wanted to protect you. This is the safest way I can do that. I have to let you go," Lucas said with a nervous smile. I stepped closer into him and pulled at the edge of his jacket. I slowly pulled him into a hug, making sure not to touch his skin so he wouldn't drain me. "You and I both know you had already made your decision, at least let me walk away like some bad ass."

I clung to him tighter. How did he know? I loved both him and Paul. But my heart and decision had fallen with Paul. I wanted to return to the human world. I wanted to pretend like none of this had ever happened. I knew that nightmares would follow me and I could never erase the things that tortured me. I needed rehabilitation to coexist normally with humans again. But I also knew that Paul was the only one that I fully believed in that could help me.

I had long ago unknowingly let him become my protector. No matter how strong I was, my mentality wasn't prepared for this war like his was.

Lucas slowly pushed me away with a cocky grin. "We don't have much time until we part ways. Wake up safely and enjoy the rest of your human years Karla. Don't waste them." He gently pressed a light kiss to my head.

"Thank you for everything," I said. He smiled and walked backwards towards the door before completely vanishing from my sight.

The outside world was now brightly lit. I couldn't handle the brightness so I lifted my hand trying to block it. I found Paul and stumbled towards him. I could now feel the effect of my body weakening and tiring.

Paul hurried to me as I collapsed in his arms.

"Paul," I whispered. I raised my head to kiss him gently on the lips. I was falling into the beauty of his green eyes. I felt safe and warm in his arms. I was reassured just by looking at him that everything would be alright. The time in this very different world was behind us. We could finally become simply- human. "Look after me," I whispered to him as my body was pulled under by the rest it had so long cried out for.

I was lighter and now free. It was only my own mind and thoughts that consumed me. Surprisingly, I didn't feel bitter towards Misfeata for everything that had happened. Everyone has their own reasons to fight. Some are simply misguided and feel like their sins are far too great to turn back from. I hoped that somewhere she found peace. I had no reason to despise her because it would only weigh on me throughout the rest of my life. I would only be allowing myself to be consumed in the same darkness that she had wallowed in if I continued to resent her.

I was surrounded in love and healing. I needed those things to move on. I needed a brighter place to fade away this darkness that once followed me so closely. I had a different fight ahead of me and that was restoring my broken pieces.

Epilogue

Seven Years Later. . .

"*I* said no," I slapped Pauls' hand away from the cupcakes I had just baked. "They're for the shop." So many times now he had tried to sneak away with my baked goods for my café below. I heard the jingle of the shop door open below and eyed Paul. "Don't touch them." He gave me a coy smile as I began walking down the stairs to the shop.

"Sorry but we are currently closed," I said. I stopped on the second last step of the staircase. "Well, it's been a while." I said with a smile. I ran to Ashley and hugged him. How long had it been since we last saw him, a year maybe?

"How's the little café shop going?" He asked, sizing up the place. I had only recently opened the store within the last six months. Coming back from everything that had happened, I didn't know how to reshape my life. I didn't know where to go or what career to submerge myself into. I originally wanted to go into nursing, but realized I felt a bit edgy with all the noise and screaming people. It brought back too many memories that I tried to block away.

"It's going really well. Your mother often helps me in the mornings, she isn't here at the moment." Ashley shrugged off his jacket and threw it over one of my small booths that were positioned along the windows. He wiped away the flakes of snow which still clung to his shirt.

"Hey, there he is," Paul said as he walked down the stairs. Paul's arms and chest had significantly bulked over the past two years since becoming a professional boxing trainer. I was grateful that he had such a physical activity for his job or I'd have to count his cupcake intake more seriously.

"Come upstairs," I said. I wiped my hands on my apron out of habit. "How long will you be in town for?" I asked. Upstairs was a small two room apartment that Paul and I comfortably lived in. We opened the shop from the savings of my full time job at another café and Paul's well paid one. The year before that he asked me to marry him. I still woke from the nightmares of my past. Only he understood and knew the words that would sooth me. Somehow Paul never broke, throughout it all, he became my pillar.

We walked into the dining room which had an open space living area.

"Not long," Ashley said looking around. The blue gem and small blade of Paige's still rested close to his chest.

"I actually needed to come and see you. I need to collect something from you," he said seriously. Ashley and Paul took a seat across from one another on our wooden dining table. I wrapped an arm around Paul worriedly. The friendliness had disappeared, this was now business.

"What do you need from her?" Paul asked protectively.

"I'm not dragging you two into anything of the sorts. It's just Lucas and I need something-"

"Lucas?" I repeated in surprise. It had been a while since I last heard his name. And last I checked Ashley still despised him.

"We need the gem you picked up from Aeisha," Ashley said. "To put simply, some other stuff is happening in the not so human world and we need it."

"What do you need it for?" Paul asked precisely. He held my hand tightly, reassuring me that it would be okay. Since my fighting days I was rather fluttery at the thought of ever having to immerse into that kind of world again.

"If I told you, it'd be an open invitation back into the institute, which I don't think you want," Ashley said honestly. I looked at Paul for comfort.

"It's up to you Karlz," he said in that soft tone that always gathered my strength.

"I'll be right back," I said. I went to my spare room which had a few paintings in it. I often liked to paint now. I found it soothing and it calmed my nerves. I had never fully recovered from everything that happened. I might even seem weak and flighty to some, but Paul reassured me that there was nothing wrong with me. I still laughed, loved, and interacted with people daily. He reminded me I was more sensitive than others, which wasn't a curse but a blessing. Hidden in one of my drawers and in a paper-thin box, I pulled out the green shard which I had hidden so long ago.

I heard light footsteps running up the stairs. They were all too familiar. I came out just in time to see Paul ready for the attack.

"Uncle Paul!" Marcus jumped on him with arms wide. He was fully covered, including his red wool gloves. It was why we chose a home which always had heavy snow. Marcus, like any Starkorf child unintentionally drained people. When we returned to my mother and Helena, we decided to raise Jennifer's and Kingsly's son. My mother and Helena became fondly attached which was the reason why Helena decided not to return to the institute.

My mother and Uncle Kyle stood at the entrance of the staircase.

"How are you son?" Uncle Kyle said with a smile as he greeted Ashley. "You've bulked."

"Not as much as this guy," Ashley teased as he pointed to Paul. Paul was distracted as he doted on Marcus. It always brought a smile to my face.

I gave Ashley the gem. I felt a little lonely to part with it. It seemed to be the only thing I had to prove that it was all real.

"Thank you," Ashley said.

"We are going grocery shopping, do you mind if we leave Marcus here for a little while?" My mother asked.

"He can stay here for as long as he wants," Paul said as he pulled Marcus up on his lap.

"I need to see my mother before I leave. Until next time," Ashley said to us all.

"Look after yourself," I said in fair warning. I was worried that they had both gotten themselves in trouble once again. He dipped his head in thank-you and walked out.

My mother and Uncle Kyle followed him shortly after.

"You're not tricking me are you," Paul said to Marcus playfully. "You always used to pretend that you could stop it and drain me."

"That was when I was a kid," Marcus said defiantly. He crossed his arms over his chest. He looked like the splitting image of Kingsly with Jennifer's beautiful blond hair.

"You're only seven," Paul laughed. "Fine but you better not be lying." Paul held out his hand and closed his eyes. Marcus shook off his little red glove. I always encouraged Paul not to, in case Marcus did it to someone else. But Paul told him even if it did hurt, it was the only form of touch he ever had. For a child, touch was important and I couldn't argue Paul's point.

Marcus very delicately placed his comparatively small hand into Paul's. Paul slowly opened his eyes in shock.

238

"Karla," he choked in astonishment. I watched on as he did.

"I told you!" Marcus said with joy. "But I can only do it a little bit."

Paul looked up at me, my wide eyes must have replicated his. "Show Karla," Paul said. So many times Marcus had unintentionally drained me. I never blamed him, but my reaction always gave him a fright. Paul reassured me that it was okay. Marcus held out his hand to me, slowly and lightly I pressed my cheek into it. I braced myself waiting for the burn, but instead I was comforted by the smooth delicate skin of this young boy.

I choked back a tear, mesmerized that this could actually happen. He pulled his hand away and put his glove back on. "That's all I can do today. I am tired," he said with exhaustion. Paul laughed at him and lifted him off his lap.

"Why don't we go start a puzzle then?" The café door chimed again and I reminded myself that I still had to lock it.

Again I stopped at the second bottom step. "Scott?" I said in surprise. He wore his usual suited attire and hadn't aged a bit since I saw him those seven years ago. He slicked back his white hair as he clicked his fingers theatrically.

"It is I?" He dramatically posed. "Look at you, don't you look all. . . grown up."

"That happens after seven years to most people," I said with a smile. I didn't expect the same kind of greeting as I did Ashley. The last time Scott and I hugged it brought him great discomfort.

"I can't stay long young one. I need to take something out of your care. The green gem you took from Aeisha, where is it." He was far more direct than Ashley. I rolled my hands in my apron self-consciously.

"Ashley came and grabbed that a little while ago. Is everything okay?" A part of me feared hearing the answer. Anxiety fluttered in my stomach.

"Oh," he simply said with a calculating look. "Never mind then, pretend I was never here." He grabbed the handle of the door before looking over his shoulder. "Congratulations by the way."

"For what?" I asked confused.

"You are carrying a child," he said with a warm smile. My hand instantly went to my stomach. Scott took his leave, allowing a sweep of cold air into the room. I walked up the stairs shocked.

Paul looked up with a smile and instantly worried by my expression. He jumped up from the floor in the living room where he and Marcus had started a puzzle. "What's wrong, who was it?"

He hurried over to me and placed a hand on my face nervously. I looked up at him with a tear in my eye. I felt overwhelmed by the news.

"I'm pregnant," I shakily said. Paul stared at me for a moment before a large smile spread over his face. The warmth filled me as his smile always did.

"Are you serious?!" Are you telling me I'm going to be a father?!" He said with excitement. He lifted me up and into the air, swirling me around. "Am I really?!" I sobbed out a laugh as I wiped away tears. I didn't know why I had a moment of panic or fear from discovering this. A loving family was all I had ever wished for. Paul pressed a warm kiss to my lips as he continued to spin me around.

The fear I had felt wasn't because of my pregnancy. I feared what now ventured into the other world. In their world. . . But gratefully I was no longer a part of it. I laughed as Paul continued to spin me in excitement pressing excited kisses on my lips.

Marcus began jumping around us and celebrating, yelling that he was about to become an Uncle. The story of my past, I might sometime sit down and tell my children as a story. Surely they wouldn't believe it, but maybe if I wrote it into a book they could pass it off as a mere journey of a teenage girl who was taken from her world, into one where monsters became real.

About The Author

Kia grew up in the Darling Downs Region in Queensland, Australia. Graduating High School, she pursued a career in freelance journalism. In 2014, having always had a passion for writing fiction, she decided to follow her dream of becoming an accomplished author.

Now living in Edinburgh, Scotland Kia has a can do attitude, a strong will and the touch of kindness that makes it hard not to fall in love with her. Announced 'The Best New Author of 2015' by AusRomToday, and being awarded numerous awards, she has no intentions of stopping. Kia Carrington-Russell is definitely the new author to be looking out for.

Learn more about Kia at www.kiacarrington-russell.com and follow @kia_crystal on Instagram.

Also Available

The Three Immortal Blades
Possession Of My Soul
Possession Of My Heart
Possession Of My Fate

Phantom Wolf Series
Phantom Wolf
Sia
Phantom Eye
Phantom King

Token Huntress Series
Token Huntress
Token Vampire
Token Wolf

The Shadow Minds Journal Series

My Escort Series
My Escort
My Exception
My Expectation

Taming Himself Series
Aroused
Taste

www.ingramcontent.com/pod-product-compliance
Lightning Source LLC
Chambersburg PA
CBHW030640110726

47901CB00002B/517